# Praise for D~'

"An extraordinary no
Pete Sutton i:
Gare ___ ɔwell

"A fast-paced supernatural thriller, Cronenbergian in its
scope, which goes straight to the heart of good storytelling.
Sutton combines first class mystery with realistic
human drama. Read this at your peril.
Once started, it's not so easy to put down."
Alistair Rennie, author of *Bleak Warrior*

"An imaginative and thrilling tale with some
genuinely unexpected twists."
Sara Jayne Townsend

## Praise for A Tiding of Magpies

"Pete Sutton has a talent for the fantastic."
Paul Cornell, author of the Shadow Police series & *This
Damned Band*, writer for Doctor Who & Elementary

" However dark their subject matter, there is a
sweet and subtle music to Sutton's stories. They take
you to strange places."
Mike Carey, author of *The Girl with all the Gifts*

"As if Raymond Carver turned his hand to
writing science fiction."
David Gullen, Clarke Award judge

# Seven Deadly Swords

Peter Sutton

kristell-ink.com

ISBN 978-1-911497-92-9 (Paperback)
ISBN 978-1-911497-93-6 (EPUB)

Cover art by Robin Scott
Cover design by Book Polishers
Typesetting by Book Polishers

Kristell Ink

An Imprint of Grimbold Books

4 Woodhall Drive
Banbury
Oxon
OX16 9TY
United Kingdom

www.kristell-ink.com

For Claire Always (again)

# Avignon, France, 2012

REYMOND HUMMED *ALOUETTE* and sharpened his sword; this time the priest would die first. The rain hammered relentlessly upon the roof of the people carrier. He'd never got the hang of identifying machinery: it smelled new and it was red. He glanced out of the window into the night, seeing nothing, remembering deserts. His hands worked, a slow circular motion, comforting. He'd long since discovered that poetry and song soothed the constant rage. What was keeping Fisher?

Muscle memory took over and he contemplated the coming violence, the necessity of it. The priest had drawn him in, initially. It wasn't his fault, as such, but he held a fair measure of culpability. This time Reymond would end it. This time.

He was aware that he smiled grimly. How many times had he sworn that this time would be different, the last? He glanced back out the window. Avignon. So near where it had all started. Seat of popes. A fitting place to find the priest. The car was parked next to an ancient wall which stretched down the road to the priest's door. Where Fisher had gone some minutes ago. The priest would have had the dream, Reymond would be expected. Or one of them would be expected anyway. Dreams and portents, curses and sorcery. Reymond spat on the blade. This time he'd end it.

The sliding door of the car rattled open. Fisher, despite his bulk, and age, moved quietly: military training honed through many years of covert operations. Reymond raised an eyebrow at the Englishman who nodded and moved off, his yellow-white hair a flag in the dark. Reymond dropped the whetstone into its velvet bag, jumped out of the car and splashed through the wet clay mud covering the road to catch up with the larger man.

Once the big man was close enough for Reymond to see Fisher's cauliflower ears he asked, "And?"

"He's still there." The Merseyside accent seemed out of place here in France.

The priest's house was modest, a window onto Passage Saint Agricole, a door on Rue Felicient David. A courtyard interior. Sand-coloured stone. The priest's church, Saint Agricole, a short walk away.

The door swung open under Fisher's meaty hand and Reymond walked in ahead of the Englishman who held the door open for him. Reymond was struck again by the fact Fisher was approaching sixty. Soon to be too old for this work. Another good reason to end it this time.

The sound of prayer drifted down the stairs as the door swung shut behind Fisher. Reymond hefted his sword and followed the chant. The stairs were narrow and slippery, the plasterwork walls cracked and scabrous. A miasma of overcooked greasy food hung heavy on the air. Reymond continued to sing *Alouette*.

At the top of the stairs a nut-brown door stood open a crack. Latin spilled out. Reymond tightened his grip on the sword and pushed the door fully open. The short hallway he walked through, past a tiny kitchen, ended in a left turn into a sitting room. Waist-high bookcases flanked the door and ahead was a well-used sofa of cracked brown leather. The Latin abruptly stopped.

"Reymond. And Mr Fisher. Welcome."

"It's just Fisher."

The priest sat at a dining table, a bottle of single malt in front of him, empty glasses waiting. "I wasn't sure if Fisher would be joining us." He picked up the bottle and screwed the top off, pouring a generous measure into each glass.

Reymond's gaze roved the room: he narrowed his eyes and tried to ignore the siren song of fury that bubbled just beneath the surface. "After everything. After..." Reymond's hand, the one not holding the sword, made an abortive gesture. "You still believe?"

The priest followed Reymond's eyes to where his own hand had picked up a set of mahogany beads and a silver crucifix. A simple enough rosary, well-made, expensive, but not ostentatious.

"It is ever a mystery to me that you no longer do, Reymond. You were always a great believer." The priest picked up his glass, his finger and thumb counting beads. The glass shook as he raised it to his lips.

Fisher crossed the room and took the offered glass. With a glance at Reymond he knocked back the whisky, then sat to one side and kicked the chair opposite the priest out as an invitation to Reymond.

"You don't think that all we've seen proves that He has no plan for us?" Reymond asked.

The priest shrugged. "We are what God has made us."

Reymond barked a humourless laugh. "And what is that exactly? *Father*."

"If your dreams and times in between are as mine then I think you know."

"You know nothing." Reymond took a step towards the table. He could feel his control slipping: he bit his lip and started reciting Dante under his breath.

The priest held out the rosary. "Come, Reymond. Pray with me, like we used to. It will give you comfort, like at Dorylaeum."

Reymond's sword flicked out, and the beads rattled across the table and onto the flagstone floor. "It is time," he snarled.

# Near Avignon, France, 1097

REYMOND FIDGETED, FINGERS playing with the small burlap sack his father had asked him to fetch. He'd spotted the armed men and a small but growing crowd as he crossed the spring market and had gone to investigate. Amid the muck and the colourful tents selling a variety of wooden and metal objects as well as fruit and vegetables, swine and fowl, the assembly stood out. In the distance cows, being sold for slaughter, lowed. A short, thin priest shouted, mid-sermon. The armed men were arrayed behind him, the rest of the people going about their business in the marketplace. Reymond watched the crowd, who placidly watched this sermon. A bitter wind reached icy fingers in exposed places despite the warmth of the sun, but yet the priest held the crowd's attention.

The priest recounted his meeting with the pope: God's representative on this Earth. How could that fail to move his audience? The priest's musical voice sometimes wheedled, sometimes denounced, using some words Reymond wasn't sure the meaning of. He strode back and forth, his feet slapping upon the baked clay. The honest aroma of the rural congregation overpowered the smell of spring. The priest's voice boomed louder as he reached the climax of his sermon.

"And the pope said to us, 'The Holy Land has been invaded by a race alien to God, and they have attacked Christians with

4

sword, rapine and flame! They have destroyed our altars! They have circumcised our men, pouring blood into the baptismal fonts!' He spoke of the vile mistreatment of women, which I cannot repeat here for it is a great evil. And what did he ask? He asked that all good men stand true in fidelity with the church and take up arms against the heathen Saracen. Charles here," he gestured, and one of the priest's armed escort, a large man with coarse black hair and an olive complexion, dressed expensively – a lord – stood forward, "is leading the men from this parish, and from the surrounding parishes. If you are a good Christian he could use your sword."

Reymond gave the man an evaluating glance. He had brought his company into the market as though there was an enemy to be rooted out, yet his men stood meekly enough. The priest carried on sermonising, but Reymond barely heard his words. He was afire with the idea. To take up arms on behalf of the Lord, to aid Christians in the Holy Land itself... he burned with the desire to join up. He wondered if his father, an older version of himself, would have felt the same pull. His father! He'd be wondering where Reymond was and he'd be angry at being kept waiting.

Reymond ran back to where his father and his tenant landsmen were selling last year's wool.

"Father?"

"No." His father didn't even turn to look at him.

"No?" How had his father even known what he was going to ask?

"You are not of age, and I need all hands." His father turned, his face drawn and strict. "I'll need you for harvest later this year."

"But Father..."

"No, Reymond. Now fetch the wool out of the cart. We only have the two days of this market to shift it, look lively now."

Reymond felt himself blushing. He turned away, walking

with his back ramrod straight. How could his father stand by when such injustices were happening, such evil? When was his father going to realise that he was an adult? That he had plans too? He'd show them. He burned with a new purpose. As soon as he could, he'd sneak away and join up.

✝

Reymond stood irresolute outside the large tent, soft sounds of sleeping men inside. It had all seemed so clear when he had sneaked away from his father's tent. Perhaps he ought to come back in the morning when the soldiers were awake? Yes, that would probably be for the best. Having made the decision, he turned to leave.

A heavy sword came down beside his throat, and something pointy and sharp pricked him, just over a kidney. A coarse voice rumbled next to his ear. "What do we have here?" There was a hot exhalation smelling of alcohol and Reymond froze. He gulped: now it had come to it he didn't know what to say, or do; sweat prickled the back of his neck and his hands curled into fists as his face burned.

A more refined voice, the owner of the sword, presumably, came from a few steps away. "Turn around, slowly, so I can see your hands."

Reymond did as he was bid, wondering how he was going to get out of this situation; he was mostly thinking of his embarrassment but a small part of him wondered if he was about to be hurt. Was this a bad idea? "Light a torch," the high-born voice ordered. He heard the scrape of flint on steel and a torch caught, flooding the area with light. There was grumbling from the figures huddled on the floor of the marquee. The skinny priest sat up, glanced in Reymond's direction. His eyes narrowed but he shuffled and lay back down.

"Did I see you earlier today?" The man, severe face flickering in the torchlight, seemed less placid than he had in the daytime;

sleek and well-fed, in well-cut clothes, the expensive sword held casually ready.

"Yes, sir," Reymond said. This was the man the priest had called Charles. He was in the right place. This was a very bad idea.

"Give me a good reason why you are sneaking in here. Come to cut our throats and lift a few purses, have you?" Charles hadn't let his sword drop.

"No sir! I would like to join up."

The two men exchanged a glance. Charles looked surprised, his comrade suspicious.

"That is if you will take me, sirs?"

Charles narrowed his eyes. Reymond imagined what he was looking at – a boy yet to reach manhood, not yet filled out, short, the ruddy complexion of a farm worker. Not expensively dressed, but not poor either. Reymond's father was a landowner but Reymond worked alongside his tenants.

"Name?" Charles asked.

"Reymond."

"Sir!" the other man barked, twitching his knife. Reymond had avoided looking too long at this man. He looked much more dangerous than Charles. Thick bull neck, a number of large scars, muscular and yet rotund. He had the look of a brawler with an oft-broken nose. Completely bald. The sour smell of alcohol drifted off him.

"Reymond, sir!"

"How old are you, Reymond?" Charles asked.

"Eighteen, sir." Reymond added a couple of years, hoping he'd pass.

Charles arched an eyebrow. "Does your family know you're here?"

"No, sir."

"Wife? Children?"

"No, sir."

Charles exchanged another glance with his companion. He

threw his sword to Reymond who caught it clumsily, trying not to cut himself.

"Well," Charles said, holding one palm up.

Reymond looked from one man to the other, wondering what they expected of him.

"Show us your sword work," the bull-necked man barked, making Reymond jump.

Reymond stumbled through the few strokes he knew. Neither man gave any sign of appreciation.

"How far away is your home?" Charles asked.

Reymond swallowed hard. He had a sudden picture of his father a few days ago when Reymond had dropped a tool in the mud. His father's face red, mouth twisted around a bellow, the feeling of foolishness he'd had. "Please, do not send me away. I want to serve God. I want to aid our Christian brothers..."

Charles waved his protests away like bothersome flies. Reymond thought furiously. "Please?" Is that all he could come up with? It was pathetic, and he hated himself for it. He sounded like a little boy, desperate to be included in the bigger boy's games.

"You sleep on the floor. Tomorrow we'll decide what to do with you. I'm too tired for this now." The bald, scarred man came back and swapped the sword Reymond still held for a coarse blanket, and Charles walked away. He must have given some sign, as the other man followed him. Reymond could hear them whispering, and he picked out a few words.

"What ... think ... stay ... need ... can get ..." he heard Charles say.

"Give him ... change mind ... tomorrow," the other man's rumbling voice answered.

The bald, scarred man came back and threw Reymond a coarse blanket. "You don't talk to Charles from now on, unless he talks to you first, and you will call him sir. I'm now the man you should spend your waking hours trying to please. You may call me Sergeant. Now try to get some sleep, lad," he said before settling on a nearby chair, watching the door and renewing his acquaintance with a jug of cider.

Reymond tried to get comfortable. His hip was painfully squashed against the floor, but if he lay on his side, his neck hurt. The floor was simply too uncomfortable to sleep on, and even if he were in a soft bed, he would be too excited to sleep. The soft sounds of the men around him, their exhalations and smells, was unfamiliar. He'd never get to sleep.

When he woke in the morning he was surprised, then the cramps made themselves known and he bit back a groan of pain. The sergeant was up and wandering about, and Reymond wondered if he ever slept. There was no sign of Charles. A few of the men looked at Reymond with interest, others feigned indifference. The priest, a thin, short man with a rat-like face, stared. A couple of the soldiers looked to be around his age, or a couple of years ahead of him, but most of the men were older. A few looked like they had been at the soldiering business for a long while.

The priest sidled over. "Come to join the crusade?"

"Yes, Father." Reymond managed to look down on the priest despite not being so tall himself.

"God bless you! I'm Father Jobert. Welcome." His pointed face cracked into a smile and he held out his hand. Reymond noticed the ink-stained fingers before he grasped it in his own. "We will see the heathen expelled from the Holy Land, God wills it!" The priest grinned and set off outside.

Reymond stretched out his cramped muscles, looking for somewhere to put the blanket. He'd used it as a pillow until he'd got too cold, then as a cover until he'd got too uncomfortable. He'd spent half the night trying to work out how to use it as both, and failing. Unsure what he should be doing, he lurked near the entrance. He was beginning to wonder if he'd made a mistake. He wondered what his father was thinking. He swallowed the maudlin thoughts and remembered the words of the priest, Jobert, that had burned in him since he heard them.

Charles strode by. He glanced briefly in Reymond's direction and took a position where he could be seen by everyone. His mail shirt gleamed in the sparse sunlight, and Reymond wondered how much it was worth, and if he would ever have that sort of money. His fingers twitched towards it hungrily.

"We have four towns to visit in this area, before we can march down and join with Robert Curthose who is leading our army," Charles announced. "This market has given us one poor excuse for a soldier," he pointed to Reymond, "so coming here was almost a complete waste of time. Let's hope there are some God-fearing men in the next village." He nodded to the sergeant, who leapt into action, striding up and down before his men and clearing his throat loudly.

"Fall in outside! Now!" He didn't spare Reymond his bellows. "You! Get outside and get lined up!" Reymond blinked in sudden confusion, not daring to wipe the fine spray of the sergeant's spittle from his face. All around him men secured their bedrolls and packs, moving outside as fast as they were able. Having nothing to pack, the blanket having been reclaimed by the sergeant, Reymond joined them empty-handed. With the recruits lined up, the sergeant walked down the line, glaring at each one in turn. Reymond gulped, what had he got himself into? Today he should have been helping his father.

At the thought of his father he suddenly had the vision of him marching angrily up to Charles and demanding his son back. Reymond blushed just thinking about it. It'd be just like his father, and it must have been easy for him to work out where he'd run off to. It hadn't taken Reymond long to find out where Charles was, it wouldn't take his father long either. He burned to be off before his father turned up and embarrassed him.

When the sergeant was satisfied with the way the men had fallen in he started them marching as Charles rode ahead on a chestnut horse. Reymond wondered why his father hadn't come for him.

"Cheer up lad, we'll soon be in Avignon," Father Jobert told him. He hadn't noticed the priest approach. Avignon? But that was at least a couple of day's walk away. Reymond wondered how long it would take to get to Jerusalem. "And don't worry about your father. I've spoken to him and he has given you his blessing."

The small troop of forty men had camped in a stand of oak and alder. The gloom under the trees relieved by shafts of sunlight. Reymond had been assigned a tent with three others, roughly of the same age – Mikael, who'd been in the troop for some time and was rough edged, Samuel with a mop of blond hair, freckles and an easy smile, and William who had a constant red nose and sniffles. Despite the cold he'd slept well; nothing like marching for many miles then drilling to give you an appetite for sleep. After rolling out of the tent to a frosty morning, but one that promised sunshine, Reymond noticed that a few men were missing, including Charles and the priest. He vaguely remembered that they'd be recruiting today, but it seemed like Charles didn't need them all.

He stood and stretched, working the kinks out of his back. He looked around the shaded woodland, counting the tents. Most of the men were already up, moving sluggishly. Mikael had left the tent before him but Samuel and William were still attempting to eke out a little warmth before braving breakfast.

The sergeant stomped past, his bald head shining in a shaft of light through the trees. "What are you doing lollygagging?" he barked. "Time to learn the sword."

"Pick it up and try again," the sergeant said indifferently. Reymond could feel himself blush, his cheeks hot, as he bent down to pick up the sword that had been knocked flying from his hands by the big man opposite.

"Pierre, you're supposed to be defending."

Pierre, easily a foot taller or more than Reymond, ten or more years his senior and much bulkier, shrugged. "Not my fault if the boy's wrists are too weak."

Reymond felt his cheeks get hotter and his eyes moisten. He snarled and leapt at the other man with an overhead swing: the two swords clanged once, twice and then silence.

"Pick it up and try again," the sergeant said through a sigh.

Later, a man with curly hair and a kind face sewed Reymond's arm, his first sword injury. Reymond bit his lip and screwed one of his eyes closed as the needle entered his flesh.

"Hush now. This is nothing."

"Sorry, sir."

"Hah! Sir, that's a good one. I'm just a plain infantryman, same as you. I'm Jean."

"Reymond." He tried not to look at the flesh puckering around the thread as Jean pulled it tight, but was fascinated nonetheless.

"Pleased to meet you, Reymond. There you are, it'll be good as new in a few days and you'll be able to show all the girls your battle scar." The older man winked.

A horse nickering somewhere in the woods signalled that Charles and Father Jobert had returned. Reymond watched them sourly: he hadn't forgiven the priest. Reymond had caught up with him and asked about the conversation with his father which the priest had at first forgotten about. It turned out that

Jobert hadn't spoken to his father at all; he'd just told Reymond he had to get him to come along without any complications. Reymond had bitter guilt whenever he thought of his family.

The familiar sounds of the sergeant shouting for them to form up drifted towards them. They packed away the tents and were ready to go in record time. Putting up and taking down the camp was becoming a routine, and the sergeant made them try to do it faster each time. After days of marching and drill and sword practice. Jerusalem seemed like a distant dream: the men didn't seem overly religious, although they said prayers together. Reymond wondered what he'd got himself into. Home seemed so far away. Every time his resolve weakened he'd get his plain crucifix out and say a quick prayer.

He was on his way to Jerusalem to oust the Saracen. God willed it! The rumour was that they'd reach Avignon on the next day.

# Near Lake Urmia, Iran, 1982

"Fucking Lumpy!" Fisher muttered, then glanced across at where the man he'd cursed sat, a dark red blossoming stain around his stomach, his face white and bathed in sweat. "How the fuck did I let yer talk me into this?"

Lumpy shook his head.

Fisher sighed and stomped over to the wounded man and checked the bandage he'd put on a few minutes ago. It was soaked. Lumpy looked pasty and sweaty. The sound of the engine of the APC firing up made Fisher whip his head around. "What the fuck is Hawksmoor up to now?"

He sprinted to the door just as the APC drew away from the side of the small two-room tumbledown farmhouse, bouncing across the scrubland, through the meagre bushes that clung perilously to life in the poor soil. No wonder the farm was a ruin, no-one could have made a go at farming out here.

Fisher grabbed his radio from his belt. "Hawksmoor!"

"What?" The growling American voice was flat against the hiss of static.

"You arsehole, where are you going with our transport? Lumpy isn't looking too good!"

"Sorry Fisher, there's too many of them. You're on your own now."

"Come back, you fuckers!"

He watched the tail lights dwindling and wondered how

close the tribesmen were. A shot rang out and the lintel splintered above his head. He ducked back inside, slammed the rickety door and thumbed the send button. "You're leaving us to die!"

"Sorry, pal. Discretion is the better part of valour. Hope to see you around."

How low do you have to be to run out on someone as they patched up their friend? Lumpy!

Fisher skidded into the bedroom of the hovel, Lumpy was lying back, eyes squeezed shut. His stomach covered in a red that glistened in the gas light.

"How the fuck did I get into this?" Fisher muttered as the bullets started zinging into the building.

"Purveyors of Rare Antiquities?" Fisher asked.

"That's what they call themselves, yeah," the former squaddie everyone knew as Lumpy, on account of his odd shaped face, replied. "We join up, they take us places, we get rich."

"I don't know the first thing about antiquities, mate," Fisher said shaking his head.

"Nor do I. But all we do is acquire them and pass them on, there's a specialist who does the selling." Lumpy grinned. "His name is Hawksmoor."

"The bloke you want me to meet?"

"Yep."

He and Lumpy had joined up together, fresh from school, in the Birkenhead town recruitment centre. Inseparable for years ever since Fisher had carried him a mile, insensible from pain with his arm bent in a sickening way, after a tumble from a tree aged thirteen.

Fisher had been given his moniker due to his prowess as a hooker in the army rugby team. Always fishing balls out of the air. Since joining up they'd done a stint in Ireland and one in

Gibraltar. When the Special Forces knocked Fisher back he'd asked to get out. As ever, Lumpy followed suit.

"Where did yer hear about 'em?"

"Rumours mainly. And other squaddies. A bloke I know, knew another fella and he introduced me to a bloke who knows this fella." Lumpy grinned.

"Hawksmoor?"

"Yeah."

"Okay, no harm in hearin' him out."

†

"A book?" Fisher asked the American who'd met them at Horseguards. They were enjoying a cigar and a brandy at the Yank's expense.

"A special book. It's been locked in a tomb for hundreds of years."

Fisher exchanged a glance with Lumpy.

"And you want us along for...?"

"The tomb is in Iran..."

Which was in the middle of a shitty war with Iraq. That was pretty hot, as far as theatres of conflict went.

"Iran?" Lumpy asked. Fisher watched the American carefully. What were they getting into?

"Are you up for it? I'll pay you handsomely."

"Let's talk about how handsome this pay packet is. Is it leading-Hollywood-man handsome?" Lumpy asked.

They got down to talking about money.

†

The transporter plane banked and the red light came on. Fisher stood as the rest of the team clambered to their feet, and Lumpy gave him a cheesy thumbs up and a grin. He counted off and shook his head. Fancy getting out of the army and then signing up to go to a war zone!

The door opened and the wind screamed in. Fisher glanced out as he lined up with the others. Iran looked like any other desert country, as far as he could tell from this height.

He hoped Hawksmoor had done his research. He'd hate to be shot out of the sky by an excitable Iraqi with an itchy trigger finger.

Hawksmoor made an A-OK sign with his fingers and Fisher nodded. He didn't trust the pock-marked bastard but he was paying well.

Hawksmoor held up his fingers. Two minutes. Fisher checked that everything was secure.

†

It had all gone to shit after they entered the tomb. Oh, they'd circumvented the stone age traps easily enough and Hawksmoor knew exactly where to look. He'd done his homework.

No, it was the hundred or so tribesmen who were waiting outside with Russian-made automatic weapons that made it tricky.

They'd made it to the APC with one man killed and Lumpy hit. Pretty good all told. Unless you were Lumpy. A mad dash across the country in the APC, leaving behind the tribesmen mounted on horses eventually – but obvious, in hindsight, that they'd be tracked. Can't hide the bloody great tracks the APC made. They'd decided to stop at this remote farmhouse, obviously a second mistake – they should have kept driving. Hawksmoor had made that decision too, but only after he'd had Lumpy carried into the farmhouse: he and Fisher were surplus to requirements. And now the tribesmen had descended, the APC had gone and Lumpy was losing consciousness.

# Avignon, France, 1097

AVIGNON WAS A riotous confusion. Reymond had never seen so many houses or people gathered in one place. There were even more groups waiting to join with them, a meeting of two armies coming together in friendship, rather than battle. Robert Curthose, who Charles reported to, gathered his forces there, planning to march to Rome to receive the blessing of the pope before he drove them on to the east coast and across the sea to the fabled city of Byzantium. A word, and a city that conjured up impossibly exotic dreams for Reymond. A legendary place where the sun glinted off golden spires.

He marvelled at the fact that he was now able to march in step and that he'd made friends with his tent-mates. Mikael showing him the rudiments of soldiering, marching, standing at attention; all that sort of thing had helped enormously. Some recruits, who'd joined the day before, were brothers: Heribert, the elder, and Pepin, who Reymond suspected was even younger than him. They'd kept to themselves so far, although Reymond had tried to make friends. There was a core of professional fighters in the unit such as Pierre, who held themselves apart and who the Sergeant accorded some leeway to, as opposed to the 'peasant recruits'. However they were all being forged into one force of *pedite*, named for the fact they would fight on foot.

They marched through the city as windows flew open

around them and women and men hung out to stare at them going past. Reymond tried to keep his eyes on his comrades, even when the onlookers tried to catch his attention. Samuel, blond-haired and handsome, jogged his elbow, leering and pointing to an attractive young woman throwing flowers to the soldiers. The streets had a particular smell; smoke, human and animal waste, mud, which made Reymond's nose wrinkle. He hoped they'd reach the barracks before the black clouds made good on their threat of a downpour.

They marched into a crowded courtyard; a chaos of chickens, horses and men met them. When the halt was called the heavens opened and the unit were treated to standing at attention as rain sleeted off them. Reymond took his cue from Mikael, the broken-nosed and streetwise one, who stood perfectly at attention, ignoring the rain – unlike Samuel who hunched his shoulders and grimaced.

The sergeant wandered up and down the lines muttering. Charles walked off with a couple of other well-dressed men, other lords.

The bitter regret Reymond had occasionally suffered from since joining up threatened to overwhelm him.

"There's a juicy chicken for the pot." A girl's voice broke in upon his reverie. He glanced to the side to see a serving girl scoop up the chicken, which protested lustily. She caught Reymond staring and gave him a saucy wink before hurrying off through one of the open doors leading off the courtyard. He exchanged glances with Samuel, who also winked. Perhaps things could be worse.

Reymond was close enough to the front of the line to overhear Charles speaking to the sergeant when he returned from his meeting. The two men were virtually shouting to be heard above the lashing rain which turned the courtyard into one large puddle. The fat drops hit the surface of the water, throwing crown-like splashes. Reymond could not think of a time he'd felt wetter, certainly not whilst clothed.

"Knights are flooding in from all over," Charles said.

"A mighty force then?" The sergeant raised an eyebrow.

"Indeed. Let us hope it is enough. It is a long way to Jerusalem."

Jerusalem! Reymond was enchanted again by the thought. To walk where Christ walked. To drive the Saracen out of the Holy City. He was fired with all the religious zeal that had faded over the long, tiring march, and he couldn't wait to enthuse about it to anyone who would listen. It was a glorious mission they were undertaking. For Jerusalem! For Christ!

†

"Christ Almighty!" Reymond spat as he felt a blister pop on his hand. Glue-like mud was plastered against his legs and the water dripped off his nose as he swung the shovel. Having to dig latrines had been a constant hardship on the march across the countryside, but he'd naively thought that in the city they'd be able to rest from digging the incessant trenches.

They'd been sent to just outside the walls and had pitched their tents in the driving rain, as the ground was churned beneath them. Reymond didn't know how they'd get dry, or sleep. William, red-nosed and malnourished, had already succumbed to some sort of illness and had been whisked off by Father Jobert to be tended.

Water cascaded down the sand-coloured walls and flooded the camp. And even so Reymond and his other tent-mates stood knee deep in a ditch they'd been digging.

"I bet we won't have to dig latrines in the Holy Land!" he said.

Mikael snorted and lent on his spade. "Jerusalem is a long way from digging latrine pits," he said scornfully.

"Why? Don't they shit in the Holy Land?" Samuel, who'd paused from digging, asked smirking.

"Why did you sign up, if not to serve the will of God?" Reymond asked. Taking his cue from his friend, he also stopped digging. The sweat itched at the small of his back.

"I only joined to get away from father, to get regular meals and a dry place to sleep. Fat chance of that." Mikael was also eighteen, or so he claimed, but he seemed to have had a rougher life. His nose had been broken at some point and set badly, he whistled through it when he breathed, and he had a large jagged ropey purple scar on his right arm, from when it had 'snapped like a twig' as a child. Mikael has spent some time building up muscle and there was something in him, like biting down on an iron bar. Reymond was impressed that the tougher boy spoke to him at all. Most of the others who'd joined before him did not. The sergeant openly called him the runt of the unit, although Pepin was even smaller and more timid. The Sergeant treated Pepin like a pet: an annoying pet that was constantly underfoot.

Samuel, blond hair plastered to his forehead, realised he was being ignored and went back to digging, muttering under his breath.

"Do you not burn to rid the Holy Land of the Saracen?" Reymond asked the taller boy.

Mikael gave Reymond a long, scathing look, the sort you would deliver to someone who was touched in the head.

"And when we have emptied Jerusalem? Will we return triumphant, to let the Saracen crawl back in? We might never come back from the Holy Land, and if we do, we'll be changed."

Reymond hadn't given any consideration to the future after the liberation of Jerusalem. He'd assumed he would return to his family when it was all over. Forced now to contemplate a future in the Holy Land that might stretch beyond a year or two, he momentarily questioned his resolve. He was glad to find the prospect did not deter him, much. Tomorrow they would commence another long march. He'd overheard that their destination was Lucca, where the rumour was that the pope would bless the crusading army. Truly they were on a historic and blessed mission. Reymond burned with a desire to meet the pope.

The rumour mill supplied new rumours all the time, some of them more credible than others. Jean, the placid long-haired older man who often assisted the priest in attending to the sick and injured, told Reymond one whilst shearing his hair. It proved to be false, but he'd heard that the pope, who was apparently in France, would come to bless the army. The second, provided by William – now mostly recovered but left with a cough and husky voice – that there was to be a grand ceremony in which every man must 'take the cross' by speaking a solemn vow to see the crusade through to the end in Jerusalem, proved to be true. Every man had to wear the cross as a symbol of this vow. Charles handed out black cloth crosses and told his men to sew them onto their tunics after taking their vows.

Reymond's lip trembled as he vowed to support his fellow warriors, live a life in Christ, and see the mission to the end by visiting the Holy Sepulchre. Even sceptical Mikael's eyes shone during the short ceremony. Now he was committed in spirit as well as intention. God would strike him down if he did not fulfil his oath, or die in the effort.

The many armies were now gathered and rumours abounded about when they would set off. Reymond was in awe at the amount of men that had arrived in the city. "There must be a hundred thousand at least."

"More like ten thousand," said Mikael, dour and unimpressed.

Even ten thousand men boggled Reymond's mind. The Saracen had no chance: not only were the Crusaders so numerous, they were blessed. Although he did wonder, how were they going to cross the seas? Feed themselves?

On the road it was clear that to feed the army it needed to break into small groups. Reymond's unit had been assigned to Robert Curthose. Reymond had no idea who that was, but knew which flag to form up under.

On the road the sergeant had them in constant practice. Reymond often marvelled at how he'd filled out. Farming wasn't exactly a leisure pursuit but he'd added extra muscle in the weeks since leaving home.

Now he was paired off with the other young men, Mikael often taking Reymond through his paces as the youngest of Charles's 'old guard' – although he also often sparred with Samuel, who was an indifferent swordsman, and William, who was mortally afraid of injury. Less and less Reymond thought of his father.

# Yerevan, Armenia 2012

MARI HELD HER father directly responsible for the death of her mother. She watched as the coffin disappeared into the small, flat tomb and cursed his name. He'd gone missing months ago and her mother had entered a long death spiral the moment it was obvious he wasn't coming back.

The maze of other tombs, many in this section of the cemetery left to ruin, surrounded her. The iron-red sand drifted across the path and the sun baked the gathered mourners.

There were several men she didn't know at the funeral: some foreigners. A Georgian, who had stood with them and that she'd seen her father with on more than one occasion waited until the mourners started dispersing, then came over. His name was Nikolozi if she remembered correctly.

"I'm sorry for your loss," he began.

"Are you?" she asked, angry with the world for taking her mother away.

"But now that she is gone, the debt falls to you."

"Debt? What debt?" She looked away from the grave for the first time and saw that he had a trace of sympathy on his face, pity even.

"Your father's debt." He handed her a piece of paper, a printout of a spreadsheet, showing an unfathomably large number, chipped away at by regular payments.

"What's this?" She didn't want to understand. She wanted

him to go away. She wanted the earth to open up and swallow the whole city. She wanted her mother.

"Your father's gambling debt. He owes the casino. Your mother was paying it off. Either you pay it, or..." He buried his hands in his pockets and shrugged. "The first payment is due."

"But I don't have any money, I've just buried my mother, I–"

"Not our problem. First payment is due. If you don't pay you'll come to work for us until the debt is paid."

"Work for you?" She hated to think of her house, small and dilapidated as it was, where she'd been born, full of memories, taken by this man.

"You're young, men will pay a good price, you'd be paid up in a few years." He grinned and the smell of his sour breath turned her stomach.

"But..." She saw it was useless.

"We'll give you to the end of the week. Out of respect. My condolences, your mother was a strong woman." He span on his heel and went to join the foreign men who she saw were now leaving.

She looked at the vast number again and cursed her father. How could he have run up such a massive debt? She'd have to go to uncle Armen.

Uncle Armen ran a car workshop out in Arabkir. He was shorter even than his brother, her father, and beginning to run to fat. He didn't seem to be happy to see her; she wondered why he hadn't been at the funeral.

She found him elbow deep in a car's workings, covered with oil, as usual. After pleasantries she told him the situation.

"Money."

"Yes, father owed them lots of money, mother had been paying. I need to find him."

His bushy mono-brow climbed. "Find him? He's been gone

for a long time, Mari. If he wanted to be found someone would have done so before. He owed me money too."

"Uncle, please. What do you remember?"

It turned out her uncle didn't remember very much and wouldn't give her any money.

She searched all the usual places, and everywhere else she could think of, but there was no more money: a few dram here and there, but she'd spent everything in her mother's bank account and the life insurance on the funeral.

She asked everyone she knew and no-one would give her any money. She went to the bank and found that the house already had two mortgages. There was no money.

She considered running, but where would she go? She considered fighting, but the men who would come were not the ones who needed to be fought. She sold everything in the house that she could bear to get rid of, which was almost everything. It didn't make so much.

She asked around for jobs but the kind that she could get were in high demand – making coffee, serving tables – and wouldn't earn nearly enough.

The end of the week came round fast. The same man came to the door.

"I'll go with you and work off the debt," she said, "if I don't have to whore and I keep the house."

The big man shrugged. "The house would pay off the debt faster."

"It's my house."

"Okay, keep it. For now."

She joined him in his beetle-black car and he drove her out of the city. She'd taken a small suitcase with a few changes of clothes, some toiletries, a couple of books and the keys to her home. She swore she'd be back. She watched it dwindle in the rear window until she could see it no more.

Nikolozi, the Georgian, wasn't talkative. She didn't feel like talking anyway. If she ever saw her father again she'd kill him.

# Lucca, Italy, 1097

When they arrived in Lucca there was another rumour that the pope would be blessing the army, and this time it turned out to be true. Reymond and Mikael had skipped camp and joined the crush of people trying to get inside the circular walls of the small town. A multitude of voices filled the air with an incomprehensible hum. The stench of thousands of men crammed together, sweating in the sun, was overpowering. Skipping out was going to land him in trouble with the sergeant too. Yet it was all worth it, if he could catch a glimpse of the pope.

He and Mikael tried to push their way further in. Reymond took every route that opened up before him, squeezing through the narrowest of gaps like an eel. They pushed and bullied and cajoled their way towards the centre, where a small platform had been built. It was impossible to hear each other over the cacophony of voices surrounding them. Mikael signalled directions with his hands, like the sergeant had been teaching them. Reymond soon lost sight of his friend and found himself swimming against the tide. He stepped in something squishy and saw a man being carried backwards in the crush.

There was a swelling susurrus ahead, and Reymond pushed through with a great effort, coming face to face with the ranks of priests gathered around the platform, their own Father Jobert among them. He blinked to see through the clouds of incense, and there was the pope, only twenty feet away. He hoped, but never really dared to believe, that he would catch a glimpse. He never in his dreams thought he'd get this close.

It was enough for Reymond to have seen him; although he felt a hint of disappointment that beneath his finery the pope looked like an ordinary man. The pope waved for silence but it was impossible. The roar of the crowd hurt Reymond's ears, and, as his initial excitement faded, Reymond became annoyed by the crowd's movement back and forward like waves crashing upon a rocky shore. His zeal was dampened as he felt in danger of losing his feet, knowing that if he were to fall he would be crushed and trampled by the restless crowd. A few feet to his right Reymond saw a limp body being passed above the heads of the crowd to the priests, who bent to lift him over the chest-high barrier.

Reymond turned, trying to force his way through the crowd but it was like trying to push the city wall out of the way. He was buffeted towards the barrier. He had visions of being crushed upon it and his stomach fluttered, his head span and buzzed as his heart raced. He tripped and managed to catch himself before being fully carried away, but it was a close thing. He swivelled his head from side to side, looking for escape; he must get out, but he was surrounded. He began to gasp, he couldn't breathe – but as the crowd ebbed he was able to clamber up, using people's arms and knees and heads to boost himself over the barrier and into the fresher air above.

He caught the eyes of Father Jobert, and grinned at him in relief. The man opened his mouth to speak, but a hand on his leg caused Reymond to twist as the next man to have fainted in the crush was pushed over the barrier. He stooped to help.

After a few minutes Reymond turned to look upon the pope once more, but the Holy Father had left. Reymond couldn't tell how: the platform with a seat upon it was blocking his view. In the distance there was an eruption in the noise of the crowd, but he saw nothing beyond the bobbing heads and waving arms. Information passed like a bad smell through the masses, and gradually the surge turned into dispersal. Reymond, hot with excitement, headed off, bursting to tell Mikael and the others that he had stood upon the same platform as the pope. But first he must find them.

# Near Lake Urmia, Iran, 1982

"HELLO?" A VOICE blared out of the radio. Not a voice Fisher recognised. The bullets slammed into and through the side of the mud-brick cabin, but most had gone high and wild. There wasn't much to hide behind, virtually no furniture: whoever had lived here had been dirt poor. He didn't think much of his chances.

"Who's this?"

"A friend. I see you are pinned down. I could possibly alleviate pressure on one front. I am above in the valley to your south."

"I see. Standby."

Fisher peeked out of the window again: he could see tribesmen advancing, running from cover to cover in a crouch. He had to do something. He thumbed the radio.

"Hello 'friend', you still there?"

"Still here."

Fisher stared down his gun, following the movements of the men in the valley advancing on the farmhouse. He glanced at Lumpy whose breathing sounded a bit ragged: he was out of it, probably for the best.

"How d'we know this isn't some sort of trap. You have a funny accent. Where you from?"

"Lots of different places. You can call me Patience."

"OK call sign 'Patience', we've got a wounded man here.

We're low on ammo and the locals may be stalling so they can get hold of a RPG or sumthin'. What's yer plan?"

"Give me as much cover as you can and I'll take out the men below me. That will give you an escape corridor."

Fisher shrugged. Cover was going to be minimal but he fired from each of the windows, crawling between them, concentrating on the tribesmen closest to him and keeping them pinned down. He took quick peeks, conscious of the return fire zipping about. He spotted an Iranian who appeared to be the leader whose head exploded in a spray of blood and brain. Patience was using a sniper rifle.

He was running out of ammo so he only fired if he saw a target. Outside he could hear handgun fire amongst the rifles. Whoever Patience was, he was good, or stupid, going against men armed with rifles using only a handgun.

There was confusion outside, tangled words of Persian shouted or hissed. A volley of shots came from behind the Iranians – an opportunely picked up rifle, he thought. He popped his own rifle up and sprayed the area that the returning fire was coming from – until it clicked onto an empty magazine.

He pulled out his pistol and waited for a lull before popping up and cracking off a few shots. He doubted he'd hit anybody. Outside he heard the rattle of automatic fire again, much closer, and he dared to hope.

The shooting stopped. Fisher raised himself up so he could see out the window without exposing too much of himself and glanced right and left. An Iranian stood up a few feet away and Fisher tried to shoot him before he could bring his weapon to bear. One of the three shots connected but not before the man sprayed the front of the farmhouse. Fisher felt a bullet nick him as it went through the wall. It stung like a bastard but he thought it had gone through the flesh of his shoulder. As he congratulated himself the door behind him was splintered open and three Iranians ran in, covering him with their rifles. He dropped the handgun.

There was a sudden burst of gunfire coming from the window behind him and two of the tribesmen dropped even as the man outside ducked down again. Fisher dived to the floor; he'd felt a bullet go through the fleshy part of his ear and he wanted to live.

A bullet skimmed the window frame showering him with splinters as the door crashed open a second time and a wailing Iranian fled into the night. The silence was shockingly loud. Someone, Patience maybe, leapt over the windowsill.

Fisher went to push himself up when a jagged pain ran down his arm – the shoulder hit must have been worse than he thought.

There was a bang and he was blown across the room. He could see the muzzle flash of the stranger's gun and he couldn't work out what was going on. Why was everything suddenly silent? Did the stranger have a sword strapped to his back? Then something hit him hard on the back of the head, and everything went black.

†

Fisher came round, groggy, in the dark and tried to get up. The place smelt musty and there was an underlying animal muskiness.

"Lie still. You do not want to brain yourself, do you? Although banging your head must be a common occurrence, so maybe you have developed head calluses or something." The words echoed strangely.

"Friend Patience?"

"That is me."

Fisher let the silence drag until he thought to introduce himself.

"I'm Fisher."

"Mr Fisher, we will have plenty of time to get acquainted later. For now we need to be quiet in case anyone is nearby. Let me have a look at those wounds."

As the man checked the two bullet wounds high on the Fisher's torso and shoulder, Fisher whispered, "Just Fisher."

"What?" Patience seemed distracted, juggling torch and bandage. In the semi-darkness Fisher's blood looked oil-black.

"Not Mr, just Fisher."

"Well, Just Fisher, it looks like nothing vital has been hit. You have not lost too much blood and all things being equal you may even live. We have to make sure we do not get caught. I'll give you something for the pain."

Fisher sucked in a whistle as the needle slid in.

"Thanks..." He was gasping, grimacing, sweating. "I owe you me life." He lay back, his features relaxing as the drugs rushed through his bloodstream.

"I will have to think of some way you can repay me," Patience said, as Fisher drifted off.

He made a huge effort to keep his eyes open. "How's Lumpy?"

The man frowned.

"The other feller, in the farmhouse with me, gutshot?"

The man's lips thinned and he shook his head.

Fuck, Fisher thought as the drugs took him.

Fisher observed Patience poke his head outside what he could obviously now see was a cave. He glanced back as Fisher shuffled up on one elbow and winced.

"So what's the situation?" Fisher asked.

"A patrol went straight on by an hour ago." Patience turned to stare out at the desert again. "It was a close thing, they searched the canyon and the farm house. Luckily the commander was too lazy to search all the nooks and crannies. Like this one." He turned to face Fisher. "I guess the army are doing a sweep, probably heard the firefight last night and come for a sniff around. Which means the local tribesmen will have scattered as well and we can get out of here."

Fisher sighed, shifted position, and winced again.

"That is, if you think you are up for a little trek?"

Fisher nodded slowly. "What you thinking?"

"First things first. Who are you working for?"

Fisher rubbed his stubble. "Well..." He blew air out of his cheeks. "I'm grateful to you fer savin' me life n' all but I don't know yer from Adam."

Patience shook his head. "I see."

"Look let's just say it isn't any army."

"Ah." Patience nodded. "Can I ask what you are doing in Iran?"

"Extraction."

"Of?"

"I'd prefer not to say just now."

"Very well. You are right, I do not wish to share my plans with you either. However fate has thrown us together, let us trust each other for now."

The man who had named himself Patience looked impatient, tapping his finger against his thumbnail. He pulled a map from his chest pocket and smoothed out the creases and shone a torch on it. "We are here," he said, jabbing at the map, "and the Turkish border is here." His finger moved an inch or so. "I will take you there and drop you off, and you can make your own way to the nearest town."

"What's this?" Fisher asked, pointing at a star scribbled on the map a few inches in the opposite direction towards Lake Urmia.

The man's grin vanished. "That, my friend, is why I'm here. I cannot tell you anything about it, except to say I hope it is the answer to a fervent prayer or two."

There didn't appear to be anything where the star was, no town, nothing apart from empty space. Fisher frowned and shook his head. "OK, friend Patience, when do we move out?"

Patience folded the map. "Right now, if you're fit to walk. Let me have a quick look at those wounds." Fisher lay still as the man took a look. "Low calibre, clean through. They might hurt like a bitch but they have not hit anything vital, so you will live. We will move by night, hole up in the daytime. Leave behind anything not absolutely essential, I will not be carrying your spare stuff, I have enough of my own to carry."

Fisher went through his pockets and dumped a few bits and pieces. "Ready."

Patience crawled outside and swept the area with his night vision binoculars, looking for campfires or similar. He put his head back into the cave.

"I would like to do about twenty kilometres tonight, but we will have to play it by ear as to your fitness. Let me know if your wounds open, or you need to stop for whatever reason, or if you are in too much pain. I do not want any macho bullshit. We will get where we are going if we are sensible." He paused as if to make sure Fisher was paying attention. "Shall we go?"

The two men headed out, in the direction of the Turkish border.

As they trudged through the night they kicked up small spurts of dust. Fisher had his head down, but was keeping up for now. He wondered how long their luck could hold. The hills were crawling with tribesmen and there was always the danger of running into an Iranian army patrol.

"Want to tell me what an Englishman is doing in Iran in the middle of a war? Should you not be trying to get some islands back from the Argentinians?" Patience asked.

"Depends."

"On?"

"What a Frenchman is doing in the middle of this war."

Patience let the question hang in the still air for a moment. "Well, that is a tale that will take some telling. There is something buried in this country, from a long time ago. Something I need to find."

"So you're like me?"

"Like you?"

Fisher held his left side a little stiffly, but he was keeping up well with the pace. He decided to trust the Frenchman, he had saved his life after all.

"A purveyor of rare antiquities."

"So you *are* here on a treasure hunt?"

"Somethink like that. Except some bastards who were supposed to be helping decided we were surplus to requirements."

"The men in the APC."

"Yep they're the bastards. Well on their way to Van by now." Fisher spat against dry rock.

There was a low rumble in the distance. The two men exchanged a loaded glance. "That's a plane," Fisher said.

"Come on, behind this ridge, lie down," Patience said. Seconds after they took cover two jets screamed overhead from East to West, red tail lights searing across the darkened sky. They gave it a couple of minutes but wherever they were going, they didn't turn back. "Okay," Patience said. "Time to move on."

Fisher clambered to his feet. "Listen, we won't, I know, but if we do, in case we do catch up with them, the stuff on the APC is worth a lot of money in the right hands..."

"And you would like my help reacquiring it?"

"Uh huh."

The Frenchman shook his head. "It seems unlikely we will come across them. If we do, it would be smarter for us to stay out of their way. I doubt whatever it is would be of any use to me anyway."

The two men walked in silence through the endless dusty landscape, grey in the moonlight.

"So what's your story?" Fisher asked.

After a long pause Patience seemed ready to trust him after all. "I am here to retrieve some writings. An ancient book, from the time of the crusades, allegedly the notes and journals of a Saracen sorcerer. They were buried with him, in a tomb hidden somewhere in this country."

Fisher laughed and shook his head. "Well, I'll be a son of a bitch. I think we just stole that book. Those tribesmen trying to kill us? They wanted to take it back."

Patience stopped. Fisher took a couple of more steps before coming to a halt. The other man's glare encouraged him to keep talking.

"Maybe. We grabbed the stuff and did a runner. Those tribesmen revere the Holy Man whose tomb we lifted it from, and they followed us. That's the fight you got in the middle of. The men in the APC? They took the stuff and left us high and dry. I should've known from yer map."

"And these men? The ones in the APC? Where would they be taking it? Who are you working for?"

Fisher stroked his chin, trying to decide what to say.

"They'll be taking the stuff to a buyer in the Middle East somewhere, Syria I think. I don't know the buyer's name. I'm working for a guy called Hawksmoor."

"And this Hawksmoor, he is an American? Buzz cut, pock-marked face, smokes cigars, ex-forces?"

"That's the feller. You know him, huh?"

"He works for someone I know, I think. Looks like you and I are on the same path, Fisher. We had better get transport, and you can tell me everything you know about who is on that APC, and where you think it will be going."

"How we going to get transport?" Fisher asked.

Patience grinned. "The Iranian army."

"The army?"

"Yes!" Patience barked out a humourless laugh.

The moon sailed high overhead like a giant yo-yo. Fisher

could see his breath in the twilight. There was a murmur in the middle distance, Iranian soldiers enjoying the night. He hawked and spat. Would he ever get the taste of grit out of his mouth?

He looked up the hillock to where Patience lay flat on his belly looking through the sniper's scope.

"How the hell didya talk me into this?" Fisher muttered, through gnashed teeth.

Patience had shucked most of his gear and was wearing only black combats. He dug in his baggage and stood to strap his sword onto his back.

"A sword?" Fisher asked drily.

"Yes."

"Okay. A sword?"

"Hopefully it will not be a gunfight. I take the sword everywhere. I may even tell you why some day." The Frenchman checked the assault rifle and handgun were loaded. "Right, do not shoot unless it is absolutely necessary. If you do have to shoot, try not to shoot me."

"Har har."

Fisher shook the proffered hand.

"Back in a jiffy, I think you would say?" Patience quipped and jogged off into the night, heading down the slope towards the Iranian camp.

Fisher took his place at the sniper and looked down the nightscope. There were several vehicles in the camp and he wondered which one the Frenchman would take: motorbike, car or truck? There were two motorbikes, an armoured car and two trucks. And lots of tents. Halfway to the camp the other man dropped to his belly in the dust and started crawling. He stopped every few dozen yards. None of the sentries seemed to be particularly alert. But Fisher was ready to drop any of them if they spotted the man crawling towards them.

When Patience got to the vehicles he checked each in turn, and selected the armoured car. Fisher clocked that it also had a couple of spare petrol canisters which would come in handy. The Frenchman used his sword to hole the petrol tanks of the other vehicles and then to let the tyres down. Cunning. He rolled under the car and disappeared from sight. Fisher wiped sweat from his forehead and put his eye back to the scope when the car roared into life. There was an instant hubbub of shouting voices.

Fisher saw at least ten men running towards the vehicles: others took aim and one man knelt bringing an automatic rifle to his shoulder. As the armoured car accelerated Fisher shot the man with the automatic – his head jerked and he sprawled gracelessly. The car jolted forward as the first shots rang out. The men scattered as it barrelled through the camp, knocking over a couple of tents, and the engine gunned as it built speed. Fisher shot a second man who was drawing a bead on the Frenchman. The Iranians belatedly realised there was a sniper and scrambled for cover.

The encampment was alive with shouts and five or six of the soldiers were still shooting. The trucks and motorbikes roared into life but went nowhere as the soldiers discovered the sabotage. Fisher spotted a radio unit and blasted it, then shot another soldier before the car drew level in a juddering halt and the Frenchman jumped out, shoving his backpack into the boot as Fisher clambered in.

Patience passed him the assault rifle, jumped in and gunned the engine and they roared off into the night as the radio blared into life.

"How is your Persian?" Patience asked.

"Piss poor, to be honest," Fisher admitted.

"Mine too. It will be an hour until helicopters are in the air, or a jet. Time to leave. I can pick up enough to know that they are looking for your friend Hawksmoor." He put his foot down and the car jounced across the rough track, throwing the two men from side to side.

"He's no friend of mine!"

"They are still in the country, they are hiding out somewhere."

Fisher hung on for grim life as they jarred to and fro. He hoped the suspension would handle the rough treatment.

"If they are, they'll make a run for the border at some point."

Patience nodded.

"What do we do when the copters fly overhead?"

"In the back, in the bag, there is a uniform. Put it on."

The car bounced and rolled from pothole to dip to trough to hill with a succession of rattles, pings, and other mechanical noises of protest.

"Surely that won't fool them?" Fisher shouted.

"It will have to. We will drive through the day tomorrow, presumably whilst your erstwhile colleagues hole up somewhere."

"We're going to drive in daylight? Won't that be a bit risky?"

Patience glanced away from the track for a second but jerked his attention back as the car lurched to one side. "Yes, we are. Yes, it is. How good are you with the sniper?"

"You're thinking of taking a copter out with a sniper rifle?"

"Yes."

"Will we hear it in time?"

Patience pointed to his eyes and then to Fisher.

"You don't happen to have an RPG hidden in that bag, do ya?"

The Frenchman shook his head. "Just a few more assault rifles and some spare ammunition." He pressed the accelerator for a fresh burst of speed, but had to ease up as the car screamed in protest. They couldn't afford to lose a wheel, or snap the axle.

"Do you know where you're going?" Fisher asked, shouting.

Patience shrugged, and Fisher fell silent, giving up the struggle to make himself heard over the rattle of the car with a throat full of dust.

They stopped to refuel as the first hint of dawn brought a blue blush to the landscape. The gurgle of the fuel can was the only sound in the stillness, and the fumes were pungent in the dry air. Fisher rubbed his gritty eyes and gargled from his water bottle, spitting a thin grey gruel upon the dusty ground. He felt done in, but checked the engine to make sure nothing had been shaken loose before digging in the bags for more painkillers.

"Your wounds have opened up?" the Frenchman asked gently.

Fisher shook his head, the muscles in his neck taut with tension.

"Let me have a look."

Both wounds looked angry, red and inflamed. The Frenchman felt Fisher's temple for signs of fever. "We need to get antibiotics, in Turkey perhaps. We had best go straight there."

There was a faint thrumming in the distance. "Into cover!" Patience grabbed the bag and made a run for the nearest bushes. Fisher slammed the bonnet down and limped after him. He aimed the sniper at the empty sky.

They saw the spotlights first and two inimical shadows squatting above them as the sound of the 'copters grew louder. Fisher sighted down the scope. Maybe, as the car was stationary and empty, they'd ignore it?

The 'copters swept past overhead, throwing temporary daylight onto the car and the surrounding scrubland. They wheeled and performed a pass, one turning whilst the other hovered. One was going to land, Fisher realised, as it hunkered down. This was bad.

The chopper in the air veered away, zooming off to the north. They heard its guns start up, a deep bud-bud-bud peppering the hills. Some poor shepherd or farmer, or maybe even Iraqi, had just been shot to shit. Daylight crept across the hills and the dawn was redolent of the dust thrown up by the 'copters.

"Maybe they'll leave now?" Fisher ventured in a whisper.

Patience shook his head. It was too much to ask. It meant they were safe, as long as they remained hidden. It didn't help them if the Iranians took their car back though. "Think," Patience muttered. Fisher tried to look keen. Patience motioned for the sniper and Fisher passed it to him and picked up the spare assault rifle. The Frenchman took a bead on the Iranians from the 'copter as they approached the car. They looked it over, trying the engine, which coughed into stubborn silence. Fisher held up a small but obviously vital piece of machinery, and grinned. "They're going nowhere," he mouthed.

The man in charge barked a few short orders and half the soldiers headed back towards the helicopter, leaving three men guarding the vehicle. None of them looked too happy about remaining behind. One lifted the bonnet and poked inside.

As the noise from the chopper faded into the distance, the first sniper bullet took out the nearest man, splashing his brains all over his companion who lent on the body of the car. The man under the hood seemed unaware of anything amiss.

Patience calmly took out the second man before he had time to shout a warning, and consequently the third man was unaware that his life was about to abruptly end until the third shot hit him beneath the armoured car. The Frenchman muttered something that sounded like a prayer.

"That was almost too easy. Three more stains upon my soul," he said. "That was very smart, about the engine. I should have been more attentive, but mechanical things elude my grasp."

Fisher didn't hold with religion, or souls, or any of that crap, but held his tongue knowing that others got touchy about it if you said it was rubbish. "Least I can do, to repay ya for saving me life." Fisher frowned. "Why didya?"

"Save your life?"

"Yeah."

"Seemed like a good idea at the time. I have seen far too

much death and maybe God ordained it."

"I wouldn't have pegged you as a God-botherer."

"There's a lot more to me than you think. Shall we move on? It will not be long before the Iranians wonder why they have lost radio reception from them."

Back in the car Fisher cleared his throat as Patience clambered in, the engine repaired and ready to go.

"What?"

"You said you've seen much death? You been in this business a long time then?"

"A very long time," the Frenchman replied before gunning the engine into life.

They were moving forwards again, as well as plenty of up and down and side to side.

A few hours later they were in border country. Fisher couldn't seem to sit still, or get comfortable. Patience's eyes narrowed every time he shifted. Both men glanced at their watches often.

"We will have to ditch it," Patience said.

"Can't we get closer?" Fisher's head had been nodding. He was struggling to stay awake.

"In a stolen Iranian military car? Are you up for a dash across the border?"

"I'll have to be." Fisher grimaced, shifted his weight, and glanced at his watch once more. As they walked away from it Fisher looked back at the car a couple of times wistfully.

They moved as stealthily as they could, despite the heat of the sun, now climbing the sky, heading in what Fisher hoped was the right direction. He wasn't sure what alerted him at first, but when he scanned the horizon he saw somewhere between ten and twenty heavily armed tribesmen, heading their way.

He clapped Patience on the shoulder and pointed, dropping

the sniper as the fighters were approaching too fast. As he pulled the assault rifle off his shoulder, Patience took aim with the handgun. His first shot slammed one of the tribesmen in the head. The rest scattered and dropped. This had every chance of becoming a prolonged firefight.

Fisher sweated and was trembling, shaking so much he doubted he could hit anything. Patience glanced at him and he shook his head. "Cover me," he said, running off at a crouch.

Fisher watched as Patience, a one man army, took out each and every tribesman with sword and gun. It was amazing to watch, a lethal ballet of steel and gunsmoke.

"You single-handedly took out a dozen or so tribesmen," he said once Patience had returned. "I've never seen anything like it. I've never heard anything like it. Are yer some kind of super soldier?"

Patience shrugged. "Just lucky, I guess. I was a farmer before I took up the sword."

Fisher sensed that there was more to it than that.

Patience put his hand on Fisher's shoulder. "You do not look so good."

"I don't feel so good," Fisher admitted.

"Try to keep with me." The Frenchman set off at a ground eating lope, Fisher stumbled after him. An hour later Fisher was leaning on the other man for support. An hour after that, he was being carried, but they were moving faster. Eventually Fisher was dropped in the scrabbly hills just across the border from Turkey. He burned with fever. Patience gave him the last of his water and stripped him of all but his essentials.

"I'm going to leave you here, with all of our kit. Stay hidden, stay safe. I'll be back as soon as I can."

"Where yer going?" Fisher hated the weakness he could hear in his voice.

"I'm going to get across the border. Get some antibiotics and get back as fast as I can."

Fisher nodded and swallowed on a swollen throat.

# Avignon, France 2012

"I THOUGHT I'D have longer," the priest said. There was a hint of weakness in his voice, needy pleading.

"You have had long enough," Reymond replied from the darkness of the courtyard. "I'll give you time to pray."

The inner courtyard of the priest's house was about twenty foot square, flagstoned and liberally scattered with plant pots with a variety of herbs and even a couple of small trees. There was a bench and the priest's washing was strung across it. Reymond cut the line and bundled the clothes to throw in a corner.

Reymond listened to the mumbled words of the prayer. Cursing God and his plan, he stalked down to the end of the yard, where he waited motionless. The priest remained by the back door of the house, tension showing in his form. He glanced at Fisher, who stood close by, and nodded. Reymond ignored Fisher. Jobert took a deep breath and seemed to stand taller.

"I am the first this time?" he asked.

Reymond nodded.

The priest sighed.

"I am ready."

With no further warning he leapt across the yard, throwing an overhanded cut with the sword that Reymond easily countered. The fight was short, silent except for the clash of steel on steel. Both men were around the same size, neither had a reach advantage. Reymond was slightly faster, the priest was slightly stronger. Reymond knew more tricks.

Reymond's sword was an extension of his arm. He was content to let Jobert take the initiative. Usually fiery angry and overwhelming, this time he was filled with a cold fury. The priest was obviously afraid and that made him desperate. He attempted a thrust that left him exposed and Reymond slammed his sword past the priest's guard and between the ribs.

Eyes open wide, the priest looked down at the sword disappearing into his body.

"Oh!" he said as his own sword slipped from his fingers.

Reymond caught him as his legs gave way.

"Will we ever be forgiven?" the priest asked the man who had just killed him.

"I forgive you," Reymond replied tenderly as he laid the other man down.

"I wish I was braver, like you... I wish... forgive..." the priest mumbled before his head dropped back and his life fled.

Reymond respectfully closed the Priest's eyes. He took Jobert's sword and put it with his own, tying them both into a cloth that he fastened across his back.

"Rest in peace."

He hoped fervently, not for the first time, that he would not need to go through this again. He wondered who the man was he had just killed. Not Jobert, the vessel. Another stain on his soul. He knew it would be another face that would haunt his dreams, another sin to be confronted with by his tormentor. He couldn't help but remember previous times: the priest always tried to atone and Reymond had cut him down time and again before he could. He wiped a tear from his eye and wondered when he lost the faith that used to succour him. It was a bittersweet victory. The first of many.

Fisher helped him carry the body back into the bedchamber and he arranged it neatly on the bed. He collected the laptop and paperwork he'd identified as useful earlier, and went through the house erasing any signs he'd been there. They left, only to return a few minutes later with a petrol can each.

As they watched the fire light up the windows like baleful eyes, Fisher turned to him.

"Why did you want me here? You could have done this by yourself."

Reymond sighed. "I wanted you to see that they are still friends. They are just as cursed as me. They have to die, but it gives me no pleasure. You had to know to whom you have given an oath."

Reymond watched Fisher turn and stare at the fire. I had to make you hate me, he thought. Then you can complete the last task.

†

On the drive to Paris Fisher listened as Reymond ran through all the possible moves ahead. Lust was somewhere on the other side of the world. Gluttony would be in the Vatican, a creature of habit. He'd decided to leave Tafur for now. Greed was possibly also in Rome. Sloth was definitely in Bristol. As usual, he had no idea where Pride was. One of the others might know; Envy's papers might hold the answer. Fisher guessed he was clutching at straws.

In Paris Fisher used his guise as a museum employee to transport the swords as cultural artefacts. Reymond was now his assistant.

Reymond phoned each of his moles and information gatherers in turn. Their information brought him no closer to finding Pride. He was more confident that Greed was indeed in Rome.

They settled in to the Emirates lounge, and as they sipped their drinks Reymond briefed Fisher.

"I hope to gain information in the next few days that will

lead me to set you upon the third task. This time it may not be something you will be able to do alone."

"Not a simple courier job, then?" Fisher wondered if the next man on the list could be prevailed upon to tell him how to break the oath.

"I am afraid not." Reymond took a sip of complimentary wine, scanning the room for danger, as was his habit.

"Where?" Fisher asked.

"Armenia, I think. Like I said, I hope to get the information in a couple of days."

"I'll await your word."

Reymond nodded and raised a glass. "To old friends." He gave a deep heartfelt sigh before drinking. Fisher gulped his.

Which of them would be next? Which of them could tell him how to break the oath? He regretted not asking Jobert.

# Brindisi, Italy 1097

"Look out!"

Reymond barely dodged the large trunk being manhandled off the ship. The chest tipped, sliding away from the two servants and dropped to the quayside. The short bandy-legged man dressed as a sailor, who had shouted the warning, rushed over. "Are you hurt, yes?"

"No, I am fine," Reymond told him, hoping he didn't look as shaken up as he felt.

The sailor looked him up and down as if checking he still had all his limbs, and turned on the servants with a snarl. "You stupid! You almost brain that nobleman, yes?" He stormed back to the two servants, berating them as they shamefacedly tried to gather up all the canvas, ropes and other paraphernalia spilling from the overturned chest. He then turned and shouted at the crew to get back to work; obviously he was not just a sailor, he was the captain.

The docks were a hive of activity: a riotous mix of colours, accents, languages, smells of spice, incense, the sour rotten stink of old seaweed and dead fish. A flock of gulls rose squawking above the boats whilst a flotilla of other sea birds bobbed about in the water. It was overwhelming to a country boy, though Reymond didn't like to think of himself as a bumpkin any more – more a man of the world.

Charles had assigned various of the men tasks in the city but several of the unit, including Reymond, were left with nothing to do. In an uncharacteristic fit of generosity the sergeant gave them the day to wander the city. Reymond felt it was because he didn't want to babysit them. The others had wanted to go and find drink, but Reymond wanted to see the sea, so had wandered down to the docks.

Brindisi was packed with crusading armies, everyone seeking passage across to Byzantium. He was surprised that even though he couldn't afford armour, the sailor had mistaken him for a noble due to his surcoat. He wondered if he could take advantage of this, and get a ship for his unit.

Reymond called to attract the attention of the captain. The man looked over at him, distracted, and the two men loading the boat clattered into him with their burden and sent him over the side of the dock. After a beat, Reymond kicked off his shoes and dived into the cold scummy water after him, hoping the sailor could swim. Everyone else seemed frozen in place.

The man thrashed about, an action that didn't even come close to swimming. Despite his heroics Reymond himself was not the strongest swimmer, and as he made a grab for the man, who floundered just beyond his grasp, he was beginning to regret his leap into the filthy water. He spotted a tall, rangy man dressed in green leather with a bow slung over a shoulder watching from the dock and waved for his attention as the captain went under. Lunging for him, Reymond struggled to get him up. He was gasping and coughing now, eyes streaming so he could barely make out the hunter's dive to join them. Belatedly the crew on deck had spotted the struggling men and had thrown a rope. The hunter grabbed onto him, pressed the rope into his hand. Then he grabbed the sailor and between them, with help from the quayside, they manhandled the bedraggled man out of the water.

The three men sat on the dockside in a spreading puddle. The hunter wrung water out of his clothes, shaking his head, a pile of his belongings including a bow and arrows safely dry on the dockside. Shivering, Reymond put his hand out.

"Reymond."

The hunter spat, shook his hand. "Jules."

The sailor looked from one to the other, put his own hand onto the other two. "Andros, yes."

"Andros? What sort of name is Andros?" Reymond asked.

Andros looked stung. "Is my name, yes? Is fine name." The little man slapped his chest and grinned. "Come, Andros has grog yes, and dry things." Andros led the other two to his boat. Despite his insouciance Reymond noticed that the little man was trembling. Grog definitely seemed like a good idea.

†

"You need passage to Holy Land, yes? Andros take. He have best boat in fleet."

In the cramped captain's cabin they'd dried themselves off and changed into borrowed clothes; Reymond's, being a little too small, exposing his midriff and calves. The little man had fetched a bottle of liquor and they passed it between them.

"Really? That is fortunate. Do you have room for my unit too?" asked Reymond.

Andros nodded, smiling.

"How much?" Jules wanted to know. "I'd also like passage."

Andros put his head to one side, thinking hard.

"You save Andros life, yes? You go free." He grinned. "But..."

"But?" Reymond prompted him.

"You take Andros with you when you go to fight, yes? Andros want to take the cross, fight Saracen, serve God." The little man put his hands together in a begging gesture.

"What about your ship? Your business?" Reymond asked.

"Is fine yes, brother is first mate, sailing is fine, yes? But can't take ship to Jerusalem, and crusade is duty of every Christian man, yes?"

"In that case we have a deal," Reymond said. "If I can convince my commander."

Andros beamed. "Come, grog!" he said.

After a glass of something fiery and tasting of aniseed, Reymond went to find his unit, dressed in borrowed clothes.

"And he has enough room for all of us?" Charles asked. Reymond was not used to being the centre of attention and stood awkwardly, his cheeks hot, trying not to stammer.

"Yes, sir."

"And you just happened to pass by whilst this sailor was drowning?"

"Yes, sir." Out of the corner of his eye he could see Pierre, stood behind the sergeant, blowing kisses at him. Reymond could imagine what he looked like in the ill-fitting sailor's costume and gulped.

Mikael and Samuel looked as if they wished they'd not gone drinking. Reymond had heard William, who was nowhere to be seen, throwing up when he'd returned.

"Well that is a stroke of good fortune isn't it?" Charles said.

"Yes sir."

Charles narrowed his eyes. "That was some quick thinking."

"Only did what anyone else would have done, sir," Reymond answered.

"Not saving the sailor, any of this lot would have done that," Charles glanced at the rest of the unit, "well most of them anyway. No, asking for passage, that was smart."

"Thank you, sir."

"I need someone quick-witted to serve me. From now on you are at my beck and call. Understand?"

Reymond blinked. "Sir, yes sir!"

"Fall out then. Sergeant, with me. Reymond isn't it?"

"Yes sir."

"Stay within earshot."

As Charles and the sergeant headed to Charles's rooms,

Mikael and Samuel came and slapped Reymond on the back. Mikael was even smiling, or maybe it was a grimace?

"Well done!" Samuel said.

"What the hell are you wearing?" Mikael asked.

"Reymond!" The Sergeant's shout made the three jump.

"Coming!" Reymond grinned at the other two and then rushed off to see what Charles wanted doing.

Reymond brought Andros and Jules into the temporary barracks Charles had created in the stables of the local inn. Mikael and Jules exchanged a long, evaluating look.

"I'd like to join you," Jules said. "I'm a good fighter and have been looking for a company to join with. Your man here," he pointed to Reymond, "seemed to be in the right place at the right time. Captain Andros has agreed to transport me so we'll be travelling together anyway."

"An archer?" Charles stroked his chin. "Well that may come in useful. Report to the sergeant. Captain?"

Andros and Charles shook hands. "My man here tells me you are going to take us to Byzantium."

"Sure. I can take, yes." The small sailor grinned.

"For free."

"No. No, him for free, yes, and him." Andros pointed to Reymond and Jules. "You? Not so free."

The sergeant sidled over and soon the three men were conducting a heated exchange about the costs of sea travel, the price of food, the difficulties of raising children with a lack of money and other such mercantile concerns. Reymond lost interest and went to sit with Jules and Mikael.

"Mikael tells me we are in Robert Curthose's army. You never told me I'd be working for the King of England's brother," Jules said.

"You never asked. Is it a problem? Are you going to join

our group?" Reymond barely differentiated the various nobles. They were all too high and mighty for him to concern himself over. He was more interested in getting fed regularly.

"Yes. I have taken the cross and sworn to serve Charles the Bold. It's no problem. It's just that I left England to get away, and here I am working for the king's brother."

He didn't say what he left England to get away from, and Reymond didn't ask. Soon they'd be setting sail, Jerusalem was getting ever closer.

Later, hanging over the side of Andros's ship, Reymond regretted drinking, regretted jumping into the sea after Andros, and regretted leaving the farm.

Andros slapped him on the back, prompting him to puke again.

"You soon have sea legs, yes?" Andros chuckled before walking on to perform one of the endless tasks necessary to get a small sailing vessel across the sea, and leaving Reymond to his misery.

His only consolation was that he wasn't the only one. William, who he thought should already have had an empty stomach, also hung greenly over the side. Mikael and Samuel sat playing dice with Jules. None of them seemed affected. Pierre, however, was groaning along the railing. The big man looked less fierce than usual, and slightly green. "Any comment from you and I'll cut your liver out and feed it to the seagulls." They both thought about that image and both heaved over the side.

A few hours later, feeling more seaworthy, Reymond watched the sandy and scrub-lined coast go past as the fleet sailed towards the Holy Land. He took a deep breath, fancying he could smell desert spices. He spotted Jules at the end of the bow, and ambled over to him, the ship rolling beneath his feet.

"What do you think Jerusalem will be like?" he asked.

"Jerusalem, is it? It'll be a while before we see Jerusalem, lad."

Reymond nodded, as if he knew what Jules was talking about, and turned his face back to the land slipping by, watching out eagerly for the Saracen horde. Reymond fingered the cross sewn onto his tabard and his hand fell to the pommel of his sword. Soon, he thought, soon he could fulfil his oath. He was on his way to the Holy Land.

Some weeks later Constantinople came into view. Reymond was stunned by the size of the city. The gravity defying buildings that seemed to go on forever, the flags in a thousand colours that snapped in the wind, the smell of a hundred exotic spices. He was therefore crushed to find that they would not be stopping but carrying on and crossing the Bosphorous as soon as possible. They were told the army was to set up camp outside the walls of the city. As they trudged to their new camp Reymond, Mikael and Andros passed on the rumours they'd heard to Samuel, William and the rest of the unit.

"Peter the Hermit had a force several thousand strong and they were wiped out by the Saracen in one battle, I heard," Reymond said.

"There was a mountain of bodies," Mikael added.

"And they took away all beautiful women, yes, and boys for slaves," Andros chipped in.

"You'll be safe then." Mikael jogged Reymond's elbow, and they all laughed.

"They say walls of city are twenty feet thick, yes, and seven miles long and inside is a thousand palaces and a hundred thousand eunuchs."

"Why do they need so many eunuchs?" Reymond wanted to know, not entirely sure what a eunuch was, but not wanting to reveal his ignorance.

"To guard harem of Emperor Alexius, yes. Would love to have tour of harem," Andros said dreamily.

"You only ever think with what's inside your pants. You'd better be careful. The emperor might need another eunuch!" The men of the unit laughed, and Reymond joined in after a beat. Andros looked pained, reflexively covering his private parts.

Charles interrupted this ribaldry.

"Robert has sworn the oath to the emperor that will allow us to move on. We are going to war..."

# Yerevan, Armenia 2012

MARI WAS BORED of roulette, and five card stud, and blackjack and oh, all gambling. But it was necessary to feign interest in her new job.

She'd never seen Andros, but she'd heard plenty of rumours. How he kept a harem of women, how he'd lift the croupiers he liked from their dull, poor lives and give them a taste of extravagant living, then dump them once they bored him. Didn't seem to deter the others though; many of them would give their right arms to be chosen by him.

Mari wondered about people sometimes. Why would you hanker for that, to be given a taste of something then spat out, poorer and with less opportunity than before? They couldn't all think they could change him, could they? Mari knew she wasn't pretty enough to catch the eye of the big cheese; not that she'd stoop to that level to pay off the debt though.

Nikolozi, the ugly Georgian, seemed to take pity on her occasionally and sent her on little errands and slipped her a tip now and then. She knew that he had a soft spot for her, and that was creepy, but she was grateful for the chance to earn extra cash. Here he came now.

"Hey Mari."

"Hey, Nikolozi."

"Want to earn a bit of extra cash?"

"Sure." She wondered what it'd be this time.

"Take this package," he handed her a small sports bag, "to Suite 7136 and ask for Ryu."

"7136, Ryu, got it." That seemed simple enough. "What's in it?"

"Don't ask questions." He gave her a little shooing motion.

7136 was in a part of the hotel the casino staff never went to. When she'd gone through induction they were told to stay out of the hotel apart from the casino. But she'd heard that floor seven was off-limits to the hotel staff too. Only those that had been hand-picked by Andros were allowed up there.

She took the lift to floor seven. When she got out it was quiet. It felt illicit. She opened the paper map of the hotel she still had to carry with her everywhere, much folded to fit in her pocket, and worked out where she was. She knew the casino and the back offices pretty well and had seen some floors of accommodation, knowing the customers stayed there. That left the vast kitchen and basement areas, the top floor, where she suspected Andros had his lair, and the mysterious seventh floor. She'd never heard of any guest staying there, but a couple of the staff who'd been there the longest had mentioned it in hushed tones. She headed to 7136.

Mari could hear voices approaching. She was totally exposed in the corridor. She hoped that being here at Nikolozi's request would be good enough.

Two burly men in ill-fitting suits came round the corner and stopped. The younger of the two leered at her and looked her up and down. The older frowned at her.

"What are you doing here?"

"Nikolozi asked me to bring this bag to 7136 and ask for Ryu."

The two security guys looked at each other.

The older fished a mobile out of his pocket and speed dialled a number.

"Yeah there's a girl on the 7th floor. Said she'd been sent up here by Nikolozi?"

He stared at her and the younger guy stared at her chest in a way that made her feel uncomfortable.

"Sure thing boss." He hung up. "You can go, but no dawdling."

The younger guy seemed confused. The older guy gestured down the corridor.

She walked on until she reached the right room. She gave the door a few knocks. She saw the peephole go dark and the sound of the chain being lifted off the lock then the door swung open.

Inside there was a middle-aged Japanese guy in a vest. He was the most tattooed man she'd ever seen.

"I have a delivery," she said, holding the bag up.

He sniffed and gestured her in with his head.

"I have to get back to work, so if you could just take the bag..."

The Japanese man scratched his bald head and sniffed again. She wasn't prepared for him to grab her and pull her into the room.

He slammed the door as he pushed her down the very short corridor, she started to struggle; too late. He shoved her into the room and ripped the bag out of her hands.

She stood rubbing her arm, which was going to bruise, and scowled at the man as he opened the bag. He pulled out a big plastic bag full of white powder. Oh shit.

He grabbed his nose and hacked as though he had phlegm at the back of his throat.

"Get undressed," he said as he pulled a knife from a pocket and flicked it open.

She stood with her hand on her arm, across her chest. She shook her head.

"You're the girl that Nikolozi sent aren't you?"

She nodded.

"Well I'm going to have some blow and then you're going to fuck me and then I'll give you some cash to give to Nikolozi and he may even let you keep some of it." Ryu said all of this with no inflection. It was matter of fact, a done deal. He jabbed the knife into the package and took his eyes off her.

She picked up the nearest thing to hand, an ugly lamp, and swung it with all her strength at his head. It took him completely by surprise. But when it smashed he merely howled and his eyes flared. She saw a piece of porcelain sticking out of his temple and one half of his face was suddenly crimson with blood. He threw the package onto the bed and all she could think was: Run, run, run!

As she turned his fist described a perfect semicircle to end up connecting behind her ear. She'd only ever been punched once before, years ago, by a girl a year older than her in school. Being punched by a full grown man was, she found, different to being punched by an eleven year old girl. She seemed to jump across the bed without trying. Her head was ringing, she smelled or tasted copper.

She landed on the package and something jabbed her in the ribs. He fell upon her and grabbed a fistful of hair and pulled. Her head jolted on her neck and her already teary eyes crossed. The knife, the thing that had jabbed her in the ribs, was in her hand. It was in his neck. Her hand let go, he staggered back.

Ryu tapped his shoulder three times before he grasped the knife sticking out of his throat. Mari backed away, shaking her head. Ryu pulled the knife out and there was a spray of bright red arterial blood across the wall. He gurgled something and lunged for her. She danced out of the way, to the other side of the bed, the other lamp. She held it out as he burbled. He belatedly seemed to realise his life was spurting all over the room and dropped the knife. He took a step towards her with one arm out, the other hand to his neck, which only seemed to direct the blood to spurt upwards.

She threatened him with the other lamp. He grinned and

dropped to his knees, his hand came away and there was another fountain of blood and then he put one hand out and lowered himself to the floor and curled into a foetal position and stopped moving.

Mari's chest heaved and she couldn't seem to let go of the lamp. She stood staring at Ryu for what felt like a lifetime. He didn't move. She put one foot out and poked him in the shoulder. Nothing.

She dropped the lamp and put her hands over her mouth and nose, then made fists under her mouth, she crouched and rocked back and forth. She'd killed him. He thought she was a whore. Nikolazi had sent her here as a whore. She'd killed him. That was the debt fucked. That was everything fucked. What was she going to do?

On the bed the white package sat like a fresh turd on a white cashmere rug. She could sell it! She grabbed it, wrapped it in a pillowcase to stop it leaking and shoved it back into the bag and slung the bag over her shoulder. She grabbed the bedding in both hands and threw it over the dead man.

What the hell was she thinking. Sell it? Who to? How'd she get out of the hotel without security seeing her? Without Nikolozi seeing her, without it being reported to the boss?

She searched the room, avoiding the blood, avoiding the body. Ryu had hung up a holster, with a pistol in it, in the wardrobe. Her father had shown her how to shoot and where his pistol was kept in the house, in case she'd have to fend off any intruders. They'd been hunting a few times: she'd never learned to enjoy killing animals, but she was a good shot. She'd not found the handgun when she was looking for things to sell. She wondered if she could shoot a man... in self-defence maybe. She was taking it.

There was a ledger, in Japanese, and three other key cards but no indication as to which rooms they were for. She took them anyway.

She went and looked at herself in the mirror: no blood on

her that she could see. Her hair was a mess; she combed it with her fingers as best she could, but she looked too pale. She splashed water on her face.

She could tell the security guards that she was on her way back to the casino. Had she been in the room long enough? She went and listened at the door. She could hear them.

There was a peephole that showed a fisheye view of the corridor. She put her eye to it and awaited the approaching men. Their voices were muffled, but they could still be understood.

"No fight left in him," said one.

"I wouldn't be so sure. Did you see that sniper rifle? That's professional, that is," replied his companion.

"Why'd he have a sword then?"

"Because the boss likes swords. Does all that duelling shit, doesn't he? Perhaps he's a rival duellist?"

The two men passed down the corridor, leaving her wondering at the reference to a sword.

Mari decided to scoot down the hall and try a few doors. She had some key cards now. She could always run back to this room if she heard the security guards coming. What she really needed was a way out.

She cracked open the door and stood listening at the gap for a while. When she was sure that no-one was about she sneaked over to the room opposite and used the key. It flashed green. She gripped hold of the gun and pushed it open.

This wasn't a standard hotel room. It was set up as a security hub. Banks of CCTV screens with a leather chair in front. She wondered if the two men she'd seen earlier would drop in on the room at some point. She took a look at the screens hoping to see that there was a clear way out. She wasn't prepared for what she saw.

A couple of the rooms were set up as cells. In one, strapped to what looked like a dentist's chair, with three men standing over him, was her father. She stared at the screen in disbelief. It was definitely him. She gripped the gun and wondered what was going on. Her father had been missing for months – if he was in the casino why had the casino been hassling her mother, and now her, to pay off his debts?

There were surprisingly few guards, although more were probably a couple of minutes away, scattered through the rest of the hotel.

She checked the clip of her gun. If she could get her father out, together they could escape. She didn't think they'd ever be able to go home but they could possibly get out of the country, to Georgia maybe.

She searched the office. She turned up a small hatchet in a drawer, and a locker held a shotgun, but no cartridges. She took it anyway. She also took a rubber torch and a walkie-talkie.

The room numbers were written in permanent marker on tape stuck onto the monitors. Her father was in 7007. She was going to rescue him. She made sure she knew how the gun worked. No-one was going to stand in her way.

Maybe the fact that her father had taken her hunting was going to come in useful after all?

# Nicea, The Holy Land 1097

THE CITY OF one hundred towers was surrounded on all sides by great walls and a double ditch. It had been under siege for a few weeks by the time Charles's unit arrived. The city was vaguely hexagonal with two walls on an adjacent lake. The crusader army surrounded it and there was a mess of tents, siege engines, half-built and finished, and throngs of men between them and the city.

The smell of smoke, human waste and decomposition was almost physical. The walls were hazy behind the ubiquitous dust thrown up by the army but Reymond could see that they were decorated with dead crusaders. Reymond wondered how they obtained the bodies, and it wasn't long before he got his answer. As one wave of crusaders fell back from the wall, leaving a number of broken bodies behind, the Saracen gathered in knots above the dead. Reymond frowned, shaded his eyes and tried to see what was happening. The Saracen lowered iron hooks on long ropes to drag the bodies up the wall. The dead crusaders, like so many carcasses ready to be butchered, rose jerkily on the ropes. Reymond was reminded of when his father used to slaughter pigs by hoisting them up by their hind legs. His stomach roiled and he shook his head. Once the bodies were dragged across the top of the wall they were stripped, anything not of use being flung back. The Saracen then held them up so that they were in sight of the crusaders forming up for another attack and cut their manhood from them, tossing them down the wall. Each corpse was then mounted on a spear and displayed, gruesome trophies to remind the attackers of what lay in store for them.

"They will pay," he muttered and Mikael tapped him on the shoulder, and silently pointed to the crusader camp.

The crusading army, having broken a sally some days ago, had plenty of Saracen heads adorning spears outside certain tents.

Charles's unit was put with the sappers. Their main task was to trundle the testudo, a siege engine resembling a tortoise, to the wall and watch for counter-attacks. The sappers would then dig tunnels and set fires under the walls. Basically they were wanted for muscle more than anything else.

Eventually their unit was called to take its turn. Reymond was so nervous he could piss, and most of the others seemed no better. Pepin looked like he was about to faint; being so small he'd be little use as muscle anyway. Pierre was the only one that seemed nonchalant, joking that they were about to earn their keep. Reymond had spent so long imagining this, both looking forward to and fearing the moment, and to his surprise it was more a nightmare than something glorious. Maybe the glory would come later?

They stood in the baking heat, dressed in padded armour, waiting for the signal that would start the attack. To his right Reymond saw the Tafurs. Holy madmen, mostly unarmoured. In the heart of their ranks, the man they called Le Roi Tafur, and what looked like a boy, dressed in a simple white robe, long golden hair flowing loose about his shoulders. They appeared to be praying, and he thought that was not such a bad idea.

Several red flags went up and waved, and at the signal the army lumbered forward. Slowly at first, but gaining pace all the while. The muscles in Reymond's shoulders bunched as he helped to push the bombardment screen towards the walls of Nicaea. He watched the Tafurs stop just outside of arrow range, their charge a ruse to divert attention.

As the testudo rumbled and bounced its way across the battlefield it took on a life of its own. A man from Reymond's unit stumbled and fell, and Reymond had to leap over him, pushing the testudo all the while. He glanced back to see an arrow sticking out of the man's throat. Only this morning the man had been complaining about the rubbish they were being forced to eat. Reymond ran and pushed hard, his mouth dry, eyes stinging from the dust thrown up from the wheels. An arrow whizzed past his face, missing his head by a foot. It was impossible to hear anything over the trundling siege engine.

When they got to the wall Reymond cowered in the cover of the testudo. It was close; the rank smell of the men combined with the hot stink of spilled blood and opened intestines made him gag.

There was a clever mechanism of leather buckets on a pulley, and he was told to pull and empty them as the sappers dug into the soil around the base of the wall. There was a loud clunk, followed by several more, rattling against the sloping roof of the contraption. The defenders were throwing rocks.

One of the ballistae scored a lucky hit, taking three men out with one bombardment. Another man was crushed by a falling rock the size of a sheep. His screams were high pitched, like a child's. Pierre, in front of Reymond, delivered a mercy blow before the noise could drive them all deeper into terror. Now the air was filled with the grunts of the labourers, the shouts of enemy soldiers, the thud of stones and arrows against wood, and the moans of the dying.

This is Hell, Reymond thought. I am already in Hell.

A massive stone landed on the front of the siege engine, causing it to leap like a slapped mule, and the order was called for retreat. They bumped and jounced the testudo back across the battlefield. It was more difficult on the way back. The engine was heavier, and there were less men to push it. When they reached their lines Reymond's knees buckled with exhaustion. All around him men were collapsing from the heat and the release of tension. Another unit was manoeuvred into place and theirs was told to go and rest. "See that wasn't so bad," Pierre said grinning, walking past.

Reymond flopped down in the camp after drinking a lake's worth of water. He looked for his friends, relieved to find them alive. Andros, Jules and Mikael were as dirty as he was. Samuel was picking splinters out of his hands. Jean wrapped a bandage around William's head where an arrow had nicked a groove through his scalp which bled like a bastard. Mikael had a minor cut on one cheek from a flying splinter of rock.

"You're lucky your nose is so squashed and broken, or that rock would have taken it off!" Reymond teased him.

Andros laughed, Jules just nodded.

Charles passed amongst his men, giving quiet praise, a word or two of encouragement to men who may have had their first encounter with bloody warfare. The sergeant was taking a tally. They had lost several of their number. Reymond made the effort to sit up. The wall was still there; the defenders still defiant.

He didn't know what it'd all been for.

"We have four hours, then it's our turn again." Charles said. He looked sympathetic as he clapped Reymond on the shoulder. "You did well," Charles said to him, before he moved on to comfort the rest of his tired men.

Three more times in the next few days Reymond took his turn pushing the testudo. The latest assault was etched firmly in his mind's eye, replayed in his nightmares. The ballistae had scored a direct hit on the men in front of him. One of Charles's men, and someone who Reymond had shared meals with, a solid, quiet presence in the unit was one of them. His neck snapped from the force of a rock striking it. Reymond was still trying to get over the loss of the one or two men he had known since joining up, even if he only knew them to nod to. He glanced around making sure that men he cared for were still whole and hearty. Everyone had their heads down. So it was Reymond that noticed the line of men on the wall lifting buckets. As something black slopped out of the buckets Reymond's eyes opened wide.

"Oil. 'Ware, Oil!" he shouted as a great splash of foul smelling bitumen rained down on the men in front of him. He barely had time to see men head to toe in black before the first fire arrow hit and the volatile mixture of oil, tar and pitch ignited. Samuel screamed as the front of his trousers and tabard were set alight and Reymond grabbed him and rolled him in the sandy mud until the flames went out.

Samuel grinned at him but Reymond stared beyond him, at the men screaming and burning like torches. The heat was ferocious. Reymond had a blistered arm. He didn't think he'd ever get the cloying burned meat smell out of his hair, his clothes or his memory. The days were going to grind on. How far now to Jerusalem?

†

There were trumpets in the distance and Reymond stood, shading his eyes to see another contingent of the crusader army arriving. They manoeuvred into place whilst the trumpets blared out a warning. Reymond looked to the west and saw a Saracen force, mounted on their swift ponies, pouring out of the wooded hills to converge on the Provencals' position. Reymond watched, horrified. If the Saracen overran the Provencals they would attack Charles's position next. So far all the sword drill had been in vain. Their unit had never seen the enemy up close. Perhaps now?

The men around him craned to see what was happening. Over the sounds of the ballistae and the cthunk-chunk of rocks falling from the walls of the beleaguered city, Reymond could just hear the sounds of men roaring, horses screaming. A cloud of dust had been churned up, obscuring the fight, but he had the impression the Provencals were holding.

To his left Reymond saw two contingents of heavy horse set off, speeding up until their hoof beats added a lower bass to the air.

Reymond found himself shouting, along with the men around him. "Trust in Christ and the Holy Cross!" They cheered their army on as the two sides came together with the force of an earthquake.

The Saracen broke, fleeing to the south. Reymond cheered as Jules clapped him on the back causing him to stagger. All around his comrades were grinning.

The sounds of the ongoing assault reasserted themselves, and as fast as it arrived, the surge of energy and hope vanished. Reymond wondered if they'd ever advance further than Nicaea.

†

The following night Charles gathered his men together. There were noticeably fewer of them now, and Reymond was shocked to see that Heribert and Pepin, the brothers who signed up together in France, were no longer in their number. He'd missed their deaths. He resolved to pray for them. Charles chewed his lip before launching into a speech. "Boys, we've been asked to perform a special task, one that isn't without danger and involves humping a heavy object." There were groans; the men were fed up with the testudo. The wall stood firm despite the fires that had been started underneath it.

"It's not a siege engine this time."

Reymond exchanged a glance with Mikael who looked equally mystified.

"We're going to help move some boats," Charles explained.

A few of the men seemed to get it at once, Reymond looked

to the lake at the westward face of the city. It had been apparent from the start that the Saracen were resupplying the city using boats across the lake. Despite some raids, the area was too large for the crusaders to control.

"Where are the boats coming from?" Reymond asked.

Charles grinned. "Where else? From the Empire." It seemed that the Emperor was going to join them, after all.

Over the next two days they marched to where the boats were, and a couple of days after that Reymond found himself amongst the men hauling specially constructed wagons with boats riding on them. He ached all over, and his jerkin had large salt rings around the armpit. Tireless boys skipped up and down the line with leather cups of water. It never seemed to be enough to quench his thirst, and Reymond had long since lost his fastidiousness about drinking water that had an unhealthy dose of other men's spit in it. He was thankful that disease had so far eluded him, having seen many of his companions fall to dysentery.

"How far do we have to take these things again?" Mikael asked.

"Eighteen miles." They were travelling barely a mile per hour.

"Tell me how we volunteered for this?" Mikael asked.

"How will this bring us closer to God?" Samuel added.

Reymond was too tired to grumble. "I wish I knew. Now, shut up and keep walking."

Two days later, Reymond watched as the boats were launched onto the lake. Charles's unit spontaneously stripped off and swam after the boats for a short distance, horsing around and unwinding from the hot, tedious walk. Reymond ducked William, whose torn ear had healed into a ragged flag of pride. Samuel floated on his back, until Reymond and William surfaced underneath him and tipped him over. Jules dived and swam out further to avoid the others. Andros splashed about like a puppy, grinning from ear to ear. Later, on the shoreline, Reymond ambled until he found Andros staring wistfully at the slowly receding sails.

"Wish you were still a sailor?" he asked.

"I always be a sailor, yes. Just now, between ships." The small man reflected. "I did not expect this."

"This?"

"War yes? It is different. Lots of boredom yes, amongst the terror. No control. No women." The little sailor grinned at last.

Reymond shook his head. "I had no thought as to what war would be like. More glorious, I expect."

Jules and Mikael walked up. "What are you talking about?" Mikael asked. Jules stared out into the distance across the water: always on guard, always watchful. Samuel and William were still in the water, indefatigable in their pursuit of relaxation.

"The glories of war, yes," Andros said, again wistful.

"Glories? Ha!" Mikael snorted.

"We'll soon be back at the battlefront," Reymond said. "Might as well make the most of this. Who wants to come for another swim?"

Charles let his men relax for the evening, but in the morning the sergeant had them up and moving early, heading back towards the city. When they returned to their lines, Reymond could see and hear an assault taking place against the stubborn east wall. He wondered if they would be asked to join it, and his heart sank at the thought of being forced under the testudo once more.

To his relief, the sergeant got them to check the camp and perform maintenance instead. Maintenance was better than the siege engine any day, and Reymond found that sewing tents and sharpening blades helped to calm him down.

"Back to the grindstone," Mikael mumbled, staring at the city, the distant sounds of battle a soft hum that belied the fact that men were dying beneath the walls.

"Maybe they'll have something else for us to do?" Reymond asked optimistically. "What can you see?" Jules stood on a crate, hand shading his eyes.

"We are attacking," he said simply.

They fell to their tasks until Charles returned, gathering the men so he could address them.

"The city has surrendered," he said. "The siege is over."

The men cheered expansively. Reymond wondered if they were the first to know, or the last. He hadn't heard much cheering from any other camp. He stood to stare at the city that had defied them for weeks.

"Has anyone told them that?"

He pointed to the east wall, which still swarmed with the attacking army.

Charles frowned. "Messengers have been sent," he said. "We won't be entering the city. The emperor has taken control here. We're to carry on into Syria and take Antioch, and a few weeks after that, Jerusalem. But tonight we celebrate!"

# Northern Iran, near the Turkish border 1982

PATIENCE HAD RETURNED and pumped Fisher full of antibiotics, Fisher hoped it would do the trick. The many hours of waiting for the other man to return, alternatively sweating and shivering with cold, were some of the worst of his life. The hours since his fever had broken stretched as the Frenchman paced, made sure Fisher was hydrated, and scanned the horizon with the sniper, although surely he couldn't see much in the starlight? Hawksmoor's APC hadn't materialised. Surely they couldn't have been that far ahead of them? Maybe they'd gone another way. People in Turkey hadn't seen the American according to Patience.

As morning broke Fisher was awake, but weak and shaky. He took more antibiotics and managed a weak grin. "Looks like saving me life is getting to be a habit."

"I got us fresher food. Do you feel up to eating?" Fisher was ravenous, but he made sure to leave an equal share of the bread, fruit and cheese for the Frenchman, in case he hadn't eaten whilst Fisher was unconscious. Patience took a chunk of bread and between bites said, "The APC will come across the border down there." Patience pointed down the hill to a forlorn looking road.

"Yeah, the border guards have been bribed. It'll be tonight. Or maybe tomorra night. What day is it?"

"Thursday, I think."

Fisher nodded. "Tomorra then. Holy day. Gerraway with a lot more."

The other man nodded. "So who is on board again?"

"Hawksmoor, you know. There's also his sidekick, Aussie bloke, and two other bad pennies." Fisher counted off on his fingers.

"It is obvious you are not going anywhere. We will hit them at the border control. Do you reckon you can hit a barn door with the sniper?"

Fisher shrugged. "A barn door? Probably."

"How about an armoured vehicle?"

"Yeah."

Patience grinned. "You keep them pinned down. I will do the rest. I only want the book."

"About that?" Fisher said.

"Yes?"

"Why's it so important? Why ya all the way out here in the arse end of nowhere fighting the Burpers for the scribblings of a madman?"

"Who said it was the scribblings of a madman? And what in the hell are 'Burpers'?"

"Carry on up the Khyber? It's a film? You French have no culture." Fisher laughed. "Look, I heard Hawksmoor describe it as being written by a mad bloke."

"I sincerely hope any insanity the author may or may not have had does not come across in the book."

Fisher was sceptical.

"It was written around the time of the First Crusade," Patience told him.

"In the twelfth century? And it's still readable? I'd've thought it would've crumbled into dust by now. My paperbacks fall apart faster than you can say 'airport special'."

"Indeed. It wasn't written on paper, but on something a little more durable. It may hold the secret I have been looking for."

"Secret?"

Patience nodded, solemn. "Yes, just that. Literally the answer to my dreams. Well, nightmares."

Strange. Fisher shrugged. "Okay, you don't have to tell me. I understand. How're we going to play this?"

"I am going to get close. When the APC shows up I will let it approach the crossing and stop, then you shoot. Bonus points if you can hit the driver. If not, I will try and get on board and make sure your erstwhile friends have a terrible day."

There wasn't much cover for hundreds of yards all around the border post, and there wasn't a lot of traffic going in and out of Iran. Tricky. The sun inched across the sky. The first faint sign of movement on the horizon, a blur in the dust, too early for sound. Fisher shook himself alert. He shaded his eyes. A car or truck, possibly even an APC, was approaching from the Iranian side of the border. Fisher wondered if Patience had the right timing. Like comedy, the timing had to be right or it would all come apart and he wouldn't be laughing. The vehicle approached. It was bigger than a car. Did buses travel this road? From a war-zone? Truck or APC? He looked through the sniper: it was the APC. He wished he could warn the Frenchman.

The APC got closer to where he thought Patience was hiding, closer still, and the Frenchman was up and running. He was half way to the border post when the guards spotted him.

The APC turret opened and a large, black man, obviously not an Iranian, popped up, clutching an automatic rifle. Fisher squeezed off a shot: it missed but made the man duck back into the APC as it rumbled to a halt.

The border guards must have thought Patience was the cause of the shot as they opened fire on him. Fisher watched as the Frenchman changed the angle of his run. The APC had stopped too far away, engine idling. The border guards might get lucky; he sighted on one of them and shot. The border guard went down, his life expelled as pink mist, the sniper silent to them at this distance. The other dropped to the ground. The APC revved, lurching forward.

Fisher watched as the turret opened again and a pair of arms holding an automatic strafed the area where Patience had been seconds before. He couldn't get a bead and Patience dived and rolled and was up the side of the APC as fast as a monkey up a tree. His sword sliced neatly through two black wrists, exposing shockingly red discs of meat.

Screams burst from the APC, tiny at this distance. The gun kept firing as it fell inside, bullets ricocheting inside the vehicle, no doubt finding metal and flesh. The APC lurched and the Frenchman was thrown flat. It came to a dead stop and the door burst open.

Two men jumped out. Hawksmoor and one other. Fisher tried to get a clear shot but the Frenchman was in the way, moving fast. He watched as Patience threw the sword and it pierced Hawksmoor through the shoulder, spinning him around. His companion shot from point blank range, but his bullets seemed to miss Patience as Fisher saw them striking sparks from the vehicle's armour.

Patience's shot did not miss. The man slumped heavily with a perforated head. Fisher scoped back to Hawksmoor who was no longer on the ground; he had the sword in his hands, which he thrust into Patience's guts. The Frenchman staggered back and slid down the side of the APC. Fisher's shot caused Hawksmoor to drop. Fisher was up and running, leaving the sniper behind, carrying an automatic.

When he got to the APC the man inside was still screaming. But there was no sign of Hawksmoor. Fisher span in a full circle, frowning, he couldn't understand it. Hawksmoor must be in the ditch running along the side of the road. He took a step toward it but a loud groan from the Frenchman stopped him. He was still alive!

Fisher jumped up on the APC and shot the screaming black man. The driver was dead, hit by a stray bullet. Patience looked down at the end of his own sword, sticking out a foot from his belly. This meant at least another foot would be sticking out the other side. Fisher wondered what happened to the other border guard. He wondered if he should go after Hawksmoor. He wondered if it would be better or worse to pull out the sword. He wondered how much longer Patience had to live.

The Frenchman was still conscious when Fisher knelt beside him. He grinned weakly. "I am not sure which of us looks worse." At least he hadn't bled to death, although the ground all around him was sticky, moist, and red.

"Bugger." As a statement Fisher wasn't sure this had entirely covered the situation.

"Get me into the APC and let us get the fuck out of here. The Turkish army will be here any second."

"Should I move you?" Fisher looked at the sword with trepidation.

"Yes. Yes, just do it."

Fisher hauled him up and Patience growled, low and deep. Fisher put him on his side in the APC and pushed the dead driver and the dead black man out and jumped into the driver's seat.

He started it up, reversed and made a U turn. It was an uncomfortable ride. After minutes of jouncing up and down he glanced back and saw that the sword was scissoring through the Frenchman's guts. Patience gritted his teeth and, panting like a dog, slowly, gradually pulled it out. As the last of the sword came out there was a gush of hot blood across the Frenchman's legs and he passed out.

Fisher put his foot down. The road led away from Turkey, but he could perhaps get some medical assistance in Urmia.

"Fisher!"

"Yeah?"

"Stop. I have to tell you something." Patience's hand was in his guts, Fisher couldn't tell if he was holding them in or the wound was swallowing it. He pulled over to the side of the road and jumped out to quickly check if they were being followed. So far, nothing.

He opened the side door and clambered back inside the vehicle. The Frenchman was slumped against the side. "Sit down or something. I do not want to spend my last few minutes with a cricked neck."

Fisher flopped to the floor.

"Look," Patience said, "whatever happens, this is not the end for me. Even if you cannot get me to medical help, and it looks like I have shuffled off this mortal coil, it's not the end."

Fisher was confused. Patience hushed him before he could start asking questions. "Promise me something."

"Yeah, anything."

"Find the book. Take it with you and keep it safe. I will come for it when I can."

Fisher thought he was listening to the raving of a dying man.

"This is very important. Give me your oath." The Frenchman coughed out, blood speckled his chin.

"I promise." Fisher said.

"Swear on the sword."

Fisher glanced at the sword, and back to Patience. He decided to humour the dying man. He shrugged. "I swear by the sword I will keep the book safe for you."

"Thank you." Patience slowly slumped lower, the intensity that had held him up fading with his life. Shit. Fisher looked wildly around until he found a battered first aid kit and threw together a compress. As he worked he tried to keep the Frenchman awake, he didn't really know what he was saying.

"Please don't die. I give ya me oath that because ya saved me life, more than once, I'll do whatever I can to save yours."

Patience's eyes flickered open. "You would swear another oath?"

"Yer saved me life, I owe you more than just the book." Fisher wrapped a bandage around the compress, it was immediately soaked with blood. "Put pressure on it."

"Swear that you will do seven tasks for me. Consider taking and keeping the book the first of those tasks. I will be back for the rest later." Patience was gasping with pain now, clammy with sweat.

"Back? How? What–" Fisher was bewildered.

"Swear!"

"I swear! Patience?"

"I accept your oath. There are others, they'll try and get it from you, you must keep it safe."

"I promise."

Patience collapsed back. "Now get me to a fucking doctor."

Fisher was up and into the driver's seat as fast as he could. He hoped he'd done enough to keep the other man alive for the time it'd take them to get to the town. The APC's wheels span, spurting the gravel out behind it as it headed for Urmia.

# Dorylaeum, The Holy Land 1097

THEY WERE MARCHING again. Reymond didn't mind the marching, although many of his unit grumbled. It was better than the mind-numbing terror of battle. Although he had yet to see a Saracen up close, he'd caught glimpses of the defenders on the walls, and he was struck most by the fact that they looked just like any other men. Outlandishly dressed perhaps, darker in skin than most of the crusaders for sure, but no different. He was troubled by this, but he didn't know who to speak to about it.

The crusaders gathered at a staging post, next to the river Goksu. Charles was with the commanders of their part of the army. Reymond and the others sat in the shade below the bridge, stealing some moments' respite.

"What do you think will happen now?" Reymond asked.

"We'll split up," Jules said.

Reymond waited for more. Apparently Jules thought he'd said enough. "Why do you say that?"

"Army is too big," Jules said.

"Isn't that a good thing?" Reymond asked, trying to draw more out of his taciturn friend.

"Coming at Antioch from two different directions makes sense," Jules said. He had always been the one in the group with the best head for tactics.

"We be in Jerusalem in couple of weeks yes," Andros said brightly.

"I wouldn't be so sure," Mikael answered darkly. "You wait and see."

When Reymond was called for and went to serve Charles a meal he found that Jules proved right.

"Half the army are to go ahead," Charles told the sergeant.

"That means we'll be in the van then?" the sergeant asked, spearing a chicken leg.

Reymond had learned to be silent in these situations. He found out a lot more and the two old campaigners and friends tended to ignore the fact he was there.

The plan was for the two armies to meet again in four days' time at a place called Dorylaeum, an abandoned Byzantine military camp.

The next two days march passed without incident. Charles wandered amongst his men on the second night. "The scouts have spotted some Saracen shadowing us," he told them. "This is not unexpected, but keep alert."

On July the first, by Reymond's hazy reckoning, they approached an area of open ground between two valleys. The area ahead of the crusaders was covered with Saracen horsemen, like a spreading stain on white cloth. Reymond's pulse quickened. Battle in the open would be a very different proposition to sitting beneath a wall and only seeing the enemy in the distance. He gulped and watched how his friends reacted. Andros grinned at him. "Battle yes?" The others looked grim faced. Jules calmly pulled his bow and strung it; he'd refused to join the other archer units preferring to fight alongside Charles's foot soldiers. Orders were yelled, counter-orders shouted back. The sergeant bellowed "Form up!" The drills they had been doing on a daily basis since leaving France kicked in and the unit closed ranks, each man grabbing a spear. Reymond could see the Saracen gathering into formation. All around him he saw panicked faces.

From a distance, he watched the horsemen of the enemy on their nimble ponies speed past the lumpish crusaders, peppering them with a hail of arrows. When that had happened outside Nicaea the force of horsemen was much smaller, and the Provencals were rescued by a counter-charge. He couldn't see that happening here. The force in front of them was at least the same size as his half of the army, and who would ride to their rescue? He fervently hoped that messengers had been sent, that the other half of the army was close by.

Charles addressed his men. "We are to stand here, as the cavalry engage the Saracen. If we are charged, we are to hold fast."

In the distance Reymond saw the Saracen moving, shouting in their strange tongue. He gulped again and shifted his grip on the spear, trying to find a comfortable position. His hands felt very hot inside his gloves and beads of sweat trickled down his face and back. The Saracen fired arrows, darts and javelins at the crusader cavalry, pushing them back. To his horror Reymond saw another Saracen force, until now concealed among the hills, charging the exposed flank of the defensive camp.

"Easy lads. Remember to trust in Christ, and we will see these beggars off!" The sergeant stood with them, a solid presence. Reymond had never been more afraid, not even under the testudo. He could see a few stragglers cut off from the crusaders, not soldiers but the followers the army had attracted in its passage across the Holy Land, and one of the nobles led a charge to protect them. In vain; all were cut down by the advancing horde, soldier and camp follower alike. The hills seemed to be boiling with furious horsemen.

"Steady lads," the sergeant said at a conversational level as the horsemen approached. "Steady," his voice grew louder as the first arrows flew.

"Hold the line!" he shouted as the arrows fell thick and deadly. Reymond hung on tight to the kite-shield he had picked up at Nicaea from a fallen knight. It had given him comfort before, but it seemed pathetically small now. Arrows peppered Charles's unit. Men that Reymond has treated like brothers since that long ago day in France were falling around him. The Saracen broke through into the camp, and Reymond found himself eye to eye with a foreign warrior whose hot breath blew desert spices in his face.

When Reymond's spear took him in the guts he screamed and fell, cursing in a language alien to Reymond's ears.

Reymond pulled his sword and twisted and turned, reacting instinctively, slicing one man across the face, not watching but trusting him to go down as he slashed another across the neck, amazed at the volume of blood that sprayed out. As the Saracen dropped to the ground Reymond let out a breath he hadn't known he was holding.

Over the cries of battle he could hear the sergeant, shouting at them to form up; he could smell blood, fear and the stink of voided bowels as he made his way towards the older man, stepping daintily over a Saracen, eyes staring at the sky, the white of bone poking through his bloody tabard.

The Saracen riders circled, sometimes dashing close to the crusaders in a brutal exchange of arrows. Dozens of crusaders fell to Saracen shots, but as many Saracen dropped from their horses, never to rise again. Priests moved up and down behind the lines, offering prayers for victory or for the dead. The women and the boys who followed after the army brought them welcome water.

"We need to hold fast," Jules said grimly.

"Whilst they use us for target practise," Mikael grumbled.

"Until the rest of the army arrives," William finished, wiping his lips and glaring at him.

Father Jobert went down the line and Reymond was struck by the sight of the clerk-like man looking totally unsuited to life in an army. "Stand fast together, trusting in Christ and the victory of the Holy Cross," the priest exhorted them.

"Today may we all gain much booty," Charles added, after the priest had passed down the line, and he offered Reymond a grin.

The sun climbed ever higher in the sky. Sweat trickled down Reymond's sides, and he wiped his forehead with the back of his hand. It wasn't clear what was happening, he could hear fighting somewhere and spotted crows circling. He could taste metal in his mouth, a bitten tongue bleeding.

The dust cleared a little and Reymond spotted Le Roi Tafur, surrounded by Saracen.

"With me!" he shouted and grabbed Andros and started him towards where Tafur was bravely trying to keep the Saracen at bay. He sprinted across the battleground, Andros at his side, Jules a step behind them.

As they got closer they could see that Tafur was protecting the blond boy from earlier who had strayed from the lines and been targeted by the Saracen. Reymond bellowed and charged the three enemies.

One, distracted, turned to look at the charging men and took an arrow through his throat for the trouble as Jules calmly stood and strung another.

The other two tried to put the embattled Tafur between them and Reymond. Tafur seemed exhausted and not willing to take the fight to them. Reymond and Andros approached and squared up. The Saracen charged and the one running toward Andros sprouted an arrow through his eye.

Reymond ducked under the wild blow and spun with his sword extended which bit into the Saracen's leg. As the man went down Reymond stood, raised his sword and thrust it deep into the man's guts.

"'Ware," Tafur croaked.

Reymond looked up and saw that between them and their lines a bunch of Saracen horsemen approached.

"Is he hurt?" Reymond asked pointing to the young man, older than he'd looked at a distance, perhaps Reymond's age. Tafur shook his head; the blond youth looked terrified but also shook his head.

"Then let's get back to our lines!" Reymond turned and saw

that the Saracen horsemen had spotted them and a few had split off and were coming in their direction. There were more than a dozen to the four of them and an unarmed man.

The Saracen went from walk to trot to charge.

There was a surge of sound behind Reymond, and he risked a glance over his shoulder to see the rest of the army approaching at a gallop

They were saved.

Reymond shared a look with the others. The Saracen charging them wheeled and sped to join their brethren.

The cavalry rumbled forward, racing to outflank the Saracen, whilst the rest of the vanguard swept past the defensive camp, gathering up the horsemen that had been harassing the enemy. As the heavy horses of the crusaders drew toward them the Saracen realised they were facing defeat, and fled the field. The army celebrated with exhausted cheers. Reymond gazed at the sad humps in the sand with arrows sticking out of them, and he couldn't bring himself to join in the cheering. No matter the victory, it was dearly bought.

Orders came down the line. The army was to camp here to bury their dead. The men around him sank to the floor but Reymond remained standing, waiting for the inevitable command to gather their tents and set up camp. It was not long in coming. The sergeant placed a hand on his shoulder as he passed, shouting at some laggard or other. He nodded at Reymond's arms and chest: Reymond looked down and saw that they were splattered with blood. He looked for a wound but found that it was all from the opposing warriors he had built up a great deal of respect for.

He volunteered to help bury the dead. War was proving unlike anything he'd dreamed of, but at least he was here doing Christ's work. Although he wondered what Christ would think of the whole affair.

Reymond stood over the grave of Pierre, a man that could always be depended upon to be in good humour despite his fierceness. He was a little numb. This was the third man from the unit he had buried today. Father Jobert offered a blessing. The man looked like a clerk or scribe, short, thin, his clothes slightly too large, as though he had shed a lot of weight since choosing them.

"You looked pained, my son."

"I am, Father. I thought the enemy would be demonic. But they are just like us. I killed some men, Father. I am ashamed, for I do not hate them. Even though they have killed my friends. I want to hate them. Why can I not hate them?" Reymond remembered that the pope looked just like a normal man as well. Perhaps looks could be deceiving?

The priest put his hand on Reymond's arm in a gesture of comfort. "Be patient with yourself. In this struggle there need not be hate. But it is best not to think of them as men. They are less than men, and they deserve our retribution. I only wish I could fight, like you."

"Do all those that sin against God deserve retribution?" Reymond asked.

"That, or absolution. Be at peace. You are not sinning in killing these Saracen. You are absolved, performing a holy task. Your heart is pure. I will pray for you."

"Thank you, Father."

The skinny priest made the sign of the cross over Reymond, and moved on to offer comfort to others in pain.

Reymond re-joined his surviving friends. They were drinking to the fallen. He embraced the chance to seek oblivion, even if it was only for a few short hours. Soon they would resume their march to Antioch, and Jerusalem.

# Rome 2012

THE LOCK WAS disengaged by the person on the other end of the intercom. Reymond pushed the door open. He was dressed for stealth, all in black, with his sword, wrapped in cloth across his back. The man buzzing him in was under the impression he was someone else. He'd hacked the security terminal earlier and had shown the picture of the young male escort he'd observed visiting the property before.

The building was in the most expensive district of the city, set in its own grounds. It had high walls, iron gates, security patrols inside and out. It had taken Reymond a month of careful, slow work, through proxies, to break the security, and he had waited for the optimal time to attempt this entry.

As he stalked into the building he pulled his gun. The guard at the desk looked up. He was expecting someone else, and as his eyes widened Reymond shot him with the tranquilising dart. The guard managed to thumb his radio, even as he slumped to the desk. There was a short pause before the other guard radioed in. Reymond answered, muffling his voice.

"Nothing happening here," he said. "I just buzzed in Marco."

"You alright, Franco? Sounds like you've got a cold," the disembodied voice broadcast.

"Fine, fine," Reymond answered.

"See you in five, just doing a sweep of the ground floor."

Reymond grinned humourlessly. He efficiently cable tied

the security guard's arms and legs and laid him out on the floor behind the desk, then settled in to wait. The second guard came through the door, unsuspecting, and was felled with a tranquiliser dart. Reymond tied him up and put him with Franco. He had an hour before they came round, he reckoned, but the outdoor guards would check in way before then.

He pushed the door slightly open and looked through. All the lights were off. If events followed the same pattern as the last time Marco had visited, there would be a private dinner laid on in the upstairs dining room, followed by a suitably erotic film and lots of time in one of the many bedrooms.

As he stalked up the sweeping staircase and onto the wide balcony overlooking the entrance hall, Reymond wondered how Greed would greet him when he was expecting someone much younger, and more pliable. At the top of the stairs he was glad of the plush carpet, hoping he had made no sound. The first door he came to stood slightly ajar and he pushed it open.

Greed sat on a couch, facing the door, pointing a handgun directly at him. In this body, she was in her mid-forties, dressed provocatively in a very short red dress. Well, she was expecting a night of debauchery, after all.

"Charles." Reymond greeted her calmly, trying not to let his surprise show. He threw his tranquiliser pistol to the floor.

"In this body? Charlotte. I should ask how you got past the guards but I'm not sure I want all the tedious details. I was told you were in town. I thought you may try something tonight. You didn't think you could turn up after I had the dream, and I wouldn't be expecting you?"

"I suppose not." Reymond shrugged.

"And Marco?"

"Having a grand time, on my money, at a private establishment."

"What if I just shoot you now, Reymond? What happens to your grand plan then?"

"Then we will go around and around the same spiral,

becoming ever more bitter, ever more degraded. I must finish this. You know that."

Charles/Charlotte shrugged. "I am rich, I enjoy life. I have never been convinced by your little mission. We are beyond absolution I'm afraid. This isn't the 1700's anymore. This time, Reymond, you will die by my hand."

As the gun spat flame Reymond dived to the side. The bullet meant for his heart grazed his ribs. Righting himself, he sprinted across the balcony and dived through another door, slamming it behind him. Two more bullets punched holes through the wood, missing him by centimetres. He pulled his own gun and checked the clip as he moved into an inner room, which was in darkness. The splintered door slammed open.

"Why delay the inevitable? Andros is a better swordsman than you. He'll take some beating. I bet you don't even know where Sebastien is; none of us do."

He could hear her footsteps, stalking towards him. Reymond crab-walked across the room, but his foot snagged a cable. A lamp crashed to the floor, the door swung open and as he dived for cover three more shots ring out. Charlotte flipped on the light. She was counting on him wanting to end this by sword.

"Have you visited the drunk yet, and put him out of his misery?"

Reymond took aim, firing up into the bulb of the overhead light. He rolled away as a bullet struck the wall, where his head was only an instant before.

"How are you going to break into the Vatican, anyway? I bet Tafur has that place sewn up tighter than last time you went for him."

Reymond shuffled behind a sofa, which exploded feathers and stuffing as a bullet narrowly missed him.

"The police are on their way. I phoned them to say I had an intruder. I am legitimately fending off that intruder, when they arrive and find you full of holes."

Her voice was very close now.

Reymond popped up and shot Charlotte through the leg. As she fell she emptied her clip directly at him. He felt a slug graze his cheek and another his arm but the other bullets flew wide. Reymond walked over and kicked the gun out of Greed's hands.

"The sword," he said.

Charlotte shook her head.

Reymond drew his sword. "It is necessary," he said. He held his own blade out and let it guide him. When he returned with her sword, Charlotte was gone.

There was a smear of blood along the wall, passing through the door into the corridor beyond. Reymond returned to the hallway to see her propping herself against the wall as she shuffled down the stairs.

Reymond threw the sword to land on the steps in front of her. "Pick it up," he said quietly.

"Screw you!"

"Pick it up," Reymond insisted.

"I'll pay you, I'll set you up for your next life," Greed begged.

Reymond edged closer.

"Pick it up." He pointed at the blade with the tip of his own sword.

"We don't have to be enemies. I can do things for you, make you someone."

"Pick up the sword, Charles." Reymond's heart was like ice, blood spilled down his face which he wiped away distractedly.

"No." She shook her head emphatically.

Reymond slapped at Charlotte's wounded leg with the flat of his sword.

"Son of a bitch! Leave me alone!" She tried to hop down another step.

"Pick. It. Up." Reymond spoke through gritted teeth.

Charlotte's make-up had smeared as the tears ran down her face. "I'm not your bitch."

Reymond put his sword through her shoulder. She gasped in pain, dropping to her knees on the stairs.

"Just fucking do it. Kill me."

"The sword," Reymond persisted. It was at her side, within reach of her hand. "I will mutilate you if you do not pick it up." He swung his sword light, intending to cut her, maybe sever an ear or scar her face.

And then her sword was in her hand, rising to block his blow. The two swords, meeting, sang out like bells.

Reymond stepped back. He had the advantage of height on the stairs, but he did not press it: he wanted the fight. Charlotte used the sword as a crutch, levering herself to her feet. She levelled the blade at his heart. Reymond waited patiently. He didn't think either injury he had given her was serious, but she was still at a disadvantage. His own injuries were slight; the bullet that grazed his face had left his cheek bleeding freely, while the wound to his arm was shallow, and self-cauterizing. The one in his side was the most serious but he felt little pain from it, and he wondered if this was a bad sign. He could hear sirens outside.

He stabbed at Charlotte. She batted aside his blade contemptuously and lunged forward, aiming to skewer him with her riposte. He allowed her to beat him backwards until he reached the balcony. She joined him and they stood together, facing each other on the same level. Reymond was stronger, Charlotte was faster, a better swordsman.

"Have at you then!" Charlotte snarled, attacking with a sudden venom that drove Reymond onto the defensive. The police were getting closer he thought they could be here any minute. He needed to end this, fast. Charlotte had no such qualms. The house was filled with the clear bright notes of metal on metal and the grunting of the combatants. Greed scored a lucky hit on Reymond's shoulder and now blood ran free and wet down both arms. He hoped it would not make the blade slip out of his grasp.

There was no banter now. They circled each other warily, each looking for an opening. Reymond flicked the blood from his hands one at a time. Charlotte limped badly now. One lucky strike could end it for either of them.

Charlotte lunged. Reymond parried, caught by her elbow on the follow-through. He stumbled and she slashed, a move he was barely fast enough to counter. His hands were slippery with blood and he almost lost his grip.

Kicking out, he caught Charlotte's damaged leg. She gasped, crumpled to the floor, and Reymond's sword took her through the throat.

No last words for Greed.

She sprawled untidily across the floor. The sirens were much closer now. Reymond had to get out. He gathered both swords, grimacing at the pain in his shoulder. He headed for the stairway.

Now he could see the blue flashing lights outside. He hoped that by going out the back entrance and across the grounds he could avoid the police, as long as they hadn't surrounded the house.

He headed back to the security station and set off the alarm at the pool house towards the front of the property, to draw the outdoor guards. He had to traipse back upstairs to recover his tranquiliser pistol in case he needed to shoot the dogs, or the guards. He checked the two guards he'd tied up, both were still out cold.

He saw the police at the front gate, and one of the guards moving towards it. The other radioed the desk; from his position Reymond could see him standing by the pool. He hoped that if he didn't answer, the man would come to check on his friends first, and leave the back of the property unguarded. He wondered how he would scale the wall with two injured arms, but he'd worry about that when he got there.

Via the camera feed, he saw the security guard at the pool sprinting towards the house, and the other opening the main gate to let the police in. Time to leave.

Reymond exited through the back door, sprinting across

the garden, trying to stick to the darker areas, the places he knew the cameras had trouble reaching. So far so good.

The back garden contained a small orchard and he was just reaching it when bright lights flared all over the property and he heard the dogs barking. He risked a glance from cover, spotting a policeman, and a single guard with a dog.

Reymond took out a flash grenade and readied it. He dropped to his belly to crawl towards the wall. He glanced over his shoulder, gauging where his pursuers were. Within sight of the wall he took out the grapple, wincing at the pain in his shoulder. They were getting closer.

Dog, man, man. Eenie meanie minie mo. He shot the dog and ditched the tranq gun, then lobbed the grenade towards the two men. The guard had dropped to his knees next to the dog and was pulling the dart out. Reymond made a run for it. The grenade exploded behind him with a blinding flash.

The policeman fired wildly, the wall bursting with dust where the bullets hit. Reymond threw the grapple and scaled the wall as fast as possible, his skin crawling, expecting one of the bullets to be on target.

As he reached the barbed wire along the top of the wall he heard shouting. Risking a glance back, he saw the second policeman running across the lawn. Only a matter of time before they called for backup, if they hadn't already done so.

Reymond dropped down the other side of the wall. He landed awkwardly and half ran, half hobbled the three hundred yards to where he'd stashed the motorcycle. He kicked it into life, hearing some chatter on a radio. Great, now they knew he was on a bike. He'd have to ditch it.

He wondered whether he should return to his hotel. His face would be all over the security cameras. He had everything that he couldn't afford to leave behind on him. Clothes and such he could ditch. His tablet was in his bag. He had the swords.

He wound his way through the streets in a semi-random pattern, listening out for sirens. He heard them in the distance, but they didn't seem to be tailing him. A few miles away he ditched the bike and walked for another mile or so before stealing a car.

Another personality he had to burn. He stopped the car and made a call.

"Fisher." The man answered on the first ring.

"I have the third sword," Reymond said.

"And the next task, I presume?"

"Yes." Reymond paused.

"Well?"

"How is the Vatican plan going?"

Five minutes later, having set Fisher on the next leg of their journey, Reymond looked for a new set of wheels. He wanted to be well away before daybreak.

# The road to Antioch, The Holy Land 1097

THE CRUSADERS SAW action several more times before they stood in front of Antioch. Reymond saw bigger, stronger, faster men than him lose their lives due to a lack of battle awareness. All the best warriors seemed to have an almost supernatural sense of their surroundings in battle, and that kept them alive. He attributed it to attention; absolute, focused attention. His sword was 'notched', as the men from Charles's unit said when a man had killed. He had saved the lives of his friends, and they had saved his, more than once. It was a more tightly knit group that approached Antioch, more than three months after the surrender of Nicea. Winter was approaching and the crusaders hoped to be inside Antioch's walls by the time it bit.

Antioch was a city of vastly different aspect to Nicaea or the little towns the crusaders had sacked along the way. Before they arrived at the city there was a garrison at the Iron Bridge to deal with first.

As the road opened up the cavalry came to a stop, gathering into formation. "Right lads, best make sure you're ready," the sergeant said, brusque as ever. "We're up after the cavalry has given them the frighteners. Keep your shields up. You don't want to be eating iron crows, do you?" The sergeant strolled among them, tightening a strap here or there, looking into the eyes of his men, offering comfort and encouragement.

He got to Reymond and gave him the stare, the look meant to convey that he, the sergeant, was much scarier than any Saracen. Reymond was inclined to agree. The sergeant moved on and Charles shouted his orders to his men.

"Close formation, slow advance, once the cavalry clears we run. Any of you that fall behind will feel my sword up their arse!"

With Mikael on one side and Samuel on the other, and Andros and William close by, Reymond moved forward at a swift march. In the distance the horses had scattered the enemy, and the signal was given. "Run! For Christ and the Cross! Run!" As they trotted forward, still in formation, the dust cleared. Reymond could see the formidable stone bridge across the Orontes river, and he had time to wonder, fleetingly, why it was called the Iron Bridge.

He noticed two distinct units amongst the enemy, a mostly unarmoured one, some hundreds strong, armed with spears, and, on the bridge itself, was a mix of lightly and heavily armoured troops. Some, the equivalent of knights to the heathens, wore scale mail and conical helmets, and they carried curved swords and round metal shields.

Reymond concentrated on the men in front, and not getting impaled on one of the long spears that thrust out of the enemy lines. He ducked past one and his sword took a man in his chest, a great vomit of blood spraying out of his mouth as he collapsed, his eyes already glazed with death. Next to him one of Charles's men was impaled on a spear which snapped with the impact.

Up and down the line, the mass of crusaders forced the poorly equipped foe back, step by step. Reymond's sword plunged into another man, high in the chest. As he pulled it free another Saracen jabbed at him with a long dagger. He saw the man lunge, screaming, before he dropped, clutching at his ruined eye. The feathered shaft of an arrow trembled between his fingers.

Reymond glanced back to see Jules stood calmly, twenty foot from the melee, unhurriedly nocking another arrow to his bow. There was no time to thank him.

Reymond slashed to the right, his sword glancing off a spear, then to the left, cutting deep into a man's thigh forcing him down to be crushed underfoot. Suddenly he was clear, open space all around him. The bridge stood just ahead, across a small gap. It was crammed with enemy soldiers.

Reymond glanced around to reassure himself that he was not alone, that the enemy around him were dealt with and his friends were still alive. The sergeant had lost his sword and was clubbing a man over the head repeatedly with one of the enemy's round shields, the crunch of his skull suddenly audible as the sounds of the melee ebbed for a second, only to crash in louder than ever.

Charles shouted a command. Reymond could see his lips moving, but his voice was lost in the chaos. Reymond formed up on him, catching a glimpse of Andros grinning like a madman, Mikael grimly determined. William and Samuel were not in sight, but he spotted Jules, blood running down his face. He must have seen Reymond's frown, as he wiped his hand across his face and shook his head. It wasn't his blood.

As the sounds of the first unit's death grew quieter and more men joined the wedge, Charles shouted for the advance. They shoved forward, shields interlocked. This would be a game of pushing. The front of the wedge crunched into the solid wall of the enemy and stopped briefly. Swords flashed in the heat haze and the dust, and men pushed and men fell and men died.

Reymond was concentrating on the right hand side of the bridge, trying to avoid the sweeping curved swords of the enemy. He was surprised to spot Andros behind and above them, on the far side of the bridge. He had clambered up to a small lip of stone the other side of the wall. He stabbed and slashed, and three men around him dropped in rapid succession. His distraction caused the right hand side of the enemy force to turn a little, allowing the crusaders to move forward and apply pressure.

An ugly, rat faced warrior turned and slashed at Andros, who stepped back to dodge him and disappeared as his step took him to the void beneath the bridge.

"Andros!" Reymond cried but there was little he could do, except kill the warrior in front of him.

He heard trumpets, shrill, from an alien throat. The fighting men struggled to disengage. The Crusaders gave chase. The enemy ranks were broken, and they were fleeing. Reymond ran instead to the side of the bridge, to see Andros's cruciform shape on the shale slope below. He wasn't moving.

Reymond sprinted around the end of the bridge and slid down the slope, scattering a small avalanche of stones ahead of him. When he reached the sailor Andros opened one eye and looked up at him with a grimace. "Ow!" he said.

"How hurt are you?" Reymond asked, worried his friend may be invalided out of the army before he even got to see Antioch, never mind Jerusalem.

Andros moved slowly. "I very bruised yes. Not broken." He groaned. "I think not broken, anyway!"

Reymond helped him up. "Let's get you to Jean, he can see if anything's bust."

They both had to crawl back up the slope to where Jules was waiting for them with a worried expression. He helped them up and over the lip and the three friends sat together at the side of the bridge, listening to the running sounds of battle as they faded into the distance. "The others?" Reymond asked.

"Samuel and William were in the main group, right behind Charles," Jules said.

"Where is Mikael?" Reymond wondered.

"Last I saw he was chasing a Saracen with his sword raised over his head like it was a meat cleaver and the Saracen a chicken running from the pot."

The three laughed at the image, and they were still

laughing as the sergeant approached, clutching his bloodied shield. "What are you three doing lying down on the job?" he demanded. "Get up and secure this bridge!"

Reymond groaned as they got up. The moment of respite had stiffened all his muscles, and Andros reeled like a drunkard. Jules grabbed his arm to support him. "We'll soon be in Antioch," he said.

"And after Antioch, Jerusalem!" Reymond shouted.

They joined the men stripping the dead of any useful items. The dead crusaders were put to one side, their tunics removed and placed over their faces, cross uppermost, while the enemy were rolled over the side of the bridge to splash into the river below. The sergeant was supervising the men when Charles returned, with the rest of the survivors of the unit. Reymond was relieved to see that Mikael, Samuel and William were among them. He caught Jean's eye and pointed to Andros, the curly haired man wandered over.

"Report!" Charles barked.

The sergeant straightened. "Ten men of our unit are dead, three are seriously wounded, and probably won't see tomorrow. Twenty are in various states of injury but still able to walk, and fight. Including this fool of a sailor here." He slapped Andros across the back, eliciting a loud groan from the little man. "What were you doing, lad? Think you were climbing the rigging?"

"It worked didn't it, sergeant, yes?"

"Well enough for you to earn some time off drill and get an extra ration for a few days, I'd say."

Andros, who had looked worried, broke into a grin. The sergeant slapped him again, making the grin turn into a wince. Jean tutted and walked Andros off. Charles, seemingly content with the report, went off to make his own to Robert, who Reymond could see in the distance talking to his knights. Reymond wondered what the burden of leadership would be like, but dismissed the idea. He was happy to be no more than a soldier.

The sergeant cleared his throat. "We're to camp here until the rest of the army appears," he said, "and then we're to march on Antioch, and God help us, somehow take it."

As the sergeant moved away Reymond turned to Jules. "God help us?"

"Antioch is going to be a bitch to conquer, by all counts. But I've been told there's a fleet out of England, coming to give us aid. It'll be nice to speak to some civilised men at last."

"Civilised? I heard in England they have only just discovered wheels." Reymond scoffed.

"And that fire is hot." Samuel chipped in.

Jules, who had spent much time in England, attempted to extol that northern land's virtues, but his arguments fell on deaf ears. The friends continued to squabble in a good-natured fashion as they built their camp.

†

Later, a unit of the army marched past. Reymond tried to make out their colours in the dusk.

"They must be in a hurry to get to Antioch!" he said to Mikael.

"Yeah, I suppose so."

Reymond was in a hurry himself. When they sat round the campfire to eat he tapped his finger against his thumbnail in a gesture of impatience.

Once the rest of the army arrived at the Iron Bridge, Robert Curthose, and therefore Charles's unit, made for Antioch. When the citadel came into sight as they rounded Mount Staurin, Reymond's heart sank.

"How the fuck are we going to capture that?" William asked.

'That' was a city carved into the rock of two mountains, encircled by a massive defensive wall, studded with hundreds of towers. Reymond whistled: nothing had prepared him for this. Avignon looked like a rude village in comparison. His heart sank further. Jerusalem seemed like an impossible dream. But then he heard a man calling upon God and he remembered that God was on their side. They would prevail.

"There are meant to be six gates," Jules told him. From their position, Reymond could only see one, but he didn't doubt his friend's words.

"Are we meant to blockade all of them?" he asked.

Charles overheard him as he rode up alongside. "No," he said. "The plan is to hunker down and wait for the city to starve. An attrition siege."

"But will they not get supplies in and out using the gates we cannot cover?" Reymond asked.

"Yes, they will," was Charles's grim reply.

Over the next few days the rest of the army arrived, and the princes divided the gates up between them. Charles's unit took up position with the rest of Robert's men, at the Dog Gate, which lay to the north of a hastily constructed bridge of boats.

Men and materials arrived from the English fleet, and the princes built a siege fort to the north of the city. Reymond and Andros were detailed to go and help build it, along with some of Bohemond's men.

Whilst they were building the fort, jokingly referred to as Malregard, Jean told them about a rumour he'd heard.

"You've heard there is a prophet amongst the Tafurs? A boy, they say, from the far northern fens, with blond hair and eyes like the sky on a summer's day."

Reymond and Andros shared a glance. "No?" they said in unison, with a tone of 'tell us more'. Tales enlivened the building work, after all. Reymond remembered the golden haired boy; was that the same one?

"It is said he has been touched by God, that he can predict the outcome of any battle. That he knows things..."

"Things? What things?" Reymond asked.

The older man's voice dropped to a whisper. "Devilish things".

He refused, despite all of the pair's best efforts, to divulge anything else. Back at their own lines Reymond shared this titbit of news with of the others, who seemed unimpressed.

"Just another rumour, lad," Jules said. "The army is full of them. Pay it no mind."

As November turned to December, Reymond discovered that winter in the Holy Land was just as awful as winter back home in France. He spent his days attempting to stay dry and warm. Many of the men came down with sickness, including William, again, who they took turns nursing according to Jean's strict instructions, which helped him make a full recovery. When food started to run out, units were sent far and wide to forage. Some fell afoul of Saracen raiding parties and didn't return. By mid-December they were running out of horses and the situation was becoming critical.

Charles addressed his hungry men, who were beginning to lose both faith and patience. "There's a force being put together to go out and forage," he said. "There will be knights going. They're asking for volunteers from the infantry, and I put us forward."

There were a few groans from the men, but only a token protest, not a heartfelt one. Some of the men looked hopeful. After all, they'd get first share of any food they found, surely?

In Reymond's opinion, trudging through the freezing rain and occasional sleet would be far worse than staying put by the fire or wrapped up warm in the communal tents, but he didn't complain. He'd long since learned that complaining didn't achieve anything.

They followed a route south, then east, of the city, until they came across a plateau and some easy pickings with a fat town or two.

The skirmish turned into a rout. Reymond's heart felt twice its normal size as he ran, doubled over, expecting an arrow or a Saracen lance to take him in the back at any second.

Reaching the relative safety of higher ground, scrambling up to a ledge above the tide of battle, Reymond stood with his chest heaving. He watched the Saracen charge towards his unit, and the sweat froze on his face with a sudden chill. The ground beneath his feet shook from their approach, and a crusader cavalry, swept in to intercept them. There was a terrible cacophony as the two cavalries collided, and Reymond could hear the yells of Christian men, and the strange alien Saracen cries.

Spotting the sergeant rallying his unit in the valley below, Reymond dropped back down and joined them, hoping they wouldn't think him a coward for running.

"Easy lads. Let's get our breath back before we charge in to help, eh?" The sergeant said, causing a few faces to crack smiles. Reymond shaded his eyes. In the distance he could see crusader colours, and beyond, horses converging upon them. He couldn't tell if the mounted troops were Latins or Saracen. Directly in front, the scarlet cross was clearly winning the day. Across the fields lay a multitude of still, broken forms.

Later, wandering numbly through the battlefield, the terror had abated, leaving a void Reymond was struggling to fill. It was impossible to sustain his hatred of the enemy; there were just as many of their dead as there were crusaders.

Reymond wondered what he'd feel like if these strange men had invaded his homeland. He found a Saracen noble who was slowly crawling away, his leg a pulp of bloody broken bones. He dragged his intestines behind him with one hand, clawing at the earth with the other. Reymond, tears running freely down his face, slashed the man across the back of the neck, once, twice and for a third and final time, blunting his sword on the stony ground even as he cut the man's head off. Now he had it, held up by the hair, he didn't know what to do with it.

Charles wandered past, looking for men missing from his unit. He spotted Reymond and put his hand on his shoulder. "You can take his armour if you like," he said. "I'll say you earned it by killing him, you cut his head clean off."

Reymond looked at Charles and nodded gratefully. His chances of surviving in battle had just increased. He stripped the man, who was a little shorter than him, but of similar build.

"I had to kill a horse once," he said, staring at the man's severed neck. "One of my father's horses fell and snapped a leg. It screamed like a child, a horrible sound. I had to put it out of its misery."

Reymond started when Charles put a hand on his elbow. "Come on lad," the older man said. "Let's get back to the unit."

Reymond sighed, lumped the armour over his shoulder and let the severed head fall. Without looking back, he followed Charles from the battlefield.

Later, as they marched back to the city, many of the supplies they had worked hard to find lost beyond recall, Reymond toyed with a writing a letter to his father in his head. One he'd never send.

*Things I saw today:*
*Two armies*
*A severed arm,*
*Fingers drumming the ground*
*Sending a message to hell*
*A dead friend*
*Crows splashing in bloody pools*
*I did not see God*

Reymond's unit was on patrol, moving to cross the Orontes and join several other units near to the Bridge Gate. Reymond suspected that there had been some intelligence indicating that the commander of the Antiochene forces was going to issue a new sortie.

Charles's quick orders were – "The men coming with supplies have been ambushed. We go to relieve them." They ran at a quick, breathless, march. Soon, in front of them were the enemy, standing between them and the men returning from St Simeon.

They approached within a few hundred feet before one of the Saracen warriors glanced behind. He raised an alarm and half the Saracen turned, they were sandwiched between the two crusader groups. Reymond couldn't interpret the faces of the men in front of him. They screamed their alien curses. They must have realised that they would be slain, with no chance of escape.

Reymond was confronted by a giant of a man, long black moustaches flying wild in the wind. He wielded a hefty axe with a bloodied blade. It clashed against Reymond's shield, jarring and numbing his whole arm.

Reymond darted forward, stabbing the giant through the thigh. It didn't slow his charge. Reymond ducked as the axe whistled through the space where his head had been a second ago.

His second thrust took the man in the belly, who was left staring stupidly as his guts unravelled towards the ground. He roared, lifting the axe high above his head. Reymond stepped in close, ramming his blade through the man's throat. As the giant toppled, Reymond heard his name called.

He turned to see Jules, standing some twenty foot away, bow and arrow picking off the enemy where he could.

Jules pointed, and Reymond craned his neck to see a further force leaving the Bridge Gate, massing on the bridge. "Commander!" Reymond shouted.

The commander was intent on the battle before him. Reymond struggled over to him, stopping to dispatch an enemy bugler who staggered out of the melee. "Sir, look!" he said, grabbing Charles and spinning him round. They were about to be sandwiched as well. Reymond stared at the warriors massing.

"We'll prevail." Samuel, close by, assured him, adjusting his grip on his sword. Reymond nodded absently.

"Shit!" Charles lunged into the fray and grabbed the sergeant as he passed. The enemy would soon fall upon them but there were now enough men aware of the threatened assault that the attack might not be too deadly.

Jules had abandoned his bow; he stood back to back with Mikael. Reymond grabbed Andros, panting heavily, and they did the same.

Reymond's world contracted down to a spear's length in any direction. It was vicious hand to hand fighting. The world was reduced to grunts, screams, the smell of blood and spilled intestines, a succession of faces: frightened, angry, hateful, lifeless. At one point Reymond received a glancing blow to his head and afterwards all he could hear was a high pitched *eeee* and had to keep wiping blood from his forehead afraid that it would drip in his eye and blind him.

The battle slowed as men tired. In one of those turning points Reymond had come to recognise, the enemy disengaged, falling back to try and cross the bridge. He could see the Bridge Gate had been closed when the force had left; forcing the men outside to be victorious or die in the attempt.

The great gates were now opening, ponderously, but there was a crushing press of men and horses on the bridge; Reymond saw many of them fall and there was a great churning in the water, which was running red.

Reymond's arms felt disconnected from his body; his sword and shield hung from nerveless hands. The dead stretched out like discarded handkerchiefs in all directions. His unit was seriously depleted. Charles, the sergeant, Reymond and his friends, and some ten others remained, out of those who'd left Europe, under the command of Charles, in another lifetime. Reymond's bleak thoughts were reflected in the stares of his comrades.

"Cheer up lads, this is a great victory," Charles said, waving his blade. "We've smashed their elite." He gestured towards the bridge. "Now we have the means to blockade the next two gates." He looked up at the citadel on top of the mountain and continued in a quieter tone. "Although I doubt we'll close the last gate until the whole city is taken."

Reymond followed where Charles was looking. Without closing the gates the siege had little chance of success. He wondered how many months they'd spend outside the walls of Antioch. He wondered what the crusaders would eat.

# Bristol 1992

REYMOND WALKED INTO the pub to find Jules waiting for him. In this incarnation, he was in the body of an adolescent girl, and she was chain smoking.

The pub was painted a dismal grey – now stained slightly yellow by years of nicotine. The central bar meant the rest of the pub was an inverted C shape haphazardly populated with broken-down furniture with broken-down people perched upon it.

Reymond raised an eyebrow. He hadn't yet been a woman, but had come across a couple of the others that had. He had no idea what that said about him. Jules was dressed in black, with long teased hair, black eyeliner, and pale skin.

"What are you supposed to be?" Reymond demanded.

Jules's pencilled eyebrows shot up and just as quickly settled into a scowl. "I am a Goth. Obviously."

Reymond had no idea what a Goth was. He made a mental note to watch more TV.

"So I got the book," he said.

Jules's eyes opened wide. "The sorcerer?"

"Yes." Reymond nodded.

"Where was it?" Jules asked.

"Iran. I secured it last time round, but a friend has been holding it for me since."

"Iran? Odd place for it to end up."

"Not really, it's a devout Islamic country. I think some

Armenians were working for the sorcerer and were trying to take it home." Reymond shrugged.

"You've read it?"

"I am slowly translating. It is bad enough that it is written in ancient Arabic, but it is also in code. But I think I have read enough to know that you were right. The sorcerer is to blame. There are plenty of references to the unicorn in there, and to eternal life. I think Pride is not reincarnating like the rest of us. I think he has drunk the draught of eternal life and it has got mixed up with the oath we took. I think he is the one bringing us back. I am just not sure why. Or how. Or how the swords are tied in to it. But I hope to find out."

"You seem much calmer, this time?" Jules ventured.

"And you are... ? " Reymond waved vaguely.

"Having a different body doesn't explain the lack of anger?" Jules quirked an eyebrow.

"No, it does not. I am getting better at holding it in, but we will have our reckoning before I leave. It cannot be any other way." Reymond had been learning ways of holding the anger in check. Like singing nursery rhymes. He was reciting poetry, in his head, as he spoke to Jules.

Jules sighed.

"The arrows were blessed?" Reymond asked.

"By Humility. But I don't think that's it. It was the ceremony afterwards, when we ate its heart. I felt something. I feel it every time we meet, every time I meet one of the others, although that has been much less often...apart from that disaster in the 1700's. It's a diminution, a dissolution, part of me leaks away. I can't explain it better than that."

"I do not feel it. I always get angrier and angrier as I go on. It is as if the curse gets stronger for each of you that passes," Reymond mused.

"For each of us you kill, you mean?"

Reymond closed his eyes. He didn't want to see Jules's face. He meditated on the memory of their first meeting instead, of

Jules as an older, wiser mentor. It helped push the anger deeper, but he could feel it growing, feeding on his denial. When it erupted it would be much worse than before.

"We do not have much time," he said eventually. "The swords..."

"What about them?" Jules asked.

"They were part of the spell, specially prepared. That is why Humility was always going on about how we had to keep them pure. That is why we all had to dip our swords in the unicorn's blood. The swords are the key," Reymond said.

"Pride is the key," Jules insisted.

Reymond took out his sword still safely inside its scabbard. The buzz of conversation in the background of the King's Head ebbed, then came back louder. The locals had spotted the weapon. Reymond sighed. Jules looked momentarily scared, then resolute. She took out her sword too.

Reymond stood. "Ladies and gentlemen, if I can have your attention please," he shouted. "This tavern is about to become a battleground. Please leave via the nearest exit." He could feel the scepticism among the drinkers, no-one moved. "Get out. Now!" he roared. A couple sat next to the door scrambled for the exit. All conversation had now ceased.

"Oi!" the barman shouted, and a couple of the locals, perhaps fancying themselves as hard men, edged towards Reymond as if to grab him. Without drawing the sword from its hard leather scabbard, he jabbed one in the guts and clouted the other across the ear with a loud thwack.

The man fell heavily across a round table, sending several pints of beer crashing to the floor. The barman snatched up the phone. Reymond heard the word 'police' before the shouting got too loud for him to hear anything at the bar. He had started a general melee.

He laid about himself with abandon, incandescent in rage. How dare they ignore him? How dare they get in the way of his mission? How dare they have safe little lives, without being cursed to come back again and again, and forced to kill your friends, forever getting more and more soiled? More and more tortured between incarnations. This must end. He wanted it all to end.

At some point his sword became bared. He didn't know if he'd done this himself, or if someone else grabbed the scabbard and pulled the blade free. He had lost the ability to differentiate between faces; they were all a blur now. He was back in Ma'Arra, in Antioch, in the desert.

He stabbed and sliced. At some point he was duelling with a young woman. At another point a balding gentleman with shaggy-haired arms tried to brain him with a bar stool. Reymond danced out of the way, slicing the man's hands off with a flick of his blade. They flopped to the ground like two stunned tarantulas. Amidst the chaos he saw blue lights and a small but important inner voice told him it was time to leave.

The pub was wrecked. Reymond had slain two of the locals and a further four were unconscious. The rest nursed their wounds, watching him with naked fear as he walked over to the fallen knight, in the body of the Goth girl. He knew, without having to look too closely, that Jules was dead. He must have stabbed her through the heart. He was glad they got to talk this time. Bygones had almost been accepted as bygones, but the curse continued its fateful turning.

Reymond felt sad beyond measure. He hoped this was the last time. He took Jules's sword and wrapped it with his own in the long black coat he wore.

He left. One of the doors was hanging off its hinges, battered open when Reymond had thrown a local through it. The same local was lying dazed outside. Reymond gingerly stepped over the injured man and made his way down the road. Two police cars, sirens blaring and lights flashing, sped past him.

# Antioch, The Holy Land 1098

A COUPLE OF months after the fight on the bridge Charles's unit was on patrol, crossing the Boat Bridge and making their way to the new fort built to blockade the Bridge Gate. The fort was named after the Blessed Virgin. There was now a fortified position blockading the last gate, too. The food situation had improved considerably and Reymond had begun to put on some weight. Coming up to the Provencal's position, they met with a knight on horseback, who directed them to join in on a bit of repair.

More and more knights were horseless; some had made themselves destitute and many were now 'Tafurs', following the former knight who styled himself 'Le Roi Tafur'. These Tafurs seemed to be drawn from all of the various armies and they were a growing force. Rumour had it they also had among their number a prophet, and that he was leading them on matters of religion.

"So we're to lug stones and wood around, are we?" Mikael complained.

"Yes, that's us, general dogsbodies," Samuel said, giving him a cheerful punch on the arm.

After their work was done, they were invited to stay and play cards with a group of Provencals. A few hours later Reymond went to take a piss. Although he'd had some ale, he hadn't drunk enough to doubt his senses. So he was confused to see a gathering of men around one of the towers near St George's gate. He finished his business, and went to find the sergeant to report what he had seen.

"That's sharp eyes you've got there, lad," the sergeant said. He led him to Charles, who was deep in conversation with one of the princes. "Gather your men now, Charles," the prince said, "and you can be amongst the first through the Bridge Gate. For tonight the Gates will open and we will be triumphant!"

Charles grabbed Reymond by the elbow, and asked in an urgent whisper, "Where are the men? I hope they're not too drunk!"

It took a few minutes to gather them all up and prepare. Charles explained that the infiltration into the city had been kept a secret from the rank and file but he'd known that it was coming fast. Just not this fast.

The men held themselves ready, Reymond's finger tapped against his thumbnail. Andros was telling a story involving a widow, a goat and a sailor, that helped take the men's minds off the coming fight. They had fought at night before, but it was always more dangerous. Reymond looked to the east, seeing the first tell-tale hints of dawn. He was beginning to think they had been dragged out here on the strength of nothing more than a rumour, when bugles and trumpets sounded in the city, over by St George's Gate.

"Men, follow closely. Let's not turn the river red when we cross the bridge." Charles led them in a swift march towards the bridge, and the gate which was still closed. Reymond looked up at the wall. He could see men moving there. Expecting an arrow any second he decided to keep his eyes fixed ahead and trust to God. There was no whistling of arrows and the gates miraculously swung open as they approached. Armenian and Greek civilians welcomed them, slapping them on their backs, gabbling in their foreign tongues. Bugles and alarms echoed through the city streets, and a force of armoured knights, all on foot, tramped past on the tight, winding road. "God wills it! God wills it!" they shouted.

Antioch was open.

The unit rushed towards the sounds of battle, passing crusaders who were breaking into houses on the way. The night was filled with clashing steel, the screams of women and children, the breaking of wood and glass. It was bedlam, and Reymond tried to keep his head down. They rushed down a small street where they had seen other crusaders running moments before, and ran headlong into the enemy.

Reymond ducked under the swipe of a curved blade, his own sword poking the man through the chest. As he pulled the blade free and turned to face the next attacker he dimly realised his unit was winning, with only one man down. He couldn't see who it was for the sweat in his eyes.

The Saracen before him turned, looking for an escape route. More crusaders were advancing down the street behind them. The remaining exchange was brief, ending bloodily for the men of the city.

There was a high pitched scream, from back the way they came. Without waiting for backup, Andros ran down the street towards the noise. Reymond shared a glance with Jules and they rushed to follow him. Someone ran behind Reymond, but he didn't spare a glance to see who it was.

On the main street there was a girl, no older than thirteen, and a younger boy. They cowered against the wall of a house. The boy was banging on the door, but no-one inside dared let them in. Or maybe the house was already empty.

Two Tafurs advanced menacingly towards the children, who looked alike enough to be siblings. Andros shouted a warning as he ran. The Tafurs laughed and held their hands up, backing away, reluctant to face down the four men running towards them.

When Andros reached the children he spoke to them in a soothing voice, phrases they probably didn't understand. Reymond slowed, so he was unprepared when he saw the glint of a knife in the boy's hand. Mikael ran past, shouting "No!" as he barrelled into Andros, just as the knife flashed.

The two men tumbled. There was a spurt of blood and the boy grabbed the girl's hand. Together they fled, and Reymond, shocked into stillness, could only watch. "They were saving you!" he shouted impotently. Jules was waving him over and his legs somehow found the power to move, to carry him across the street to his wounded friend.

Mikael clutched his neck, blood spurting from between his fingers. Andros shouted "let me see, let me see!" as he tried to pry Mikael's fingers away. Reymond slid to a halt, falling to his knees as Jules stood guard. Mikael smiled, or at least bared his teeth, gurgling, trying to say something as he slumped into Andros's arms. His hand fell away from his neck and Andros blinked at the hot arterial spray striking his face. Reymond tried to staunch the bleeding, but could see the life leaving Mikael's eyes. Andros shouted, "We need a healer!" But it was already too late.

Mikael had gone.

Reymond sat next to him. Blood, like a pair of ragged gloves, covered his hands and arms. He stared at his friend in incomprehension. He had seen plenty of death since coming to the Holy Land, but this seemed so arbitrary, so unexpected. Jules laid his hand on Reymond's shoulder. He tried to shrug it off. He didn't want to move, he didn't want to leave.

Jules pulled his tabard off and placed it tenderly over Mikael's face. "We must return to our unit," he said, voice steady, quiet. Andros wiped his mouth, smearing blood into a gory beard.

Reymond looked up at Jules. "What do we do now?" He wanted someone to take charge, to tell him what to do next.

Jules looked like he wanted to look away, but he held Reymond's gaze. "We carry him," he said. He shook Andros's shoulder and between them the three gathered up their friend and went to find their unit. Reymond and Andros carried Mikael, whilst Jules stalked ahead.

As the sergeant saw Jules his face reddened. "Where the hell did you think you were going?" he shouted. "I'll..." he tailed off as he spotted Reymond and Andros, carrying their burden between them. "Is he...?" the sergeant asked.

Reymond shook his head. The sergeant rested a hand on his shoulder and gave it a squeeze. Andros looked stunned, white-faced under the mask of blood. Jules was silent and grim. They gently laid the body down, and the sergeant sent one of the men off to find a priest.

Charles returned. "Orders from the top," he said. "We're to secure the city and gather at a certain church, ready for an assault on the citadel."

The sergeant gave Reymond one last pat, and cleared his throat. Finding his voice, he bellowed, "You heard the boss. Let's form up and show this city what it means to take the cross. Do your fathers proud, don't embarrass your mothers and save the best loot for me!"

"What about Mikael?" Reymond asked.

"Let the priests sort it out. We'll catch up with him later. We have God's work to do," Charles told him. Reymond saw Jobert hurrying towards them.

It was not until much later that they said their goodbyes, over a hastily dug grave.

✝

For days following Mikael's death, flashes of that night came disjointedly to Reymond.

There was little in the way of extra food, little in the way of riches. They had failed to break into the citadel; the populace had mostly fled or was barricaded away. The city wasn't safe unless you were with a group. What he remembered the most, vividly, was the street running with blood. He'd never seen the like before, the streets carpeted with corpses, men from both sides killed in the fighting; city dwellers too, women and children.

Reymond made his way to the top of the wall, bearing a message. He stalked towards the Dog Gate, occasionally stepping over makeshift board games or men playing dice. He avoided looking down towards the river.

He eventually found his unit. Charles was propped up against the wall; he'd been stabbed through his left leg during a skirmish. He perked up noticeably at the sight of Reymond.

"What news?" he asked.

"Nothing much new. Curthose wants us to remain on wall duty for now. We're expecting another major advance from the citadel. There is no food for us; we're on our own in that regard."

"How did he seem?"

"Grim, like everyone else." Reymond glanced over the wall at the Saracen army that had arrived the day after the city fell. What he could see would have been the view the city defenders had suffered of the crusader army for many months. They would not have months to look out on the Saracens, because there was no food left. Many of the horses had wasted away, the rest were weak because men had taken to drinking their blood to survive.

Charles's unit was down to ten men now. Many crusaders had deserted, dropping over the walls under cover of darkness and making their way south and east, away from the army of allied Arabs and Saracens.

Reymond looked back at Charles. "Any return message?"

Charles stared down at his hands. When he looked up Reymond was surprised to see anger in his eyes.

"No, no message. I've heard there will be mass tonight, at St Peter's. I've a mind to go. The man in charge of that lot is getting ready to attack. We'd best be shriven. Help me up, lad."

Reymond helped him to his feet and handed him his crutch. The sergeant came over to help. He was the only one of them who didn't look gaunt, his great bald head still rested on a neck that had a fold of fat at the back. But even he, Reymond noticed, had cinched his belt tighter.

"Gather the men, we're going to Mass," Charles ordered his number two. The sergeant bullied the men into line and they set off for church.

When they arrived, there was already a crowd of men both inside and outside the church. Priests stood ready, upon pedestals built for that purpose, to relay the Mass to the faithful.

Also present were many Tafurs, most of whom still eschewed armour. The man they called Le Roi Tafur stood with them, like a stork amongst crows. Next to him was a boy, golden haired, dressed in a simple white shift. Reymond was surprised to see Father Jobert next to the leader of the Tafurs.

Mass finished. Reymond, who had been tapping his thumb throughout, felt calmer. Charles relayed his latest orders to what was left of his unit. They were to make ready in the hills above the city as they expected a sortie from the citadel at any moment.

As Charles was speaking Reymond noticed that the blond boy in the white shift, the one they called the Prophet, had drawn a crowd. It was hard to tell at a distance what for, but there was a murmuring. Reymond edged closer, until he could hear the man's shouts, and saw that his eyes had rolled back in his head, leaving two egg-white globes staring blindly at the crowd.

"... St Andrew and Christ! It is here! Here!" Le Roi Tafur caught the boy as he collapsed and the Tafurs carried him away from the church.

Jules, who had appeared silently by Reymond's shoulder, muttered, "Nothing good can come of visions." Reymond was too tired to respond. The two returned to their companions and tramped up the hilly streets towards the citadel. Charles was propped against a wall, and they settled down to wait.

They had barely had time to break out the dice when the gates of the citadel creaked open, and trumpets and bugles sounded from both sides. Pouring out of the citadel like woodlice from an overturned rotten log came the enemy. At the same time in the city below Reymond heard more bugles. The attack was coming from both sides. They would be overwhelmed, Reymond had heard that there were three of the enemy for every one of them.

When he mentioned this to Jules, the tall hunter bared his teeth. "We'll have to kill three times as many of them as they do us."

The taciturn archer stood apart now, with an arrow notched, ready. The enemy rushed forwards, bellowing, a sound to strike fear into Christian hearts.

"We are surrounded on all sides by the cross!" Charles was shouting from somewhere behind Reymond, out of sight. Father Jobert rushed down the line blessing the men, as battle was joined.

The next few hours passed in staccato flashes. Reymond concentrated on arm, sword, dodge, stab, duck, slash, arm, sword, to the exclusion of all else. He was aware of the man next to him crumpling as a sword met his brain.

Reymond himself was stabbed through the arm so that his shield hung mostly useless, but the man who stabbed him felt Reymond's sword through his bowels.

The sword swung up and down, heavy on his arm, sometimes meeting resistance, bone and gristle and the twang of muscle, or the clang of metal shield, sometimes a swish through the air as his target danced backwards. The unit was jammed together shield to jowl, getting tighter and tighter. Reymond's arms were sheathed in gore. Somewhere he heard a crusader calling out for his mother, many men prayed whilst they fought. The sweat stung his eyes but he dared not try and wipe it away as he'd then replace it with blood, and worse.

This was it. This was the end, death on a hill above a citadel very far from France.

Reymond took his last few breaths, and then he heard hooves on stone. A ragged group of knights, hardly a cavalry charge at all, exploded against the side of the ranks of the enemy, tossing them beneath their steeds. The crush around Reymond eased a little. He was aware of more bugles, over the ring of metal echoing in his ears.

The enemy retreated but the crusaders had no energy to follow. A small boy, a local by his appearance, was suddenly next to Reymond with a dipper of water which he accepted and drank in one draught. He reached for more but the boy had already moved on to the next man.

The enemy were reforming; their reinforcements had arrived. Reymond was ready to drop, but he raised his sword again. His shield arm still refused to obey him properly. Father Jobert was by his side; he felt his arm raised and a bandage wound tight around it. He was blessed again.

The bugles sounded. The enemy screamed as they poured down the hill towards the little knot of crusaders. Reymond looked up, into a sky so clear and blue, studded with small fluffy clouds. It seemed hard to believe he was going to die under such a sky, a glimpse of the heaven that awaited.

The first man to reach him was slain with a thrust through the neck, the second to the chest. Reymond's sword clanged harmlessly off the shield of the third, but the impact was enough that the Saracen stumbled, and the backslash crumpled his helmet. The man fell beneath the feet of the next in line, and the next.

The next time Reymond had the chance to look up the sky was a much deeper blue. They must have been fighting for hours.

He looked around. The gates of the citadel were closing but the walls were still crowded with the enemy. In the square they'd been protecting, the dead were piled up in their hundreds. Taking advantage of the lull in the fighting, Reymond sought his friends. He saw the sergeant stood with his chest heaving, his hands on his knees. Charles had abandoned his crutch and was using a spear to propel himself forward. He was covered in blood.

Everyone was covered in blood.

At first he couldn't pick out Andros, Samuel, William or Jules, but eventually he recognised the little sailor. He was talking to a woman who was giving out water, while Jules was sat propped against the wall of a house. Done with his drink, he walked over to Jules and slid down the wall, leaving a great stain of wetness, streaked red. Neither man spoke, but their eyes were on the citadel. The walls sprouted spears like the spines on a thistle.

"Is this all that is left?" Reymond eventually asked as the remnants of the unit gathered. He didn't recognise his own voice; it emerged as a wheezing croak. Samuel propped up William who appeared to be wounded, holding an arm awkwardly across his chest.

The sergeant nodded. There didn't seem to be anything else to say.

Somewhere in the city below, harsh trumpets blared. Enemy trumpets, brazenly defied by friendly bugles. Above them the gate creaked open to reveal a mass of fresh enemies. The survivors of Charles's unit exchanged glances and dragged themselves to their feet. Robert Curthose trotted past, riding a horse that was all ribs.

"Let us not forget that Christ is with us and that we will see victory," he cried. "God wills it!"

"God wills it!" his men shouted in reply, and the shout was taken up by crusaders up and down the line, until a thousand throats shouted it. And for a brief moment they drowned out the ululations of the enemy, until the clash of steel replaced the sound of faith.

†

Later, deep in the night, there were still sounds of battle across the entire city. Reymond and the others were in a house, snatching a few fitful hours of sleep. The smell of smoke woke him and he roused the others who complained sleepily. He came to Jean and shook his shoulder and the man didn't stir. "Jean?" Reymond shook him harder, then felt for injuries. When it came to the man's head, beneath the curly hair there was a tell-tale fist-sized lump on the back. Jean was still sleeping with long deep breaths, but nothing Reymond could do roused him.

Charles put his hand gently on Reymond's shoulder. "I do not think he will awake again. I have seen such injuries before."

Reymond shook his head as a couple of tears tracked down his face. "He's still alive, we can—"

"We can tell the priests and they'll take him to where they care for the injured, and we can pray."

Reymond turned to look at Charles, seeing Jules stood at his shoulder grim-faced. He rubbed his mouth and chin. "I'll go and get a priest," he said.

Charles nodded. "The fire, wherever it is, we'll need to go help fight it. Find us when you can."

Reymond made sure he had his equipment and slipped out of the door and ran down the streets to the makeshift infirmary. In the southwest of the city a district of houses blazed.

Once he had helped the priests move Jean, he joined the chaos in the southwest. When he arrived he was shoved into a relay of water buckets. The night was as hot as if the desert sun had returned. The fire screamed with a thousand angry throats, a giant rushing noise as a great wind howled around the burning houses.

The crusaders had given up trying to put out the flames; they were tearing down houses, trying to create a fire break, soaking the resulting debris in water. Reymond's world was running bucket after bucket after bucket a number of yards: each time he handed one off he got a few seconds of blissful lightness before another leaden bucket was thrust into his arms.

There was singing? Screaming? Coming from somewhere outside the immediate area and Reymond came back to himself as the man who was supposed to be handing him a bucket stopped and stared towards the walls. Reymond turned stupidly, too tired to comprehend what was happening. It was another attack.

Every other man in the bucket relay formed up away from the firefighters. Reymond wondered if his face was as befouled with black ash as the other men around him. His clothes were certainly smudged. He wondered where his unit was, where his friends were, whether he could summon enough energy to fight for his life. He watched indifferently whilst the enemy ran towards them. When the men around him started shouting for God and the prayers started up he lifted his shield and sword.

# Bristol 1826

THE PLACE PROVED to be a deceptive fortress. Ostensibly an inn, the back rooms were locked up tight. Reymond fought his way through several guards to get to the door, and when it opened he was rewarded with the sight of his quarry.

Reymond paused in the doorway, squinting into the thick fug of blue smoke. The scent of tobacco, mixed with a heady, sweeter smell, almost overwhelmed him.

*Opium.* How like the Slothful knight to lose himself in a drugged haze. He entered the establishment carefully. In a far corner he saw Sloth, sat at a table, an opium pipe at hand. He was drinking tea. Reymond took his cloth-wrapped sword from his back and advanced through the smoky air.

Jules gasped as the sword crashed down on the table, sweeping the opium paraphernalia and the tea set to the floor with a clatter. Some of the patrons looked shocked, but most were too stuporous to care. The bar man lifted a club, but relaxed and put it away as Jules shook his head. The two women Jules had been talking to stood without being asked and sashayed away.

"Patience!" Jules opened his arms wide, to show he was unarmed.

"Apparently not anymore," said Reymond sadly.

"What should I call you then, Sir Wrath?"

"You could always call me Reymond. It was once good enough for you. "

Jules smiled, equally sadly. "Then, of course, you may call me Jules."

"The curse?" Reymond asked.

"Indeed," says Jules. "Please, sit." He indicated the other chair.

With a great sigh Reymond sat down.

"You have a short amount of time before I am unable to control myself and start swinging my sword. I hope you have yours." Reymond felt a vein throbbing in his forehead. His finger tapped his thumbnail.

Jules nodded wearily. He reached under his chair, and pulled out his sword, placing it gently on the table. Reymond could feel his knuckles whitening and his eyes widening at the careful movement.

"When Humility had his mad idea, I welcomed it. I was a hunter. I had hunted all sorts of animals, I enjoyed it. I wanted to find it. The creature. If I hadn't been so keen, would you all have still done it?" He looked speculatively at Reymond who was holding himself still. The vein throbbed harder at his temple, and he breathed loudly through his nose. Jules obviously thought he may not have had much time, and skipped to the end.

"I was first sword. I slew the beast; you all just dipped your swords in its blood whilst it died," Jules spat.

Reymond shook his head. Jules's eyes widened. "I remember – the second sword. That was you?"

"We. All. Ate. Its. Heart." Reymond bit off each word, and his hands shook as he reached for his sword.

"The curse is not our fault. Humility–" Jules could get out no more words. Reymond leapt to his feet, flinging back his chair. Jules snatched up his sword and parried Reymond's first blow.

"Remember the sorcerer," Jules gasped, shaking his arm at the shock from the sudden blow. "The one in Ma'Arra," he rasped, barely dodging the next blow, flinching as Reymond's blade scored his arm.

"The first siege," he panted as Reymond pushed him back. His heel hit the wall, and he had nowhere left to go. He dropped his guard and Reymond ran him through, sword grinding against the bones of his ribs. "The sorcerer," he managed, but when Reymond stepped back and the sword left his body Jules slid to the floor. Reymond cradled his head.

"Ma'Arra." Jules coughed, huge wracking coughs. Intent on the Slothful knight, Reymond didn't see the club as it swished down, cracking the back of his head.

# Antioch, The Holy Land 1098

REYMOND WAS DULL from three days lack of sleep and food, awaiting orders his brain was having trouble processing. Jules jogged his elbow, and Reymond winced. He had some movement back in his arm but it was stiff and painful in certain positions.

He glared at Jules, who pointed with his chin to the rooftops. Reymond saw men with flags on the roofs. One looked south into the city, another north towards the citadel. Reymond understood that they were now in a flying sortie, ready to take aid where it was required most. His brain told him he could safely zone out a bit and his eyes lidded slowly. If anyone had told him he'd develop a knack for sleeping on his feet he would never have believed them. The snap and flap of a flag roused him, and he saw the man on the roof facing north waving with all his strength.

Curthose gave orders to his commanders and the few knights who still had horses cajoled them up the steep street as the men on foot trotted after them. When they cleared the houses Reymond saw the blood red cross on white, surrounded by the enemy.

Part of the army poured in on one side, and he could see more coming from another direction. In amongst the soldiers were the Tafurs, fighting like possessed men. The crusaders bashed into the line of the enemy, and time slowed down to the measure of a breath, the thrust of an arm, steps forward, steps back...

Le Roi Tafur and his men were separated from the main force and the men around him were being whittled down. Grabbing Jules, Andros and the sergeant, Reymond bore down on the attackers from the rear. Tafur yelled his gratitude, almost lost under the sounds of fighting. They turned and, with Tafur's men around them, battled their way back to their own lines.

The enemy retreated. The crusaders had broken the attack, for now. After four days fighting, most hours of the day, Reymond could barely move. He slumped down in the street and stared dully ahead. He tried to count how long they'd been in Antioch, but gave up. The days blurred into one endless fight for survival.

Charles hobbled over, still using a spear, although the blade had snapped off – in the belly of an enemy most likely.

"No rest for the wicked," he said, with brittle cheer, "we're going to make a defensive wall."

Reymond groaned, forced himself to his feet and trudged after their leader as they joined the work crew throwing up a hasty defensive wall between the city and the citadel. Reymond joined the chain of men passing stones up the line. His neighbour, a Provencal with ginger stubble, struck up a conversation.

"I hear they're digging in St Peter's."

"Digging? What for?" Reymond asked.

"That prophet from the north, he's said there's something holy in there."

"Like what?" Reymond took a quick break, wiping his hand across his sweaty brow.

"I heard it was the spear of Longinus," the ginger soldier said.

"The Holy Lance?"

"The very same."

Reymond shook his head. Another rumour: the army

seemed to live on them. He wished they could eat rumours, then the whole army would have had full bellies.

A few hours later and sat in the shade Reymond was grateful to accept a bowl of greasy water with lumps of unidentifiable grey meat in. It was more meat than he'd eaten for several days. "What is it?" he asked the man slopping it into bowls all around.

"Camel," was the short reply.

Reymond dug in without a word.

The rumours abounded: the Holy Lance had indeed been found in St Peter's, and the crusaders had demanded that the commander of the Saracen army surrender. Robert Curthose directed his men to the Bridge Gate, and up on the wall Reymond was shocked to see that despite four days intense fighting, and the piles of dead bodies both within and without the city, the army camped on the plain still dwarfed the number of crusaders that had first arrived in the Holy Land all those months ago, never mind the pitiful number that must have remained at this point.

Charles, limping but more mobile, came straight from a meeting of commanders.

"What is the plan?" Reymond asked him,

"We wait," came the uninspiring answer.

"For what?"

"For word of the emperor. We have the Lance now; we cannot be defeated, but we may not be able to break out of the city!"

# Yerevan, Armenia 2012

MARI KNOCKED ON the door.

"Who is it?" a voice asked. There had been three men in the room with her father. He'd been strapped to a dentist's chair. They were obviously not good guys.

"It's me," she said.

The instant the door cracked she kicked it open in the face of a man with a lazy eye she immediately labelled as Droopy. A second man loomed over the first that she labelled Gorilla, the third was out of sight.

"Get back," she said, threatening them with the gun. Droopy put his hands up and backed into Gorilla, who grunted and curled his lip. "I know how to use this. I won't hesitate to do so. I want the man strapped to the chair."

The third man in the room was long and thin, like a stick insect, so she mentally labelled him Lofty.

"Unstrap him," she ordered.

Lofty hovered behind the chair; Gorilla still hadn't put his hands up and Droopy turned to look at his friends.

"Or what?" Lofty asked.

"Or I'll shoot you!" she said, with all the toughness she could muster.

"That'll bring the rest of the guards running," Lofty said.

Gorilla lost patience and lunged for her.

She shot him in the chest. She was more surprised than he was.

That should have slowed him, but Gorilla roared in pain and lunged forward even as she shot again, which struck him in the neck with a bright arterial spurt.

Lofty ducked, Gorilla slapped his hand to his neck with barely a flinch, and pulled his own gun. Droopy seemed to be in molasses. Mari dived to one side and the shot that Gorilla got off slammed into the door.

Mari's next shot took Gorilla in his jaw, whipping his head to one side as if punched by a giant's fist. His last shot went wild, through the ceiling as he collapsed.

From the floor she shot Droopy through his lazy eye. As he toppled she wondered how many shots she had left. And how she was so calm. She was killing people. Bad guys...but still people. This was her most surreal day ever.

"Drop your gun or he dies!" Lofty stood behind her father, pressing a gun to his head. Mari aimed, squinting down the barrel. Just as Lofty opened his mouth to speak again, she blasted a hole in the dead centre of his forehead. He went down like a sack of wet cement.

"I am eternally grateful to you," her father murmured, as she took the hatchet and cut the cable ties holding him to the chair. He stood stiffly and stalked over to a cabinet against the wall. He slid it open and retrieved a sword. Mari frowned.

"Papa?"

Her father spun and weighed the sword in his hand.

"My thanks for freeing me. Who are you, why did you free me?"

"Papa? It's me, Mari."

"Mari?"

"Your daughter. Remember?"

He looked blank. He was obviously traumatised. Best to just get him out then they could catch up. Then it hit her. She'd been in a shootout. She'd now killed four men. Her teeth chattered as she suddenly had a full body tremor. "Oh, God!"

"God?" her father responded. "God will not help you."

He grabbed her from where she'd dropped to her knees, and gently raised her to her feet. "Come on, we need to get out of here."

He'd remember her soon. She would keep reminding him. He was talking funny though, not like he used to.

They collected the guns and ammunition from the bodies. "I expect someone will have heard that little gun fight?" Mari asked.

Her father shrugged, stalked to the door and looked out. He glanced back at her, still without any sign of recognition and walked silently out of the door. She hurried to catch up with him. Her father really didn't sound like he usually did. He sounded formal, his accent was different, he moved differently. What had happened to him the last few months? Why didn't he recognize her?

✝

Twenty minutes later, Mari sweated as three security guards come down the corridor towards her, guns out and ready. As they passed a certain door a shotgun blast took out two of them. As the third spun in response he received a sword in the guts.

Her father emerged, wiping his blade. "I am guessing that is the last of them. I need to be on the dock to meet Andros's boat when it returns," he said.

"Why?" Mari asked. She'd followed the trail of bodies and had finally caught up with him. She'd wanted to get him out but he seemed to be going further in. He ignored her question and hurried off, not waiting to see if she followed.

They left the hotel via the service entrance onto the marina. The yacht was just docking. Her father cursed. "We are not in the best position." He shrugged. "We will have to make it up as we go along. It has been working so far."

Mari watched the yacht. There was plenty of movement,

but no-one had disembarked. They were probably wondering why they could raise no reply from the hotel.

"We will not get a better chance," her father said, and moved at a crouch towards the yacht. He got twenty foot before being spotted. Mari still dithered behind him.

The goons on the boat opened fire at her father as he zigzagged towards them, Mari provided cover.

Her father reached the boat, picking off three of the goons in quick succession. Mari was impressed: when had he become such a good shot? She was usually a better shot than him, although that could have been down to his drinking. She pulled off a lucky shot and another goon took a dive into the marina. There was a pause in the firing, and the yacht's engines coughed into life once more.

Her father made a dive for the handrail, dragging himself over it and onto the boat as another goon emerged from below decks and aimed a gun at him. Mari's long shot took the goon in the head, and he flopped to the floor as the yacht began backing away from the pier. Her father gave Mari a salute before he stalked around to the back of the boat.

She was on her feet and running before she could think about it. She wasn't going to lose him so quickly. She leapt across the divide and heard gunfire from the back of the luxury yacht.

†

Her father dropped the shotgun, which was out of ammo. He cocked his head trying to listen carefully, but it was hard to hear anything over the throbbing of the yacht's engines. He hadn't seemed pleased to see her on the boat but obviously had little choice now. She wondered how many bad guys were on board.

A goon popped around the corner as if summoned by the thought, gun extended. Her father crouched and swept the man's legs from under him, then picked him up and threw him overboard. The sea around the foaming propellers turned red. She'd never have expected her father to know martial arts. Where had he learned that?

He picked up the man's dropped gun, checked the clip, then lay down and looked around the corner at floor height. The yacht approached the harbour wall and the open sea beyond.

She mouthed, 'what can you see?' He held up two fingers then rolled out into plain sight and as the bullets whizzed about him he let off two shots. She watched a red line suddenly appear across his arm scoring his skin, but the wound was shallow.

The man driving the boat threw panicked glances over his shoulder and shouted into his radio. Mari ignored him for now, ripping her father's shirt so she could bandage the worst of his wounds. He gritted his teeth. Once they were done they went below.

†

Inside, Andros waited, his sword on his lap, relaxed. "What took you?" he asked. "And who's this?"

"Oh, you know, *you* cannot get the staff. This is Mari, she's my daughter. Mari, you should have waited outside."

"I am not the first this time, yes?" Andros arched an eyebrow.

"No, the priest was," her father replied.

"Was? Shame. Where was he hiding?"

"Hiding? Not sure I would call it that. He was in Avignon." Her father took darting glances, around the small room: fixed table, leather bench seats along the wall, everything shipshape and Bristol fashion. She was having a hard time following the conversation.

"And Greed after the priest, yes. Sloth? Still wasting his life in the arse end of nowhere?"

"Jules is still on the list."

"Well, well. Gluttony is deep in the Vatican, yes. But I bet you'd like to know where Pride is?"

Her father nodded, narrowing his eyes. She looked from him to Andros. What were they talking about?

Andros's eyes flicked for an almost imperceptible moment to Mari where she stood behind her father – who reacted, pushing her aside, ready to defend himself from two fronts.

The swift look was a feint. Andros's sword arced to meet her father, who was wrong-footed. He was immediately pushed onto the defensive.

Mari checked her gun. It was going to be impossible to get a shot off in the small space. She could do no more than watch from where she retreated into the corridor. When had her father learned to swordfight?

Her father recovered quickly. The two men circled, exchanging exploratory blows. Andros was fitter, faster and probably more skilled, and her father was losing blood, still battered from the earlier beating he'd received, as well as the few flesh wounds he'd taken making it onto the boat. In between blows, they talked.

"Give up, Wrath, enjoy the curse. Live a lifetime for every seven years you get. I do. No-one can do anything to us. We are gods." Andros moved like a cat, lithe and dangerous. Overhand strike, swift retreat, sweeping blow.

"Is that what you tell the women you kidnap, rape and torture?" her father countered.

Head block, riposte, leg block.

"Torture? Really, Reymond, would one break a precious artwork yes? Remember when I was Don Juan? How Mozart followed me around like a puppy, yes?" Andros smiled in reminiscence.

Thrust, feint, move.

Mari wondered what they were talking about. Reymond?

"Is that what people are to you? Objects for your amusement?"

Her father scraped his sword past Andros's guard but Andros

revealed this was a calculated manoeuvre, and his blade scored a long gash down her father's side. He gasped in pain but instead of disengaging he stepped into Andros's reach and head-butted him, connecting with Andros's nose with a satisfying crunch.

Bleeding profusely, Andros dropped, but rolled out of the way of the follow up with the sword. Blood trickled down her father's side, making its way down his leg. He stepped after Andros. Mari continued to point her gun as best as she could at the boss of the casino. Both men now ignored her.

As her father tried to adjust his swing with a grunt of effort Andros dropped his sword and tackled him around the knees, bringing him crashing to the floor. Her father's head glanced off a bench. Andros scrambled for his sword, but her father still had hold of his.

His thrust pushed through Andros's back, the tip emerging from his stomach. Andros grunted in surprise. Scrambling up from his knees, her father pulled the sword free.

Andros flipped over. Blood ran from his mouth and he coughed once, spraying red across the cabin.

"I'll see you next time." He grinned. The spark left his eye and his muscles relaxed.

Her father spat. "There will not be a next time."

"What the hell is going on?" Mari asked. Her father staggered as the yacht changed course. He stumbled into her arms and she realised he was terribly hurt. "Never mind, tell me later."

The yacht was still powering out to sea; her father was tired and bleeding heavily. She searched for another gun. As he picked up Andros's sword he shook his head and sat heavily.

He took a deep breath, and with a massive effort forced himself to stand. He swayed for a few seconds, and glanced back at Andros's body.

"Come on, let's take control of this boat."

Later, driving the yacht back towards shore, she wondered if any of the men she'd killed had families. The man driving the boat, now floating towards the bottom of the sea, had worn a wedding ring. She wondered if they had brothers, sisters, wives, children. She wondered if their parents were still alive, if they were expecting a call from their son in the next couple of days. She wondered if their families knew what they did. She blamed Andros for their deaths. She didn't wonder why her father looked so grim. He'd been the one to pause when he'd seen the wedding band.

'*This has to stop*,' he'd whispered before rolling the man into the sea.

"Papa," she asked, "what's going on?"

Her father sighed and scratched his head. He looked like he'd like to avoid this conversation, but he sat beside her.

"I am not your father," he began.

# Antioch, The Holy Land, 1098

REYMOND STALKED THE wall; Jules, Andros and Jobert following. His unit now down to seven. Samuel and William had slipped away in the night, or were killed by city dwellers; certainly nowhere to be found. Reymond worried over that, imagining a number of gruesome fates. He assumed they'd been killed, as he'd have thought they'd have asked him to join them if they were going to run away. Charles's men were now absorbed into another unit. He sought out Le Roi Tafur who welcomed him as a friend.

"You saved my life, and I am in your debt. All of your debt," he said, "Come, I'd like you to meet Sebastien."

He led them to a row of houses the Tafurs had claimed as their own; smashing down connecting walls and enlarging them.

Reymond's heartbeat sped up and he scanned all around him in swift darting glances. He had spent little time around the holy beggars. Their fervour, and their poverty, unnerved him. Jobert also looked uncomfortable. The fastidious little priest was far out of his depth, in the Holy Land, and his expression of distress had become habitual. The others looked equally uncomfortable.

Tafur led the way, threading through the multi-coloured, multi-patched, lean-to tents the beggars had woven out of scraps. He headed towards an impromptu recreation of the crusader leader's command tent, a place Reymond had seen, but never been called to himself. Jobert leant closer to speak and Reymond craned to listen. "Remember, Le Roi Tafur expects respect. Not even the commanders of the armies can control him. He is a holy madman." Andros opened and closed his mouth, obviously thinking better of whatever it was he had been going to say. Reymond's palms were sweaty and he wiped them on his tunic. Jules patted his sword and dagger and a pouch of coins below his belt. Reymond squared his shoulders and nodded for Jobert to lead the way.

The five were stopped by beggar knights, wearing a motley of discarded armour that other knights must have thrown away on the long journey. They still managed to exude menace, and the swords they were armed with could kill a man as well as any in the crusader army. Better perhaps; the fanatical Tafurs held less compunctions, drawn as they were from the dregs of crusader society.

A small man minced over to greet them. He barely glanced at Reymond or his friends, but drank in the sight of Jobert with a covetousness Reymond found disturbing. His filth-encrusted hand reached out, and Jobert took a step backward.

The small man grimaced in displeasure. "My Lords, honoured guests, well-dressed gents, this way, this way. You are expected." He led the way obsequiously. Reymond glanced at Jobert, who shrugged and shook his head. Reymond wondered how they were expected. Probably the magician's powers.

They were led into a wide semi-circular camp around a great fire, where some priests were dispensing food and medicine, and taking confession amongst the beggars.

The 'king' of the Tafurs hurried across the room and took his place on a massive chair, cobbled together from driftwood, bits of cart and other oddments; he was lost in the seat, being one of the thinnest men Reymond had ever seen. Le Roi Tafur watched them approach, as if he hadn't escorted them in personally. To his side, partly in shadow was a young man, with sharp features, long blond hair and piercing blue eyes that stared deep into Reymond's soul as he approached. Bearing the priest's advice in mind, they sketched a bow.

Reymond stepped forward.

"Your Majesty, I am honoured to have been granted this audience. I–"

"Patience," the boy intoned. His voice was surprisingly deep and strangely accented. He hopped up and approached them.

"I, er, what?" Reymond was brought up short, nonplussed.

"Your Virtue. I can smell it upon you. Be welcome, Sir Patience. With your companions, Kindness, Diligence, Chastity who saved the girl," he said pointing at Andros. Although Reymond couldn't place the accent, somewhere from the wild northern lands, he began to get the drift. So far Le Roi Tafur seemed content to let his companion do the talking.

"We are not without means," Reymond started again, obviously flustered. "I'm sure in return for your blessing and support we could arrange some, er, charity and kindness."

Le Roi Tafur stood lazily. Around them, the beggar knights fell to their knees, the friends, caught out, were left standing for a moment before they belatedly followed.

"Sebastien, are these the ones you foresaw?"

"Indeed they are."

"The seven, the 7 are gathered," Tafur said, striding over to the fair-haired man in white and throwing his arm around him. "This is Humility. He found the Holy Lance, you know. The Holy Lance! I am Temperance."

Le Roi Tafur covered the ground in front of the throne in two great strides and clasped Reymond on the shoulders, lifting him off his feet. "Brother, brother, welcome, welcome!" He kissed him on both cheeks. He then did the same to Andros, who looked a little stunned and disgusted. Tafur's breath was repellent, and he emitted a rank, sour odour, overwhelming at such close quarters. He grabbed each of them, bringing them to their feet.

"Where are our manners? Drinks, drinks for our guests, our honoured guests."

Filthy blankets were brought forward, and Tafur invited them to sit. Reymond dreaded what vermin he was about to acquire. The one they called the Prophet, the boy with blond hair, sidled over and stared at them. Reymond was sure it was impossible to go without blinking for so long, and his own eyes watered in sympathy.

They were brought simple wooden goblets, filled to the brim with what looked like red wine, but smelt suspiciously like vinegar. "Drink! Drink..." Tafur prompted them, before he drained his own goblet, a thin red line escaping to run down his chin and onto to his eccentric clothes, joining a host of previous stains. "My magician, my seer," he pointed the goblet at Sebastien, "foretold your coming, your arrival and what it would mean. Your forces and my forces will join together in our attack, our assault upon Antioch. For we have been appointed a great task, a holy mission. From God. God!"

As he finished this speech his goblet, which he thrust out, was filled again and he drained it in one. Reymond took a deep breath and took a gulp. The potency of the astringent alcohol took his breath away. What in hell had the beggars been fermenting? Jobert, who had taken a swallow from his own goblet, couldn't seem to stop coughing, trying to hide it behind his hands.

"We are the Virtues. Humility saw it all. He saw it." Tafur held his goblet out to be refilled. "To the Virtues," Tafur toasted, and downed the contents.

"The Virtues," the men echoed, and drank. Reymond took a polite sip, feeling the liquid coat his teeth and burn his tongue. His empty stomach roiled in protest.

"Come, let us eat, let us feast." Tafur led them into another room and within was indeed a feast, impressive by the standards of the city, but one which would still have been a meagre meal on any table in France. Tafur and those he had named as Virtues were invited to the table. Reymond glanced with distaste at Tafur's men, who stared greedily at the food.

"Shall we not share this?" he asked.

Tafur, a bird's leg in his mouth, shook his head. Pulling it out he spoke with his mouth full. "They are fasting, for tomorrow we are going to win a great victory. A historic victory."

Jules was already eating, cramming dried figs into his mouth, and Andros munched some nuts. Hunger got the better of Reymond and he joined in. He was shocked how little it took to fill him up, with his stomach vastly shrunken.

"We seven, we 7. You and I. Your noble Charles, Sir Charity. Sir Kindness, your priest, my sorcerer, Sir Patience, the Hunter, the Sailor. We will be triumphant. It is our fate, our very fate." Tafur looked them all in the eye, one by one. "Truly our God given fate, to be triumphant in these Holy Lands. We, we the chosen, we will bring Virtue back. Bring. Virtue. Back!"

Reymond was impressed by the fervour behind Tafur's words, even though he was unsure of their meaning. This was why he joined the Crusade, after all. He felt he had been touched by God.

Later as they made their way back to their lines with some gifts of provender, Reymond asked the others, "What did you make of that?"

"This war has made us all strange," Jules said.

Andros appeared happily drunk and didn't give a coherent reply, chattering away in his own language. They shared the food they'd come away with amongst the few survivors of Charles's unit. Reymond thought it might be the last meal they saw for some time. Reymond spent some time explaining to Charles Sebastien's vision about the virtues. Charles was sceptical but in the end it was decided. They would join forces with the Tafurs.

# Yerevan 2012

THE BIG MAN her father had called Fisher drove her home. He'd turned up at the docks after they'd landed the yacht, and her father had called for him. He'd supposed to have been with her father but they'd become separated and her father, who now called himself Reymond, had been captured. The two men had exchanged heated words. Fisher had been given the babysitting duty and her father had taken another car to the airport.

She'd overheard enough to know that they were heading to Rome to find 'the next of the 7'. Her father had told her that his spirit had flown from his body and had been replaced by the spirit of another, this Reymond, a man from ancient history. Crazy talk. He promised that he just had to complete his tasks and her father would return.

Fisher had been uncommunicative on the drive to Yerevan's suburbs. She'd peppered him with questions that he'd given single word answers to. Did he believe that her father was this 'Reymond'? Apparently, yes he did.

As the car pulled up to her house she noticed that there was a light on. She hadn't left a light on.

"Can you come in?" she asked.

"Why?"

"There's someone in there. And there shouldn't be."

Fisher sighed, and pulled a handgun from a shoulder holster hidden beneath his light jacket. "Very well."

They crunched along the gravel and she took out her keys.

Fisher held his gun in both hands and nodded. She turned the key, pushed open the door, and stepped aside to let the big Englishman go first.

In the small kitchen, at the rough wooden table, sat Nicolozi; her father's gun on the table in front of him.

"Who's this?" he asked pointing at Fisher with his chin.

"A friend of my father's."

"A passerby," Fisher added.

Nicolozi's little finger tapped the star etched on the grip of the Tokarev pistol.

"There is still a small matter of debt," the Georgian said.

"I could just shoot you," Fisher replied.

Mari looked from one man to the other. She opened her mouth to speak but Nicolozi spoke first.

"You won't. There'd be the noise, then what would you do with my body? Plus I am but one man in a much larger organisation."

Fisher shrugged. "So?"

"So leave. The girl and I can discuss business." Nicolozi smiled at her.

"No, Fisher, please," she said.

Fisher gave her an enigmatic look. "What do ya want?"

Nikolozi's smile grew broad.

†

She'd watched Nicolozi getting into his car and waited until his car had disappeared before returning inside. Fisher had bought him off: the debt and more. She wasn't convinced that the Georgian wouldn't be back. Although he knew her father was back, he also knew her father was fleeing the country after killing some men in the organisation Nicolozi worked for. Although Andros had been the local boss, bosses change.

Fisher had then answered some of her questions on Reymond. The big man was convinced that her father's spirit was gone and another man inhabited her father's body. A man who claimed to be from the time of the crusades. It was crazy. She'd convinced Fisher to give her a contact number, just in case the Georgian came back, she'd said. Once Fisher had gone, to join her father to fly to Rome, Mari flicked the banknotes in the envelope he'd given her. There was enough for a flight to Rome, she thought. If they thought they'd be able to keep her away they were dead wrong.

# Bristol, England 1770

JULES HAD THE dream again. Knee deep in sand made sticky with blood, the expanse of brilliant white in front of him. Besmirched with bloody hand prints. The intelligent eye, as big as his fist, regarded him with an expression of pity, compassion and worst of all, forgiveness. The others didn't know; his sword was first. His arrows had brought the beast down; it had flown from him across the sand.

He'd had no hope of catching it if not for the cruelly barbed arrows he had hit it with; once, twice and, as it stumbled, a third. It was the third shot that brought it down, helpless, flanks heaving. He had strode across the unforgiving sand in what at the time had seemed like an instant but now, in his dreaming mind's eye, took an age. Each step he took his reflection grew in the brown, sad eye until he was all it encompassed. In the dream he relived the moment his sword arced down and there was a great splash of blood on the sand and he woke sweaty and nauseous.

He was unsurprised to wake in the inn, at the table, his head in yesterday's ale. He had soiled himself again. With shaking hands he lifted the mug and drained the dregs. He needed more.

He looked blearily around him. There were other forms sleeping off their drink on benches and in corners. They had all toasted the comet, and he secretly hoped it would crash into Bristol and set it all ablaze, destroying everything in a great fire.

He swayed over to the latrine and emptied his bladder, his insistent awakener. As he stumbled about kicking pot shards and other debris the door opened. The bright sunlight streamed in to blind him, and all he saw was a silhouette. But it was enough. Always the dream, then the avenging angel.

"I bid you welcome, welcome..." He stumbled over to his table and fumbled to draw the sword from the belt slung nonchalantly on the back of his chair. "I'm afraid we won't be having a repeat of lasht time as I can hardly shtand." He gripped the back of the chair and swallowed a wave of nausea, bile clawing at the back of his throat.

"You wished to talk?" said the silhouette.

Jules grimaced and let forth a long fart.

"Maybe nexsht time," he muttered, weaving from side to side, trying to focus.

"Hell's teeth, man, have you no pride? How did you end up this way?" cried the Wrathful Knight.

"First sword," muttered Jules, straightening up and looking contemptuously at his harasser.

"I was the first fucking sword!" he roared, sweeping his sword from its scabbard and running towards his friend and enemy. His wild charge ended on the point of a blade. He looked down at his chest, at the spreading red stain on a filthy shirt. He stared at the Wrathful Knight, and his voice was tortured.

"I was first sword. There was so much blood."

Reymond didn't know what to think as he lowered the body to the ground. He had spent two days trying to quell his rage before coming here. He wanted to talk. He had not talked to any of them before. He always just attacked. The longest conversations had lasted a handful of seconds between grunts of exertion and swordplay. He looked sadly at Jules, again a wastrel, a sot, a body at his feet. Next time, he thought, they could talk. There would always be a next time. Unless he could break the cycle. But he didn't understand it. Maybe Jules had known. But he didn't even know if the others were tortured between lives, like he was. He assumed that they were. He knew that the others could stand to be in the same room as each other without it coming to blows. Unlike him, although he was getting better at controlling the anger. Childhood rhymes, songs, religious tracts, all helped. But rage pressed at him all the time. He needed to end the curse.

# The Vatican, Rome 2012

"You never said I'd have to walk through shit," Mari complained, as the three of them made their way down the tunnel. Shining a torch under his chin, Fisher gurned until Mari was forced into a smile. Reymond was a few hundred yards away and he stood at a junction, shining his torch first one way then the next.

She'd turned up in Rome and phoned the number Fisher had scribbled on a piece of paper in case any of Nicolozi's goons had come after her. They'd not expected her to follow them. But now she was in the city Reymond had decided that she was in less danger if she was with them. They'd met and taken a trip to the sewers. Reymond had seemed to weigh things up, and eventually gave her a handgun.

She'd overheard another argument between Fisher and the man she couldn't help but see as her father.

"What the hell Reymond, she's just a girl!" Fisher had said. She'd be having words with him about that once they were in a comfy hotel somewhere.

"I have a feeling that she will have a part to play," her father had replied.

"A feeling? You'll get her killed, fer a feeling?"

"The curse works in mysterious ways. Besides, if we don't have her with us she'll only track us down, probably at an inopportune moment."

In the end what Reymond said went. It seemed that he had some power over the bigger man.

They caught up with Reymond. "Problem?" Mari asked.

"I thought I heard something, that's all," Reymond said.

"Something?" Mari wasn't sure she wanted to know.

"Large, splashing. Not sure which way it came from."

"Alligator found under Vatican!" Fisher joked behind them.

"It is possible," Reymond deadpanned.

"More likely to be a guard of the two legged variety. We'd best be quiet," Fisher said.

They came to the junction that Fisher had marked. They ascended the red ladder one by one. Reymond came last.

"This section has guards," Fisher warned them.

As if his word had summoned them, a trio of guards came round the corner some thirty foot away from them and performed a comedic double take. The guns they pulled were less funny.

The first bullet shattered Reymond's torch. The three scattered. Reymond hugged the wall next to Fisher.

"Go!" Fisher hissed in his ear.

"Are you sure?" Reymond asked.

"I'll hold them here."

Reymond didn't need to be told twice. He raced off into the darkness, turned a corner. Mari struggled to follow, less used to moving about in the dark. Shots rang out behind them, she ignored them and pressed on, deeper into the Vatican. She had soon lost Reymond, but carried on in the direction she'd last thought he was in.

She thought back to the casino and Reymond, the man she'd come to think of as Reymond, saying that he wasn't her father. That was a long and difficult conversation.

She didn't understand it all, even now, but had come to accept that the spirit inside her father's body was not her father. She'd first thought that it was an act but when Fisher came to take them away from Armenia he corroborated a lot of it.

Were the two men insane? A collective hallucination/psychotic break? It seemed the more likely option, but not one she could believe.

Voices and sporadic gunfire echoed around the darkened labyrinth and brought Mari back to the present. She had to catch up to Reymond.

Reymond had his eyes closed, to enhance his other senses. With one hand trailing along the plastered wall, he advanced carefully. He could hear sounds of fighting, but it was impossible to tell if they were coming from in front of him or behind. A sour, pervasive odour was noticeable in front. He made his way towards it. Rotten garbage. Tangy fruit, something much coarser, and the sweet sickly smell of rotten flesh. Reymond was literally following his nose.

When the wall ended he walked on for a couple of paces, thinking he had found another corridor. A subtle change of acoustics alerted him to the fact that he was in a much wider space.

He opened his eyes, and now he could see the source of the smell. Before him was an oak table, so huge it could easily seat forty people. He couldn't understand how it could have got here, down the narrow corridors. Upon the table was a mass of food, in various stages of decay. Sat at the head of the table, his sword in front of him, was Gluttony.

Gluttony had been many things in many bodies but this was the first time Reymond had seen him so thin since the Crusade. Vermin crawled upon the table, in and out of the cornucopia of rotting food. Maggots, cockroaches, other less identifiable creatures. Across the floor dripped a foul leachate. Rats scampered in throngs, skipping out of the way of his feet. Reymond felt his gorge rising.

"Sir Wrath. You took your time, it has been a long wait," Gluttony greeted him with a smile.

"Tafur." Reymond mentally ran through another verse of Alouette.

"No-one has called me that for some time, for ages," Gluttony said, making no move to stand.

"You still have delusions of royalty, though. Although now you pretend to be the power behind the throne."

"I *am* the throne. Their holiness's rule because of me, of me," Gluttony responded.

"The papacy is becoming an irrelevance."

Gluttony merely shook his head. "Poor Reymond. So angry, so cross."

He stood, the table between them.

"What is all this?" Reymond asked, making a sweeping gesture taking in the table, the labyrinth, the Vatican, everything. "What have we become?"

"I am hunger. But I refuse to be dictated to by the gaping hole that demands more. More food. More drink. More. More. More!" Gluttony was shouting now, ranting. "I gorge and purge and it only gets worse so I gorge more and purge faster. I blame you. Killing the others makes the curse stronger. If I kill you it will be stronger again. But needs must."

The tide of battle in the labyrinth behind Reymond changed pitch, constant gunfire now. Reymond pointed at Gluttony with his sword. "You brought the curse down upon us. That is what I have always believed. When I came across you at Ma'Arra, you and your men. But I know now. I should have known from what happened with Andros. I found the book. The sorcerer of Ma'Arra. Everything is in there. He cursed us. Sebastien was the unwitting instrument of that curse, and its greatest effect."

Tafur stopped moving round the table, allowing Reymond to approach a little closer. "What are you saying? What book? What writing?"

"The sorcerer of Ma'Arra wrote it all down. When Sebastien had finished with him the Armenians fled east with his body, to Iran. I found it there."

"But Sebastien had a vision, a prophecy. From God," Tafur said.

"No. He caught himself a sorcerer. You remember the bird?"

"God spoke through him." Tafur sounded so sure, still.

"No man! Think! Why are we cursed?" Reymond suddenly felt it was important to convince Tafur. The song in his head finished, he started another. He wondered again if he was trying to convince himself, as well.

"Because of Ma'Arra," Gluttony said.

"No, Ma'Arra was a symptom. The curse fell upon us as we besieged it. As the walls fell. Was that not when your hunger overtook you? That was when Wrath first overtook me."

"I am not responsible for the curse? It is not my fault?" Tafur asked. For the first time he sounded uncertain.

Reymond inched closer. "No, you are not. But you will help me lift it."

"How?"

Reymond raised his sword. Tafur cocked his head.

"By the sword it was started, by the sword it will end. I must face Pride and defeat him."

"You'll never get into his lair, his fortress," Tafur said, after a beat.

"Fortress? You know where he hides?"

"If I tell you, would you let me go?" Tafur didn't look hopeful.

Reymond shook his head. "You know I can't."

"I thought not." Quick as a snake, Tafur struck.

It had always been a challenge to get inside his circle of guards, therefore Reymond had fought him much less often than some of the others; he was less aware of Tafur's strengths and weaknesses. The two men exchanged half a dozen quick, sharp blows before disengaging.

Tafur skipped backwards. Moving swiftly, he dropped, rolled under the table and popped up on the other side.

"You always were a sloppy swordsman, Sir Wrath. Any of us could best you. Except perhaps poor Envy. Fancy you making him the first. A crueller man would make him jealous of the release you afforded, the relief."

"Come then Tafur, if you are so eager for release." Reymond let the rage flood into him, filling him with speed, strength, and deadly purpose.

Reymond bounded onto the table and skated across it, struggling to keep his feet as the rotten mush squelched beneath them. Tafur leapt out of the way. Jumping down, Reymond brought himself within striking reach, with no barriers between them. He took the required steps, almost a formal dance to bring his sword up.

Tafur executed a set of precise and devious moves that Reymond was hard pressed to counter. As the two disengaged, having more of a sense of each other, Tafur's eyes flicked to something behind Reymond, out of his line of sight. He manoeuvred, side on to his assailant, never taking his eyes off him. He could see a Cardinal, standing stock still in the doorway, watching.

"Don't just stand there, do something!" Tafur barked. His voice seemed to break whatever spell the man was under, and the Cardinal drew a small handgun from his robes and pointed it at Reymond, his hands shook visibly.

Reymond danced around, trying to keep Tafur between him and the cardinal with the gun. They exchanged blows, the clash of metal ringing in the chamber. Reymond must have left himself open as a shot rang out, closely followed by a second – but it was the cardinal that stumbled and fell. Reymond risked a glance behind him to see Mari had evened the odds.

Another figure turned the corner. Reymond was too busy to see who it was, but hoped it was Fisher. There was a shot and Reymond glanced away from Tafur. Mari had seen the gun and had thrown herself bodily into the path of the bullet aimed for Reymond's heart.

Her mouth worked soundlessly as she tried to prop herself against the wall. She slithered to the floor, leaving a vivid red smear across the white plaster.

Reymond watched Mari fall, as if in slow motion. The man who'd shot her, a random Vatican guard, cursed, fumbling to reload his gun for another shot.

Reymond had to concentrate on Tafur again, they exchanged a few more blows. Reymond was aware of the man behind him with a gun and his back itched, expecting a shot any second. He manoeuvred so that Tafur was side on to the man who was drawing a bead on Reymond.

Another shot rang out and the guard sprouted a third bloody eye in the dead centre of his forehead, before toppling like so much lumber to the floor.

Mari, behind Reymond, sitting propped against the wall, said, "Seriously, it's beginning to be a habit." There were no more sounds of gunfire in the labyrinth.

Tafur took advantage of Reymond's inattention, diving forward to score a deep cut down his side. Reymond tried desperately to fend him off and took a second, more serious, wound in the meat of his thigh.

Reymond stumbled. He dropped back, crashing into the table. Like a shark smelling blood, Tafur pressed forward irresistibly, only to discover Reymond was not as wounded as he appeared.

Reymond thrust, and Tafur was unable to fend off the blow. Reymond's sword trembled in Tafur's chest. Tafur coughed, spraying blood.

"You asshole..." he grunted as he fell to the floor. As famous last words went they were not the best.

Reymond fell to his knees. The air in the chamber seemed to have grown darker with Tafur's death. He clutched his side where Tafur's sword had struck and winced, his hand coming away hot, like a burn. Head swimming, he forced himself to his feet and gazed over to Mari. Her eyes were open, and she blinked at him, but she was bleeding heavily. She tried to sit up and hissed with pain, and slumped back to the floor. "I always seem to be pulling your arse out of the fire," she said, her smile sweet and kindly. Her eyes closed.

Reymond himself was seriously wounded. The heat had spread all down his side. Deciding he'd best deal with his own wounds first, he was wrapping a bandage around his torso when Fisher arrived.

"Holy shit..." Fisher took in the scene. He checked Mari, arriving at her side at the same time as Reymond. "What happened?"

"Too much." Reymond handed Fisher a strip of material. "We had best get out of here before we discuss it."

"The way we came in is out of the question. Even if the Italian army are not breaking down the door, the Swiss Guard are everywhere." Fisher was covered in filth and his clothes were torn but he appeared uninjured.

"We can only go deeper, then," Reymond said.

Fisher nodded.

"Can you carry her?" Reymond asked.

Despite his age Fisher was still powerfully built. He lifted Mari easily. Reymond bent to pick the swords up, and whirling black dots invaded his vision. When he straightened he had to take several deep breaths before he could see clearly again.

Reymond followed Fisher through the tunnels until they found themselves in a sewer outlet. They followed the sluggish water until they saw daylight and sped up, although still hampered by Reymond's injuries. They came to a large gated entrance above the river. Fisher took a few seconds to open the gate whilst Reymond attempted to swallow the fresher air, a slight breeze wafted the worst of the sewer away.

As they scrambled down the bank and into the faster-flowing cold – but clear – water, a great weight seemed to lift from Reymond's shoulders. He was one step closer to his goal. His joy was tempered with the knowledge that his nightmares would now include the noisome tunnel fight.

†

Fisher thought he was the only one awake. Mari and Reymond had been given painkillers and rough and ready first aid. Fisher headed towards a discreet clinic he knew in Switzerland where they could get treatment, with no questions asked – if Reymond could cough up enough cash. The headlights picked out the winding road and the thrum of the engine was soothing.

"Tafur knew where Pride is." Reymond's voice was scratchy, his eyes red.

"I thought you were asleep." Fisher glanced over his shoulder at the back seat. Mari was still sleeping, but he didn't like how pale she was.

"Too much on my mind. There may be something in the Vatican that will lead me to Sebastien. We have to go back," Reymond said.

Fisher gave him a sidelong glance.

"When we are recovered," Reymond amended.

Fisher said nothing and the silence stretched on.

"I am so close," Reymond muttered.

Fisher nodded. The car sped on through the night, towards mercy and rest.

# Bristol, England 1665

REYMOND SLAMMED OPEN the door and drew his sword. The inn was full of the pestilent and those too poor to follow Charles II, who had fled to the countryside to get away from the plague.

Reymond was determined; this time he would have satisfaction. He had a cloth tied round his face to evade the sickness that had scuppered him in the past. He glanced around the interior of the inn. It was dark with all the shutters closed; some shafts of light picked out lazy dust swirling in the breeze he'd ushered in by opening the door. He spotted the man he wanted, hefted his sword and strode over to the table.

The man he had come to kill was sitting quietly, mazed by the drink. As expected, Jules was unprepared, but he scrambled to his feet and pulled his sword as Reymond approached.

With an overhand strike Reymond drove Jules before him. Jules looked ill, dissolute, in his cups, and he barely managed to block the angry blade. He put up what fight he could, but it was obvious he was outmatched from the first stinging blow. The resulting clash was short and deadly, and ended with Jules pinned to the wall on Reymond's sword, twitching his last.

"Curse..." he managed to say, before his life drained away.

Reymond was triumphant. Jules was the first of the 7 to die at his blade. This time, he thought, he would be victorious.

With a swirl of his cloak he stomped out of the inn and ran to his horse, hastening to get out of town. He had a ship to catch. He was heading for Rome, where he knew the Greedy Knight would be, just as he knew the Slothful Knight would be in Bristol. God-given knowledge.

He had less time than he'd have liked. The damn plague made travel difficult.

He'd heard rumours about 'Don Juan' in Spain, so expected that Andros was somewhere there. As his horse picked its way through the muddy street, splashing through the filth, he pondered what he'd learned so far.

They came back at odd times; he'd tried to discern a pattern but couldn't see one. Sebastien would know, but it didn't matter who he paid – he could find no sign of the man he'd once known as Humility. The man who'd brought the curse down upon them. It didn't matter if he found the other five if he couldn't find the Prideful knight. His revenge, and the curse, would not be done until all fell beneath his blade.

In his dreams, his nightmares, he'd pieced together some information. Let slip by the masked man, the man with his own face, his original face, his tormentor. The swords were important. Every one of them, when they returned, always returned with their sword. Although, once returned, it was possible to lose them, deliberately or accidently.

The horse chuntered a greeting to another and Reymond looked up briefly to meet the eyes of a man wrapped up against the weather and the plague. His hand hovered near his sword, as did the stranger's. There was little trust in this plague-ridden land.

Every time he awoke into a new body he was filled with a burning rage, and a purpose. To slay the others. He knew, without knowing how he knew, that it was his purpose to end the curse, and to do so he had to kill the other knights.

This time he had wasted six years. He had struggled to forget the curse, to forget his revenge, but it would not let him rest.

As the seventh year dawned he was filled with purpose, unable to relax until he was revenged. He had seldom made it to the seventh year before, and he doubted he would again. His soul felt like it was being torn apart. He knew he would most likely fail again, but he was helpless to stop trying.

He had been guided by his nightmares, and the periods in between lives where he was mercilessly tortured by himself and all those that he'd ever killed. And there were a lot of them. Saracens, women, children, his former friends in various incarnations.

But over the decades he had come to the realisation that the curse could be broken. Underneath the horror the clues were there to see. He had to end the others and then God would let him rest.

He arrived at the docks and sold the horse. He had enough money to book passage to France; once there he would buy a new horse and make his way to where he suspected the others were. Again their locations were revealed in dreams and portents. All except for Sebastien. That sorcerer knew how to hide!

The periods that he was lost in a red rage were getting longer. He knew that eventually he'd become a creature of pure wrath, killing indiscriminately in a frenzy and tortured for each death in between lives. He had to end the curse, and he had to do it before that happened, whilst he still had some semblance of rationality.

This time. Maybe this time he'd be successful. If he could find Sebastien. He wrapped his cloak around himself and waited to board the ship.

# Antioch, The Holy Land 1098

ROBERT CURTHOSE ADDRESSED his commanders: there was now a flatter structure to the army. Reymond and the sergeant were also at the meeting, although Reymond wasn't sure why he was there.

Curthose looked around his men, seemingly trying to gather his strength, or find the right words. He might have eaten better than the rank and file, but he was still lean with hunger.

"We're out of options. Their army has us caught fast. We have limited horses, not enough men, and not enough food to last a prolonged siege. We can't run away, not that we want to, so we're going to attack."

This got the men's attention.

"Attack? But the enemy is three times our number, at least. They are well fed, and on horses that are better fed than our men. It's suicide." The speaker was a man Reymond knew by reputation, a fearsome warrior for all that his beard was shot with grey.

"What is your strategy then?" Charles asked quietly.

The man blustered, but had no retort.

"As I said, we attack. We shall be in the vanguard."

This seemed to surprise some of the assembled commanders. Most of them had retained more men than Charles, although Charles had now been given stragglers from units whose commanders have died.

"To what do we owe that honour?" a man Reymond didn't know asked.

"I asked for it," Robert said. There was a moment of stunned silence, broken by the sergeant's bass rumble.

"Why?"

"It is better to die in battle than to starve to death. Besides, we have the Holy Lance. We cannot be defeated."

The rest of the meeting was given over to planning.

In a few short hours, after another Mass, the army gathered at the Bridge Gate. Reymond was near the front, and he found it difficult to see how many men the crusaders had, but it seemed a substantial force behind him. There were few horses, so few, in fact, that he could see one knight mounted on a donkey. There was the usual nervous waiting, men touched private relics and prayed.

"It's clever," Jules said.

"What is?"

"To go out of the Bridge Gate. It means the river is between us and the majority of the enemy. We'll be able to fight our way out and not get stuck like a cork in a bottle. That's sound thinking."

Reymond nodded. His finger tapped his thumbnail and he jiggled a foot. A whole line of priests in full regalia strode past, carrying crucifixes and candles with banners the colours of each of the princes amongst them. It was like a festival.

The priests climbed the stairs onto the wall, and as they did so the gates swung open. The horsemen trotted out first and with a collective sigh, as men shouldered spears and got into line, the whole army snaked its way out of the gate.

As Reymond passed under the shadow of the arch he intoned the Lord's prayer, which was taken up by several men around him. As they wheeled to the left, so the four contingents were fully deployed, Reymond could already see that their army was vastly outnumbered. He hoped there were more men waiting inside the walls of the city, ready to rush to their aid, although such a defence wasn't in the plans that Robert had discussed with them this morning.

The familiar trumpets and wailing started up as an enemy battalion, numbering in the several hundred, charged across the plain. There was a thrum and whoosh as a contingent of archers unleashed three flights of arrows, which winnowed the numbers before they met the set spears and thirsty swords of the crusader's line.

Reymond was intent on staying alive, braining one man, cutting another until bone showed shockingly against the rent armour. Trumpets blared and flags fluttered in the distance, their meaning lost on Reymond, although he assumed they signalled the main body of the enemy force.

There was a thundering that Reymond realised he had been feeling, then hearing, in between the sounds of battle. The pitifully small cavalry crunched into the enemy flank, which bent, buckled and collapsed. The Saracen turned and fled and Reymond's sword took a final soul before the order to stand fast was bellowed down the line.

In the vanguard, they were treated to the sight of an enemy in rout, colliding into men on their own side, racing to relieve them. The Saracen army was in disarray.

Robert Curthose sounded the advance and the men marched forward in a quick step. The enemy were panicked now, and a great gout of smoke gusted in from another part of the battlefield. The smell of smoke made Reymond turn briefly to glance back towards the city, blinking into the haze above the dry fields. Someone had torched the grass.

Crusaders and some of the enemy raced towards the river. Other men of Reymond's army were in full pursuit of the Saracens. Although they vastly outnumbered the crusaders, they appeared to be in full retreat. Reymond scanned the battlefield for Jules, catching Andros instead and gesturing for the sailor to come with him. The three friends were reunited by the river, where Jules was using his helmet to douse himself in water. Reymond and Andros followed suit. Reymond's mouth was dry with ash. The wind blew to the south, taking the grass fire with it, so they were able to return to the city with relative ease.

"Two hundred men were left to guard the city. They could easily be overrun by the force in the Citadel," Jules informed them. The priests, who had been chanting blessings, were all cheering. Reymond hoped this meant that they were triumphant.

"The Lance! We cannot be defeated, yes, if we hold the Lance," Andros shouted, a big grin on his mired face.

"Yes, but that was too easy. They must be preparing some ruse, surely?" Reymond found it hard to believe the siege was broken and the battle over already.

They headed to the rally point and waited, whilst stragglers arrived in ones and twos. The sergeant found them idling, but for once he failed to bawl them out over it. Instead he pulled out a waterskin and passed it around. "I hear the Citadel surrendered," he said. "Took one look at the massive army scattering to the hills, and decided they'd had enough too. Next stop, Jerusalem!"

†

"Horse?" Reymond was hungry. He seemed to be hungry all the time.

"Yes, horse," the sergeant said, "it's perfectly good meat. We're all out of goat. We're out of most things, if I'm honest."

Reymond put his hand to his forehead and closed his eyes.

"Fine. I am hungry enough." He squatted next to the man who had brought him out of France and accepted the stringy meat.

"How bad is it?" he asked.

"It's gone from shitty to utterly pissing diabolical," the sergeant said.

"But how can we have run out of food? Wasn't there plenty left by the rout?"

"So we thought. What about our new friends?" The sergeant looked hopeful.

"Not sure. The Tafurs play it close, you know?" Reymond glanced across the camp, to where the Tafurs were gathered. His attention was brought back to the sergeant by the older man's hand on his arm.

"Listen Reymond, I've heard some rumours. About Tafur. And his magician."

"Rumours?"

"I'm not sure if they are the best people for us to be involved with. Charles won't listen to me, but I thought you might."

"According to rumours?"

"They're pretty hefty rumours."

"Jules and Andros are with me," Reymond protested. "We saved Tafur, and he owes us. He is going to knight us. I thought you would be happy for me." Reymond wondered why the sergeant was trying to spoil things.

"I am, lad. It's just..." The sergeant opened his hands, lost for words.

"They are just rumours!"

"Well..."

"Thank you for the meal. I will pass the message on." Reymond stood.

"Message?" the sergeant said to his retreating back.

"That you have no food," Reymond said as he walked away. He didn't look back. As he approached the Tafur's camp he reflected on the sergeant's concern. It was well meant, he supposed, but patronising. Although he had heard certain rumours too, and sometimes he wondered if he was doing the right thing.

Jobert welcomed him as he approached. Andros and Jules

chatted with Charles, while Tafur and the odd creature who had brought them all together were nowhere to be seen. The four men were sitting around the remains of a meal.

"I have just been speaking to the sergeant," Reymond said.

"And?" Jules asked.

"And the unit has no food." Reymond said.

"Many have no food," Charles added.

"He asked me about the Tafurs," Reymond said, turning to the nobleman.

"What about them?" Jules asked.

"If they had any food." Reymond stirred the remains of the meal pointedly with the toe of his boot.

"Yes, but only to share amongst themselves," Charles said.

"Where did it come from?" Reymond wanted to know.

Jules glanced furtively at Andros before he answered. "The same place all the army's food comes from. The surrounding land."

"Of course, it is just that..." Reymond broke off.

"Go on," Charles prompted.

"It is just that there are these rumours..."

"That the Tafurs are lying, cheating, robbing vagabonds with a welcome for any disease-ridden son of a whore who wants to join them?" Charles asked.

"Yes, that. And more specific rumours too." Reymond was glad he'd broached the subject.

Charles and Jobert exchanged a glance. "We've heard them all too," Charles said.

This surprised Reymond. "But are we not, well, 'with' the Tafurs now?"

"Yes. But we didn't start out with them. Despite their lack of equipment they are a formidable fighting force, and of course Sebastien is touched by God." Jobert had started sheepishly but was firm at the end. "All the princes together cannot tame Tafur," he added.

Reymond glanced at Andros and Jules. "It is best if we

know everything." Reymond hoped Andros and Jules would back him up.

Charles hawked and spat. "There's nothing more to know. Apart from that the man is from the fens high in the north, and he has uncanny senses. We've been at the heart of fighting several times since joining them and lost no more men. Certainly those that stand closest to Tafur seem to bear his protection."

"Although the common Tafurs die quickly enough," Jobert muttered.

Charles paused, contemplating this, or some other imponderable. "We have the protection of the Tafur king and his Holy Man. That seems to count for something."

Talk turned to the campaign, to food, to the battles to come and the friends that had been lost on the road.

# Bristol, England 1547

Reymond stalked the filthy street, trying not to step in the ordure. He kept a posy clamped to his face to cut out the foul stench. He was following a tip-off that there was a foreigner bunking at the White Hart. Reymond hoped it was the man he was looking for, the one he'd once known as Diligence. He approached the sprawling inn and paused. Best not to alert the man he had come for. He spotted a grubby child and beckoned him over.

"A coin if you go into the inn and tell me if the foreigner is there. Do not be obvious about it, mind." He held up the coin and the urchin tried to snatch it, but Reymond palmed it skilfully.

"Once the task is done," he chided.

The urchin stared, then turned and scampered towards the inn.

He returned a short time later.

"The Frenchy is in the inn, on the right of the main bar, sat by hisself. He's all dressed in black." He held out his hand. Reymond smiled and placed the coin in it and the urchin was off in a streak. Towards where, Reymond didn't care to imagine.

He loosened the sword at his side and stomped over to the inn. He breathed in a measured way, preparing for the fight ahead. He crossed the threshold, looking for the man he'd once called brother. The man who'd lost his heart, his hope, and his drive when he killed the creature in the Holy Land. The man he now thought of as the Knight of Sloth. It was time for God's Wrathful vengeance.

He strode into the main bar. No sign of the Frenchman. He addressed himself to the barkeep.

"Have you seen the foreigner in here, the one dressed in black? He was sat at a table."

The bar man grimaced and sneezed. Reymond wiped mucus off his face in disgust. The bar man hawked and swallowed. "You've just missed him. He spoke to an urchin and then he left quick sharp."

Reymond cursed. "Did you see which way he went?"

The barman gestured toward a side door and moved to serve a customer.

Reymond burst through the door and was confronted with a long narrow street, with a busier intersection at the far end. He spotted a beggar and dropped a coin into his bowl.

"See anyone dressed in black come from this alley?" he asked.

The beggar turned eyes clouded by cataracts towards Reymond. He broke into a hideous smile, full of teeth long gone to rot.

"Can't say I've seen anyone in a long while, sir."

Reymond cursed again.

"But a gentleman did drop a coin in my bowl a few minutes ago and when I thanked him he said something like rain, sounded foreign."

"De Rien," Reymond said.

"That's the phrase. You foreign too?" The beggar blinked his egg white eyes.

"Which way did he go?" Reymond asked looking around.

"East, towards the market."

Reymond dropped another coin in the bowl and hurried east along the street. He spotted several men wearing black, but none that identified as Sloth. When he got to the market it was obvious he was out of luck; he would never find him amid the jostling crowds. He asked a few of the stallholders if they'd seen a man dressed in black who looked French, whatever that would look like, but no-one had.

Giving up in frustration, Reymond returned to his lodgings. He would search again in the morning. At supper he began to feel an ache, deep in his bones. His neck was stiff, his head sore, and a foul taste gathered at the back of his throat.

"Are you alright, honey?" The landlady asked, noticing his discomfort.

"That damn barman has given me a pestilence," he said.

"Best have a posset and get to bed." She bustled off to make him the hot drink.

Reymond sneezed, inwardly railing at the prospect of any delay. He'd thought this time was different, certainly not like the time, was it in 1322? When he was a cripple? Plenty of penance, but not of the kind he sought.

So many times he had come back and been unable to find the others, losing himself in endless bouts of anger and recriminations. Random fistfights and duels. Arbitrary killings. He felt his humanity like the sand in a timepiece, slowly running down each time he returned. Each time he seemed to spend more and more periods in the red rage. He'd hoped that this time would be different.

This time he knew tracking down Sloth to whatever piss-poor tavern he had chosen to drown himself in, to ward off the inevitable, was but a matter of time. He shivered, feeling utterly wretched. How typical that he should fall ill just as he was getting close.

The curse continued to beat in his veins. Find the others and exterminate them. Deliver God's Wrathful vengeance. Whilst on the mortal plane it was clear that this was his purpose. Which was why it seemed utterly cruel that his tormentor in his own personal hell should punish him so for slaying his friends.

When he remembered that they were his friends, and

chained together in mutual guilt over their crime, he burned with shame, but always under the shame was a deeper heat. Rage boiled his blood.

He took the posset to bed with him. Three hours later he was bathed in sweat, with a raging thirst, his head splitting. He called for the landlady and gave her explicit instructions regarding what to do with his effects. The sweating sickness had been visited upon him this time. Death from an unexpected quarter. Not much time to plan and now the 7 would go unpunished.

Once the landlady had gone the fever carried him away. He was neither alive nor dead he felt. The curse was still there, a siren call, a castigation. And now he was fully immersed in his dreams, the room was populated by all the people he'd killed. The friends he had, in the past incarnations, tracked down and slain, given speaking parts, a chorus of condemnation.

He railed and raged, dimly aware that the landlady, amongst the ghoulish forms of the dead, was real. Eventually the man in the mask arrived.

"I did not know!" Reymond shouted, his throat raw from screaming. "Please."

The figure, whose face, un-masked, was like looking into a mirror, shook his head and held out a hand. Andros, the original one, with several other incarnations gathered like shadows behind him, handed the masked man a dagger. Turned edge on it was guilt and remorse sharpened.

As the masked man turned back to Reymond the gloom behind him took the shapes of wings which beat the air. Reymond realised that death had taken him once again, and his tortures started anew.

The landlady burned all the bed linen after she had sewn him into the sheet. She sent the boy to fetch the undertaker.

Luckily Reymond had left her with substantially more money than he was paying her for lodgings. When the boy returned she sent him out again to fetch the lawyer. When he arrived he spent some time reading the letter Reymond had penned before he'd lapsed into unconsciousness. He took charge of the Reymond's belongings.

"He had a sword," she said.

The lawyer, in the act of bundling up Reymond's clothes turned to look at her, a question upon his face.

"It's gone," she added.

"There is no mention of a sword in his letter, madam. It can't be very important."

Relieved, she forgot about it.

In the morning the landlady was arranging for the body to be taken away when the news broke that the king was also dead. He had left an infant to take the throne. She crossed herself, shuddering with a sudden foreboding of evil. As the shiver ran down her back she turned to go inside and was surprised to see a short man approaching her. At his hip was an identical sword to the one Reymond had worn, the one that had gone missing. The one she'd decided to forget about.

The man had long dirty hair and a sharp nose. He questioned her closely and at some length; he had a French accent. His eyes were trying to dissect her, looking into her soul. He seemed satisfied with her recounting of the life and death of the gentlemen who had been lodging with her, and she told him what had happened to the body, and to Reymond's effects. He asked her if there were any correspondence left, and she told him there wasn't.

As he rose to take his leave she looked upon the sword.

"Sir?"

He regarded her with an eyebrow raised. She took a deep

breath for courage. "What about the sword, sir? You have the exact same blade the gentleman had, looks like a cross it does. His went missing when he died. I think someone may have stolen it."

"No madam, no-one would have stolen it. If anyone comes here after me asking about your lodger, or his sword, you tell them nothing about me. Do you understand?"

She nodded vigorously.

She was relieved when he departed, and hoped she never had to see anyone with a similar sword again.

# Ma'Arra, The Holy Land 1098

THEY MARCHED SOUTH from Antioch. Jerusalem was a still distant target. Robert Curthose had been given the task of gathering more supplies.

"Three days march to the south is the city of Ma'Arra," Charles said. "We're to sack it and bring back as much food as possible. Until our supply lines are more secure we won't be marching on Jerusalem. So let's get into this city and grab whatever we can." Charles's men were unenthusiastic about the prospect of another siege. "Come on, boys," he encouraged them, "think of the booty. Besides, it'll be easy; our scouts say there isn't much of a garrison at this place."

Reymond was only half listening. The previous night he'd been inducted into a strange new brotherhood. He glanced over to the ragged army following the newest 'Prince', now even acknowledged by men such as Curthose as worthy of respect, as a brother in arms. Reymond also knew Robert had made some sort of deal with him. He wondered if this was all due to the weird man called Sebastien. The Fenlander. He thought back to the odd meeting a couple of evenings ago, with Jobert leading them in prayer.

"My Lord Tafur has determined we each represent one of the heavenly virtues. He is Temperance, Charles is Charity, I am Kindness and Sebastien is Humility. You three have also exhibited the virtues. You, Reymond have embodied Patience, Andros, you are Chastity and Jules is Diligence. We have each taken the cross, each sworn sacred oaths. It is time for a new oath. A bond of friendship, of fraternity, that will be impossible to break. We 7 shall henceforth be known as the Knights of Virtue. Le Roi Tafur will knight each of us. Our bond will be witnessed by God and He will grant us victory."

"It has been seen," Sebastien added solemnly.

Reymond was not sure about all the mysticism, but if it was fine for the priest then he guessed it was fine for him. He hoped he could live up to his new name, a Virtue, and that it would see him achieve grace.

Charles, Sir Charity, addressed them. "Some of our number follow Robert Curthose, others follow other princes. I suggest we split from our former allegiances, amicably of course, and join with Le Roi Tafur, who is independent of the other princes. We will join with this expedition to, where was it?"

"Ma'Arra," Sebastien provided.

"To Ma'Arra, there to join in with its sack for the Glory of God."

Not a breeze stirred the sands, but there was a black dot moving in the sky. As it came closer it resolved into the shape of a bird, one of the Corvid family. On the horizon there was a hint of darkness, some far away dust clouds roiling. The sun had risen a scant hour ago yet the desert was scorching. The sky was cobalt and the sun an angry yellow. The bird swept towards the small town.

As Reymond watched it fly, his eye was drawn across the sands as the bird wheeled above the hastily-built fortifications. Carts had been turned over and debris piled on top to create barriers outside the gates, facing the approaching army. Ma'Arra was like many of the towns they'd plundered before except that rumours abounded of a shapeshifting Saracen sorcerer who made the town his own. He was supposed to be able to go abroad as a bird, which was why Reymond was watching the crow. What intelligence the sorcerer could have gleaned by flying over the army that the men on the wall wouldn't be able to see with their own eyes he didn't know. They would make camp and assault the town in the morning.

Many of the men were receiving communion. Reymond arrived back at camp to see that Jules, 'Sir Diligence', and Andros, 'Sir Chastity', had arrived. They fell to small talk and passed a bottle of sour wine between them as they awaited the rest of the group.

They didn't have long to wait. Sir Kindness, the priest, Jobert, should have be the natural one to lead them in prayer but it always seemed to be the young one, Sebastien – the one they used to call 'The Prophet', now renamed 'Sir Humility' – who led them and devised the rituals. Reymond knew that Charles, Sir Charity, was still of the mistaken belief that he led the group, when anyone could see that they did nothing without the say so of the Prophet.

Temperence paid little attention to the ritual, and Reymond wondered if the man would try to find a camp follower to share his bed tonight. He had often demonstrated he was not the most virtuous of them. Reymond found the thought of paying a woman abhorrent, but he tried not to judge. He wondered if Tafur was a proper Christian, and fluffed his line, caught out in his inattention. Sir Chastity, Andros, coughed to stifle a laugh, and instead of skipping over such lapses as he usually did, Humility hissed a curse. Reymond blinked; all the others were looking expectantly at him, bar Jules, who he still struggled to think of as Sir Diligence, who stared at the stars, looking bored with proceedings. Reymond said his line in a clear, loud voice.

"Amen," they said in unison.

Humility gestured at the priest, Kindness, who brought forth seven bundles.

"These swords have been made by the best sword makers in Europe, at the request of the Holy Father himself. I have secured seven for us, seven blades of virtue. They are yet to be blooded." As he spoke Kindness handed them out.

They had a striking design; long swords with a cross guard making them a cruciform shape apart from the tapering end. The pommels bore carvings of the Christian cross and Pax symbol. With ceremony, each knight was given a sword. Reymond hefted his, examining it critically. If it was from the best sword makers in Europe, then he was a heathen Saracen. The swords were well made, but not of the best steel. He kept quiet, knowing the men needed a boost before battle, and they would swagger a little thinking they carried special blades.

He grinned at Sir Charity. "Guard yourself, Sir Knight!" Reymond threw a half-hearted overhand swing. Charity easily blocked it and the two swords struck with the surprisingly sweet tone of chiming bells.

"They are not to be used against each other!" cried Humility. "They must be blessed! Today we wash them in holy water, tomorrow in blood!"

Reymond sighed. That sounded like yet another ritual.

The 7 awaited the call. Each had been shriven, each had prepared as best they could for the day. Reymond prayed fervently, while his stomach cramped and a knot of tension crawled up his back. His skin itched. The damn sand got everywhere. He was always irritable before a battle. He hated the waiting. He hated the fighting too, but at least he was good at that part. He reflected that it was only his outward appearance that seemed cool and collected and this was why he'd been renamed Patience. It was not a fitting name, not before a battle.

Especially not when there was no real plan. There were no siege engines at Ma'Arra. The crusaders were expected to run towards the city, climb over the debris into the killing ground and up rickety ladders onto the walls. It seemed the men in charge thought the defenders wouldn't put up much of a fight.

The 7 were assigned to a squad in the second wave. Could have been worse, could have been better. It meant they'd run over the corpses of the first wave. Each of the 7 waited in his own way; some prayed, some paced, some rested. Reymond may have appeared to be resting but inside his thoughts raced.

The commander for the attack on this section of wall, a noble Reymond didn't know, asked them to get ready. He had thought he'd be with Curthose, but somehow they were separated from their old command.

It wouldn't be long now. The men who rested now stood, preparing to run at the wall, in baking heat under heavy armour.

The command was given. Reymond started slowly, neck and neck with the others, but sped up to make the shelter of the ring of debris around the wall. He panted and chafed; deep damp patches spread beneath the armour making it even more uncomfortable.

Broken carts, furniture, doors, even dead animals had been stacked haphazardly. At this barrier the crusaders were at the outer limit of the range of arrows. Reymond looked up and across, his eyes followed the first wave. A fraction of the men who had set off in the charge had made the wall. There were many corpses.

He climbed the debris mechanically, ready for an arrow to strike at any moment. One clattered down at his feet. It had gleaming white feathers, strange and gory as they fluttered against the staring black eye sockets of a sheep's rotting skull glaring at him from the debris. He slithered down the other side of the barrier, and now the steel rain of arrows sleeted down around him. He rushed forward, past a man who screamed, three arrows sticking from his torso. Reymond hoped another would take him fast. It would be a mercy.

The commanding noble pulled ahead and Reymond studied the wall. It was topped by defenders who peppered the crusaders with arrows. This was a shambles, a bloodbath. The commander was hit and fell heavily, an arrow sticking out where his neck met his shoulder. They reached the wall, and now there were heavy stones to avoid. There weren't enough ladders.

Charles, Sir Charity took control. "We must retreat," he said.

"Retreat?" Reymond dodged a rock thrown from the wall. "That is madness surely?"

"This, this is madness." Sir Charity swept his arm, taking in the dead and dying, the chaos beneath the wall, the organised, stubborn defence.

The sergeant, stood next to them, did not need to be given explicit orders. He filled his lungs and bellowed. "Retreat, retreat!"

Time to run across the killing ground again, but this time with their backs to the enemy. It was long minutes sprinting, the skin on Reymond's back crawled with every stride. Once they reached a safe distance the 7 gathered, heaving and panting, mouths dry and limbs aching.

Tafur, Sir Temperance was the first to regain his breath. "Well that was a fucking disaster," he spat. Many of his men were still lying on the open ground beneath the walls.

It was a humiliating defeat. No-one seemed to know who was in charge anymore. The demoralised troops departed, trudging back towards Antioch in ragged lines. Above their heads a black crow circled, golden bands on its legs. Almost none of the crusaders paid it any attention. Reymond noticed it, but only because Sebastien, Sir Humility, watched it so carefully.

He remembered the rumours of a Saracen sorcerer and wondered if the bird was him in a shapeshift. Maybe the magic of the Saracen had saved the city? Reymond shook his head. The sorcerer must have mazed the commanders; everything beneath the walls had seemed more chaotic than usual.

Reymond looked to Sebastien again. Maybe they needed magic to fight magic?

Reymond pitched his tent for the night. Sweet–smelling incense wafted from the open door of Humility's tent as the black bird swept directly overhead. Reymond jumped and swore at the unexpected motion. The bird swooped down, flying directly into Humility's tent and there was a loud squawk, immediately cut off. The 6 exchanged glances. Jules shrugged, and indicated that Reymond should have a look in the tent.

"Everything alright in there?" he shouted, glancing back at the others who were watching him expectantly.

"Fine." Sebastien gestured inside the tent. There was no sign of any bird inside.

The next night, after a full day of marching through the heat, Reymond was dog tired but had managed to drag himself to the meeting. When he'd agreed to become one of the Knights of Virtue, he hadn't expected to spend so much time in ritual obeisance. To worship God, yes, but the other more esoteric stuff he could have done without.

"Patience, welcome, welcome," the elder of the order said as Reymond approached.

"Greetings, Humility."

"You are the last to arrive. We can now begin."

Reymond nodded to the rest and received a mixture of responses, some more friendly than others. He wished Humility would just get on with whatever tonight's ritual was. His fellow knights all looked as tired as he felt.

Humility called for silence.

"Virtues, we have before us a historic opportunity. I have had a prophetic dream, God's hand has touched me. I can give us an edge in our next battle. I can give us an edge in all battles. God has decreed it. There is a creature we must hunt. We must hunt it and kill it and use it. If we do this in the proper manner, then the victory of the Lord is assured."

Later, Jules took him to one side. "That was pretty weird, right?"

"More than everything else?" Reymond watched the others breaking camp.

"You saw the bird." Jules seemed intense, uncharacteristically nervous.

"I saw *a* bird. Well I thought I did, entering his tent. It wasn't there when I looked inside."

Jules nodded. "It was the sorcerer. I know it was. He's got this new idea from the captured sorcerer."

Reymond frowned.

"What are you two gossiping about?" Le Roi Tafur asked, having arrived soundlessly.

"How the tide will turn once we've slain this beast," Reymond said.

Jules hawked and spat. "I know hunting. We'd best prepare," he said. He gave Reymond a meaningful glance and went to give the others a hand packing up.

"God wills it!" Tafur said, hand on sword.

Reymond turned to stare into the desert. Were they doing the right thing? Leaving the army to hunt a mythical beast. He wondered if Sebastien had captured the sorcerer. The desert looked vast, and lonely.

# Bristol, England 2012

REYMOND WALKED THROUGH the doors of the King's Head, noting where they had been repaired from the last time he'd been there. Jules was inside, as he expected. There was a long wrapped object on the table in front of him, plus several empty pint glasses.

"Jules."

"Reymond." Jules touched the wrapped object.

"Buy you a drink?" Reymond asked.

"Same again." Jules pointed to the glass with a logo on it.

When Reymond returned from the bar they drank in silence for a long moment.

"Each of us that are gone increase the burdens of the others," Jules said eventually.

"To absent friends." Reymond raised his glass.

"I'm afraid—" Jules started.

"Do not be," Reymond interrupted.

Jules gave him a sharp glance. "I'm afraid we are working to different scripts. Mine is a love story."

"What do you mean?"

"I am in love. I can't leave her. I won't surrender," Jules said simply.

Understanding came to Reymond. He had been viewing this as a necessary, sad step. But not a difficult one. Well, not difficult in this way.

"If you win, you will only have another few years," Reymond

pointed out.

"I will take whatever I can get." Jules smiled sadly.

Reymond's anger was sudden, incandescent and uncontrollable. To be denied, at this stage, was unimaginable. He sprang to his feet, throwing the glass to one side. The sound of his chair cracking the floor and the glass smashing were cacophonous. He swept his sword out of its wrapping as Jules scrambled to do the same.

"I am sorry I–" Jules managed to get out, before their swords met with the familiar clear bell-like tone. They both ignored the eruption from the shotgun, and the call for them to drop their swords.

The bar maid frantically dialled on the phone as the other patrons rushed to leave, except the foolhardy ones filming the clash on their phones. Reymond concentrated, every sense bent to his sword, his opponent, and the fighting circle that had opened up around them.

Jules was the cannier swordsman. He always had been. Until now, his sin had always been his biggest handicap. He looked determined to throw off the shackles of sloth this time. Reymond cursed himself for taking things for granted. Tired from travel, his recent wounds still aching, he tried to put all thought out of his head, to regain his combat meditativeness, but a vein throbbed angrily at his temple and his mind ran over and over how unfair this was. Railing against the childish emotions that squeezed him in their grip made it worse. Better to channel the feeling, as he had been able to before. But the wrath was too strong this time.

He jumped away from a great overhand blow which smashed a table to splinters. He was peripherally aware of others around him and he calculated angles even as he forced another thrust away.

This was possibly the most closely matched the two had been in their many encounters. Reymond flicked a riposte that Jules countered, earning himself a red stripe on one shoulder.

Reymond was hyper-vigilant, knowing small cuts could be decisive.

They circled each other, moving with quick, small steps. Reymond executed a flurry of quick moves that Jules barely countered and earned a brand of his own as one riposte came too close for him to fully knock away.

Both men breathed heavily now. Reymond didn't want to wager that he was in better condition; he just wanted to end this quickly. They exchanged more stinging blows and Reymond remembered Jules, older, before the curse took hold, teaching a younger Reymond how to fight. It was a tiny distraction of memory overlaying reality, but it was enough.

Reymond was caught by an elbow across the face. His nose cracked, and pain shot across his cheeks. His head felt heavy and uncomfortable. He tried to breathe out through his nose, spraying thick strings of blood. He shook his head and backed off, desperately trying to fend off Jules's renewed attack.

His heel smacked against the skirting board and his head smashed against the wall as Jules's sword took him through the shoulder, pinning him to the plaster. As Jules tried to pull the blade free, Reymond dropped his own sword into his left hand and rammed it up. It pierced Jules's chin and was driven into his brain, killing him instantly. As Jules crumpled, the sword was wrenched out of Reymond's hand by the movement. He was left stranded, pinned to the wall by his dead friend's blade.

It was at that moment the police stormed the pub, charging through both front and rear entrances. They were armed. The first through the door was a bear of a man, Afro-Caribbean with a no-nonsense face.

"Don't you fucking move," he said as Reymond struggled weakly, caught like a fish on a hook. Blood poured down Reymond's face from his broken nose, and there was no feeling in his right arm.

He grimaced, tasting blood, eyes wide with pain. "Could not if I tried, officer."

The first policeman rang for an ambulance whilst two more checked Jules. Reymond saw a young WPC, white as a sheet, and he wondered if Jules was her first dead body. He was ashamed. They took a few photographs, both of him and the body at his feet.

When the ambulance turned up, he was handcuffed to the stretcher by his good arm, and the paramedics cut away his clothes. He had refused to answer any questions.

"What's your name?" the policeman asked him again.

"Patience," he replied through gritted teeth.

The two paramedics shared a look.

"Right, I'm going to give you something for the pain," one of them said. Reymond felt a needle, a sharp scratch followed by an icy bloom in his vein.

The ambulance wailed through the traffic, taking him to hospital. He could hear other sirens, so he knew the police were following close behind. He wondered if Mari had seen this on the news.

🗡

Mari knocked back another vodka. This was her third. She resented this 'man must do the thing alone' deal, and at the moment she felt like a spare wheel. It didn't help that there was football on the telly. She toyed with the idea of phoning a friend in Armenia, trying to work out the time difference and whether it would be incredibly rude to do so, when a young man strutted in and addressed the barman in a loud voice.

"Hey, my cousin Harry just texted me to say he's watching a sword fight in Fishponds!"

"What, a staged thing?"

"No, real life. Two blokes trying to kill each other. He sent me a photo, it's brutal!"

Mari, who had leapt up at the words 'sword fight', snatched the phone out of the man's hand as he held it up to show the bartender. "Hey!" he yelled in protest.

Mari threw the phone back at him and rushed outside, scanning the area for a taxi. Across the centre she could see a rank of blue cars. She ran over to them.

"Fishponds, please," she said to the driver, throwing herself into the back seat.

"Okay. But just to let you know, there's been some sort of incident, and the police have closed Fishponds road," he told her.

"Shit. Okay then, take me as close as you can to the King's Arms." As the car pulled away she texted Reymond.

"ARE YOU OK?"

The taxi joined the stop-start traffic leaving the centre.

Mari texted Fisher – "REYMOND MAY BE IN TROUBLE."

"WHERE? HOW?" The response was almost instant.

"BRISTOL. POLICE."

"SIT TIGHT. SEND ME THE DETAILS. I'LL GET THERE AS SOON AS I CAN."

She felt panicky, but there was something about the solid presence of Fisher that gave her comfort, even when he was on the other end of the phone. It would be better if he had been here now, but she was happy he was on his way. She looked out the window at the slow-moving traffic. She Googled Bristol News and located a 'Breaking News' feed which even had a video. She watched it, heart in mouth as she saw the two men, fighting to the death. It faded to black and skipped to a reporter who said something about disturbing images.

*Don't be dead. Don't be dead. Don't be dead.* She re-ran the footage. It did look like Reymond had the advantage, at least by the end of the video.

The taxi dropped her a short walk from the pub. As she followed the directions the taxi driver gave her she found the road blocked by police.

"What's going on?" she asked the policewoman, innocently.

"There's been an incident at the King's Head. Everything is over but the lab guys have to do their thing so it'll be closed for a while yet."

"My boyfriend was in the pub. Is he alright?" Mari asked.

The policewoman looked at her properly for the first time. "Who is your boyfriend, miss?"

"John. John Farmer." She had no idea where that name had come from.

"They've taken the witnesses to the nursery opposite the pub. He'll probably be in there. You can get there over that way." She pointed. "Talk to the officer over there, and tell her WPC Dorset sent you."

"Thank you. What happened here?"

"I'm not at liberty to say," the officer said primly.

"Is my boyfriend likely to be okay?" Mari asked.

"I expect so. There were only two casualties."

"Casualties?" Mari feared the worst.

"I've said too much as it is, Miss. Go and talk to the officer; she'll see you right."

Since the policewoman was watching her she had to go through the motions. Mari trotted over to where she had been directed, and introduced herself to the officers in charge.

"PC Dorset sent me," she said. "I'm looking for my boyfriend, John Farmer. He was in the pub when it happened, he texted me. I want to make sure he's okay."

The female officer looked Mari up and down. "You'll have to wait, Miss. What was your name again?"

"Smith. Mari Smith."

"OK I'll go check. Farmer wasn't it?" she confirmed.

The police officer walked away from the yellow tape. For a mad moment Mari considered ducking under it, but there were far too many police around to get away with it. It seemed eons before the petite officer comes back.

"No-one of that name there, Miss Smith," she said crisply.

"You sure?"

"Yes, I am. I don't think I can help you any more, Miss Smith."

She scanned the street, wondering if she could find a way in to the locked-down pub. Perhaps if she squeezed past the ambulance which was parked across the road?

The sight of the ambulance made her realise the casualties would have been taken to hospital. A quick Google brought up a couple of hospitals in the local vicinity, to her mounting frustration.

She turned her back on the scene and walked back down the road the taxi had brought her up, looking for a cab firm.

Twenty minutes later she was almost back where she started, next to Bristol town centre at the Stalinist concrete edifice of the Bristol Royal Infirmary, where the cab dispatcher told her was the most likely place her fictitious boyfriend would have been taken if he'd been hurt in the fight. The building was dirty, like a smoker's lung, absurd next to the happy pastel colours of the children's hospital.

She asked for A&E at reception and was given directions. Once she arrived there she stood in the queue behind an old man in dish-dasha, being held up by two younger men. His ankle seemed horribly swollen, and he was having trouble understanding the instructions he was being given. Mari hopped from one foot to another, trying to plan out what she was going to say.

"Next!" the nurse called out.

"Hi. My boyfriend was stabbed. I think they brought him here." Well, it was worth a go.

The nurse tapped away at a hidden keyboard with gaudily-painted nails. "Name," she barked.

"Mari Smith."

"No. Your boyfriend's name." The nurse gave her a long-suffering look.

"John Farmer."

"We've only got one stabbing. Seems he refused to give his name. He's in police custody. John Farmer, you say... Wait here." The nurse levered herself up and trudged out of a door behind the counter.

Two casualties, but only one survivor? God, let it be Reymond, let him be okay. She was about to take a seat in the waiting area when she saw a policeman step through a door at the back of the ward, and the nurse returning. Changing her mind about taking a seat, she instead walked out of the back of the ward and down a long corridor, taking random turns until she ended up in the main shaft of the hospital where the elevators were. She rode one to the floor where she'd came in. She found the café, and ordered tea.

As she drank, a man and a woman bustled in. They didn't look like a couple. He was short, and scruffy, probably in his fifties, while she was tall, attractive, and at least two decades younger. Mari idly watched them. When they sat down and took out notebooks, Mari fetched a refill on her tea. When she sat down again, she made sure it was as close to them as she could get.

"Obviously we will lead on this story. Two men have a proper sword duel and one ends up dead. It's gold." The man's voice was wheezy and high pitched. His fingers looked like they've been dipped in yellow paint they were so stained with nicotine.

"The editor's a daft cunt who doesn't know his arse from news dynamite," the woman said. "Read over what you got from that copper and let's see if we can beat it into shape."

"Witnesses say the two men shared a drink, then one of them said something the other didn't like and they both drew swords." The man read out. "Hold it. Why were they carrying swords?" The man wheezed.

"Dunno. We'll come back to that."

"Do you reckon we can get to speak to the survivor?" the man asked hopefully.

"Doubt it. Not for a while at least. He won't be talking to anybody who isn't in a uniform, or his brief for quite some time."

Of course. A lawyer. She texted Fisher. HOW DO YOU FANCY PLAYING A LAWYER?

Then she went back to A&E to watch and wait.

A woman marched in. She was wide eyed, and could have been beautiful under different circumstances, but she looked like she hadn't slept and had pulled her clothes on in a hurry. Mari listened to her side of the conversation with the receptionist.

"Where is he? ... Jules ... what? ... Lombardy ... No I will not calm down, where the fuck is he? ... Tell me now or so help me God I'll ... Okay! Okay! ... Please?"

Mari spotted the policeman as he entered the reception area, in an instant the distressed woman rushed over to him.

"What have you done with Jules?" the woman demanded.

The policeman seemed nonplussed to be accosted by a mad woman.

"Calm down, miss," he said. "And you are?"

"My partner was in the sword fight, I saw it on TV. I went to the pub but they said the casualties had been brought here. Is he here? Is he alright?" The distraught woman reached out to the policeman with pleading hands.

"Perhaps we should find a private room, Miss," the policeman said, looking around for assistance.

This seemed the wrong thing to say. The young woman burst into fresh tears. "That means he's dead, doesn't it? Doesn't it!"

"Now miss, let's get you in a private room." The policeman led her gently away, pulling out a small packet of tissues and pressing it into her hand.

Mari felt more hopeful. Although her heart ached for the young woman, she hoped Jules was the one that was dead.

She decided to go back to the hotel to wait for Fisher.

The ambulance wailed past them as they stood in front of the hospital, finalising their plans.

"Have you got it?" he asked.

"Yes. I'm not an idiot."

"Just checking you were listening." He smiled, taking the sting out of his words.

Mari gave him what she hoped was a dirty look and headed into the hospital. She marched straight past reception, making it look as if she had the right to be there and she knew where she was going. Which she did. She went directly to the ward where Reymond was being kept under armed guard. With Fisher posing as Reymond's lawyer, and her as his assistant, they'd found all the information they needed to get into the ward.

When she reached the ward she snagged a nurse.

"We're here to see the John Doe. This is the court appointed brief," she informed her.

The nurse looked harassed. "Talk to the bobby," she said pointing, and hustled away. Mari approached the policeman, wondering why she was able to walk into the ward without anyone challenging her. She also wondered why Fisher hadn't followed her.

The man had a beefy face, she could imagine it with whiskers and a cigar.

"Yes?" he said, slowly standing.

"I'm Annabel Jocelyn-Smith from Fisher Associates. Mr Fisher has been assigned to the John Doe you are guarding. Would it be possible for him to speak to his client?"

"I've not been told to expect anyone, Miss Smith." The policeman reached for his shoulder radio, and looked at her uncertainly.

"Jocelyn-Smith," she said automatically. "You should have been told we were coming. My boss will be along shortly."

"Of course. I'll need to pass this by a superior. Hold on a second." He talked into his shoulder, passing on the request.

Mari smiled politely at him. There was a gap and a garbled voice delivered the news.

"I'm afraid there's no record of a brief being allowed to visit at this time," the policeman said. "Who did you speak to at the station?"

"The secretary made the arrangements," Mari extemporised.

"Well, can you give her a call and find out?"

"Yes, I'll certainly do that." She whipped her mobile phone out, and the policeman pointed to the strident 'No Mobiles' sign above her head. "Damn," she said.

A doctor approached while they talked, and flashed his badge at the policeman.

"I'm here to check on the patient," he said.

The policeman, still occupied with Mari, waved the doctor in. He winked at Mari as he walked past. She tried to keep the surprise out of her face, and kept the policeman talking.

"I'll have to make the call outside. Are you sure you've no record of my appointment?" she asked sweetly.

"I'm afraid not, Miss. You see... erk!" A meaty arm wrapped around the PC's throat in a sleeper hold. Mari saw that a couple of the more compos mentis patients on the ward were urgently pressing their buzzers.

Eventually 'Doctor' Fisher dropped his arm and propped the unconscious policeman back on the seat. They hurried into the room and unhitched the bed, and Reymond, from the various monitors and electrics. He was groggy, but awake, and handcuffed to the bed.

"OK let's wheel him out to the lifts, and I'll get that handcuff off," Fisher told Mari. "You okay to walk after that, Reymond?"

Reymond nodded vaguely, his eyes unfocussed. They wheeled the bed out, Mari opening doors and Fisher steering Reymond through.

They were nearly out of the ward when they were confronted with a small, angry nurse.

"Where are you going with that patient?" she demanded.

"It's okay, nurse. Carry on here, I'll be back with the paperwork in a minute," Fisher said, without slowing down.

Mari sweated; she hoped the perspiration didn't show on her nice silk suit that they'd bought to make her look more like a legal assistant. The main doors to the ward provided no resistance as they scooted out into the main artery of the hospital and pressed the button for a lift.

Fisher made short work of the handcuffs, and together they helped Reymond off the bed. He was wearing a hospital gown, and beneath it his shoulder was swathed in bandages. He still seemed considerably out of it, so they walked him up and down in the lift.

They got out on the second floor and Fisher pressed the button for the twelfth, sending the empty bed up to the higher floor. They moved as briskly as they could to the stairs and down, both helping to prop Reymond up. The stairs bustled with nurses, doctors, patients and members of the public, but no-one paid them much attention.

On the ground floor Mari left Fisher and Reymond. She jogged out of the hospital, to the loading area where they'd left the hire car. She pulled up to the hospital entrance just as Fisher was emerging. He bundled Reymond into the back, and they drove away from the hospital at a sensible speed that wouldn't attract attention.

"Now what?" Mari asked, glancing at the big man in the passenger seat.

"We ditch the car and get another one. Get Reymond into some clothes and get to a little place I know a few hours up the motorway," Fisher said. Mari looked in the rear view mirror and was relieved to see no signs of pursuit. So far.

†

Mari was worried about Reymond, who barely stirred as Fisher exited the motorway and guided the car down ever smaller roads until they reached a single track lane with tall hedges either side. Eventually they came to a set of iron five-bar gates, and beyond them, a small farmhouse. Fisher clicked off the lights and killed the engine, and darkness covered them like a blanket.

Fisher asked Mari to help Reymond out of the car, and went to unlock the place. As she shook him awake he murmured something that sounded like French.

"It's Mari. Come on you big lump; don't make me carry you, you can pee inside." She tried to lift him, but he was a dead weight.

"No, Mari, *où sont les épées?* Where are the swords?"

In getting Reymond away she hadn't given a thought to where the swords were. "I'm not sure. Come on, let's get you inside, and then you can ask Fisher?"

She offered him her arm. Once he was standing he seemed to draw strength into himself from some inner well. "It is my arm that is wounded. My legs are fine," he insisted.

"We cannot!" Reymond bellowed.

"Do you really need them before we confront Pride?" Fisher asked. Mari had so far been silent in the argument that had been popping for five minutes.

"Of course I do!" Reymond was flushed. He'd warned them many times about angering him, Mari wondered how to calm him.

"Well, I don't know how this works!" Fisher was red-faced too.

"Just stop it!" Mari shouted, breaking the deadlock as both men turned to her. Reymond drew a breath, about to launch into a tirade against her, but she held up a hand to forestall him.

"We will get the swords," she said.

"What?" Fisher shouted. Obviously she hadn't mollified him by choosing Reymond's side.

"We return to Bristol. We break into evidence, we take the swords, then we drive to London, get on a plane and go and confront the last of them in his evil lair."

"Yeah, it's that simple." Fisher threw up his hands in disdain.

"Well, no. Obviously not, but what else do we do?" Mari asked.

Reymond sat back down. Now she had cleared the air she watched his anger drain away; he seemed to deflate, before making an effort to sit up. His arm was still wrapped. They had no idea if it would heal fully before his confrontation with Pride.

"That's a heavy sigh," Mari said. Reymond looked up; Fisher had banged out of the room.

"It's a heavy sort of day," he replied.

"Look, I..." Mari tailed off. She paused, and Reymond gave her the time to get whatever was on her mind out in the open. "I've kind of tagged along, I realise that... I don't know what I'm trying to say. Just that I'm there for you, I guess. I just want my father back." She seemed embarrassed, staring down at her fingers.

Reymond gave her a smile. "I appreciate that," he said.

Fisher returned, phone in hand. "Okay," he said. "I've spoken to a contact, and for a hefty fee they'll do the job and bring the swords here."

Reymond frowned. "Just like that?"

"It's what they do. It's apparently no longer what I do, though."

"We wait?" Mari asked.

"We wait," Fisher and Reymond said at the same time.

"The key is the book." Fisher paced up and down. Reymond

looked more alert after sleeping for several hours. Mari perched on the chunky kitchen table. Something bubbled on the stove, filling the farmhouse with the delicious smell of lamb and herbs.

"What do you mean?" Mari asked.

"If Pride is looking for the book, we can use it to lure him out," Fisher said. "I know a few dark net places where we can advertise that we have it. Sebastien will no doubt work through proxies, but we can follow the trail back to him if we're clever."

"Okay, do it," Reymond said.

† 

"Syria?" Mari's voice was low, deceptively mild.

"Yeah. In a place called Ma'arat al-Nu'Man." Fisher read the name from his phone.

"Ma'Arra." Reymond stalked across the room and stared out into the darkness outside the window.

Fisher glanced at Mari and shrugged. "Yeah? If you say so..."

"Then that is where we must go. Where it will end." Reymond spoke without turning to look at them.

"Syria?" Mari repeated more forcefully. The two men looked at her, Fisher's eyebrows forming a question. "There's civil war there, or had you forgotten?"

"It will not be the first time we have walked into a war zone," Reymond said. Mari looked anxiously at Fisher, who nodded.

"But... Syria!" she tried again.

"How do we get there?" Reymond asked Fisher. It seemed the decision has been taken.

"Through Turkey?" Fisher asked.

"I think the Turks will have that border locked down," Reymond said.

"Wait. Will you listen to yourselves? Syria!"

Reymond ignored her completely. "How about Jordan?"

"Maybe Lebanon," Fisher replied.

Mari gave up, sat with her arms folded and a scowl on her face.

"Do you need a visa to enter Lebanon?" Reymond asked.

"I think it's the same as Jordan?" Fisher shrugged.

"We could take a boat from Cyprus?" Reymond suggested.

"Okay, leave it with me. I'll come up with a route." Fisher stabbed at his phone.

Reymond walked over to Mari and rested a hand on her shoulder. "You do not have to come with us," he said.

"Just you try to fucking stop me!" Her voice was sharp, her eyes felt full of tears.

Reymond splayed his hands in a conciliatory gesture.

"But just so you know? I'm really not happy about it!" Mari leapt to her feet and stormed out of the room.

# The Syrian Desert 1098

THE BEAST FLED across the desert. Birds wheeled in the sky far above. Across the dunes the 7 followed; Jules, The Hunter, Sir Diligence leading them ever onwards. He was armed with a bow and sword. His was the honour. Three arrows he had been given by Humility, for Humility had dreamt it thus. Any of them could have followed the beast across the sand, if not for the wind that erased its tracks. Sir Diligence, uniquely, could follow it across rocky places, seeing signs none of the others knew how to interpret.

On the first day Reymond thought they had taken a measure of the sun. On the second day he discovered that they had barely endured its glance. On the third day the thirst took them. They veered away from the trail to find water. At night, after filling their waterskins, the others made their way to where Sir Diligence had built a fire. Footsore and half blind from the sun, they sank to the floor one by one.

"We set watch, we don't let the fire go out. Naked steel, or the ghouls of the desert will come and steal our souls," Sebastien, Sir Humility, ordered.

Reymond was accustomed to the night sounds of the desert by now; birds, snakes, the yapping of desert foxes. In the night they each stood watch, on his Reymond heard cries that made the hairs on the back of his neck stand up. Like children being tortured, the mewls of giant cats, the rush of wings from some gargantuan bird. Naked steel glinting red in the firelight seemed to keep away whatever it was out there. But Reymond orbited nervously around the camp.

In the morning there was no spoor, no signs at all that any creatures had circled where they'd slept, although all had clearly heard something. Sir Diligence was in a quiet place, utterly absorbed by the hunt. Reymond sought out the priest, Jobert, Sir Kindness.

"It may be the Devil himself you heard. Did he not tempt Christ in the desert?" The priest's words did little to allay his fears. "This is but our third day," he went on. "Christ endured many more. We must do as he did, walk in the faith and no harm can come to us."

Humility, who had overheard, chimed in. "The beast is evil and ancient," he said. "It will not be taken easily. Daylight is our cloak, as night is that of the beast. Diligence is like unto a hound with the scent of the beast in his nostrils. We will take it. If not today then tomorrow, if not tomorrow then the next day, if not the next then the one after. We will be triumphant. God wills it."

This was the most Reymond had ever heard the young man say all at once that was not a prayer. He wanted to ask about the sorcerer, but truth be told he was afraid of the mystic.

"The beast runs to water today," Diligence said before he hastened from the camp, leaving his companions looking at each other in surprise. They followed him at a more sedate pace, but never let him out of their sight. Indeed in a few hours they saw a smudge of green on the horizon, the sure sign of an oasis.

Charles had wanted to bring the sergeant and some of the men with them but Humility wouldn't hear of it. So Charles had left the sergeant in charge and agreed to meet the army wherever it had got to by the time they'd finished on the hunt. "The beast needs to drink, as much as we do," Charles, Sir Charity, remarked to Reymond as they jogged along.

"And yet it leads us ever further from our army, and deeper

into the desert," Reymond replied.

It was not long before the cramps and headaches started again. The sips they allowed themselves just made the thirst worse. Reymond held the tiny amount of water in his mouth, imagining that it was evaporating from his ears. The disc of the sun crawled across the sky as they ran across the desert. The beast drew Diligence on, and Diligence drew the rest of them.

Reymond was surprised to realise he could smell water. He dragged his eyes from the stony ground, which he had been looking at to avoid the burning glare of the sun. One by one his companions came to a stop at the edge of an oasis. In front of them there were a couple of scrawny trees, a brown puddle, and several Saracen.

It took a moment for Reymond to realise that Diligence had his bow out. The Saracen sat around a blackened circle, and they were all much thinner than Reymond expected. Closer still, and they resolved into desiccated corpses, stick like. Their eyes were empty black sockets in their drawn faces, their rictus grins silently mocked the 7.

"How did they die?" His voice was cracked, throat dry. Diligence lowered his bow. Reymond looked at the oasis. "Bad water?" he croaked.

Diligence shook his head. "No dead beasts," he said.

It was true, there were no desert dwellers around the water hole. Not a guarantee the water was good, but not a bad sign.

"Ghouls," Humility said. None of them argued with him.

"How do we test the water?" Reymond asked, his hand on the depleted waterskin hung over his shoulder.

"We draw lots, yes?" Andros, Sir Chastity, said. It was ironic that he lost and was first to drink. They waited for an hour to see if there were any bad effects, Chastity taking the opportunity to drink his fill. If it was going to kill him, he might as well die with his thirst quenched.

The water was fine. They drank and filled their waterskins. Reymond glanced at the Saracen bodies. Their unquiet spirits might still haunt the oasis, and the thought made him shudder. "We should bury them," he said.

"Why? What for?" Tafur asked.

"It is the Christian thing to do," Reymond replied, frowning. None of the others said anything.

Andros was the first to rise. He took a round shield from near the bodies and started digging a hole. The others joined him one by one. Jobert, Sir Kindness, uttering a prayer over the graves. As soon as he finished, Jules took off. The rest of the brotherhood shrugged their packs on, made sure their waterskins were full, and set off after him on their weary quest.

The desert was endless. Reymond tried to save moisture by not talking; the sun stole the energy that rolled off him in great waves. Sir Diligence seemed indefatigable. Reymond plodded along, often at the back of the other knights.

At sunset the heat fled and, after being too hot all day, the brotherhood had to make a fire. They were running low on faggots as their packs became emptier. The land didn't yield much to their searches; it was a place where life had but a tenuous grip. Around the campfire, throats too parched to speak during the day were loosened, and they spoke about their former lives, the crusade, Christ and many other things.

A scream split the air, chilling Reymond's blood. Humility got them to face outwards with bare steel again. "As last night. We sleep and guard in shifts." So saying they organised them-selves for guard duty and Reymond found himself with the prospect of several uninterrupted hours of sleep.

Reymond was exhausted but none of them could sleep. He saw that Diligence was oiling his bow, Charity sat staring into the embers of the fire, Kindness paced up and down. He considered relieving Chastity, who was on guard, but decided against it. Lying down and resting was doing him some good.

He turned the idea of the hunt over in his head. Just because a thing was possible, it wasn't always necessary. He lay awake, watching the wispy clouds as they raced past, highlighted by the moon. The strange sounds echoed through the wilderness and each one sent shivers down his spine. Each howl, each low grumbling bark, made his hair stand on end. There was something primal, atavistic about them. Something that spoke directly to the ancient mind, the prey mind. He felt that he would not get to sleep, that perhaps he should get up, when he felt a hand shaking him. He had fallen asleep after all, and was dreaming of being awake.

He stood watch over his companions, and the cries of the creature were not a cause of his shivering. His waking mind found them of concern but they were not terrifying, not now he had become accustomed to them. He was also curious as to the nature of the beast producing the sounds. It prowled closer tonight, he thought, and his suspicion was confirmed in the morning when Diligence said, "We may see it today, if we are lucky and we can keep up."

Reymond looked around the group. They were all tired, all dirty, all concerned or nervous about what the day would bring. They were all relying on Diligence. Reymond looked to the older man, who shaded his eyes against the early morning light and gazed into the distance. Their fate rested in his hands.

Diligence came to a decision and trotted off in a northerly direction. The others packed up and took off doggedly after him.

At mid-day there were flashes of light in the distance. Something at the limit of sight, lost in the heat haze, something large and white. Reymond ran, his thoughts in suspense. Only when the men in front stopped did he consciously apprehend what his mind had not yet grasped. In the distance was the creature. Majestic, brilliant white, untamed, it skipped over the landscape at such speeds that it swiftly moved out of sight. It seemed impossible that they were hunting it, that they could possibly ever come anywhere near it.

Without a word Humility broke into a run again, Kindness and Charity following. Reymond shared a glance with Chastity, seeing his own awe mirrored in the other's eyes. They jogged after the others. Reymond felt doubt in this enterprise again. Had they the right to hunt this creature? Had they even the power to do so?

That night, when they finally caught up with Diligence, he said, "It is looking for water again."

"And so should we," Chastity voiced the concern of the whole band.

Diligence looked at them, one by one. "We can find water before it does. We can set a trap, if we travel through the night."

"What of the ghouls?" Reymond hated himself for the fear he could hear in his own voice.

"Bare steel and fire will keep them away," Humility reassured him.

"But if we have fire we will be seen. We need to travel with stealth," Diligence said.

"Bare steel will have to do, then," Charity said.

Reymond's mouth was dry, and not just from the knife-like desert wind. He didn't want to meet whatever made the sounds he had heard the last few nights. Chastity and Temperance also looked uncomfortable.

"So be it," Humility said, and they were decided. Reymond swallowed his fear. "Naked steel." Humility pulled out his sword. One by one the others drew. They turned to look at Diligence, who hastened away, following his incomprehensible signs by the wan light of the moon.

Luckily, the night was cloudless; unluckily that made it chilly. Reymond saw gouts of his freezing breath expel moisture into the desert air.

There were moths, pale flitting things, that bumped into his face or he occasionally inhaled. Reymond wondered where they had come from, where they were going, what they ate, where they found moisture in this desert. He guessed there were plants here, marginal, liminal life. The first yaps from the small foxes pierced the night, but so far, no ghouls. No noises from the great beast that he felt must be stalking them, just as they stalked the creature Humility had dreamt about.

One foot, next foot, marching, one two, one, two. Reymond was half asleep, reciting nursery rhymes as he plodded along, barely jogging now. The others were spread out in a ragged line, in front and behind him. The journey seemed to be in a suspended time, running slowly across a lunar landscape hypnagogically lit by the moon. One of the others uttered a sharp barking cough, a sure sign he had inhaled a moth. Reymond had the first intimation of the smell of water; his tired body yearning to drink. It was a constant need that he had, until this moment, been keeping in his subconscious. He restarted the counting song he'd been reciting in his head. 'One for sorrow. Two for mirth..."

The line came to a sudden stop as a strange warbling roar split the sky. Reymond looked wildly about, remembering to lift the sword he had been carrying limply all this time. There was another huge roar – it was louder, closer?

Charity shouted "To me! Form up, on me!" They formed a rough circle, Humility protected in the centre, digging in his bag. There was a third roar, massive and close, and a sudden charnel smell, mixed with an animal stink like old urine, blood and rank sweat. Reymond gagged, pressing his hand over his mouth and nose, breathing shallowly. A large shadow slunk past them as they heard a grinding growl.

The night behind them flared into light as Humility lit some alchemical potion with a *phoosh* and a roiling smoke ring that drifted slowly on the windless air, out past the circle of defenders. There was a final, overwhelming roar and the creature bounded away into the night.

"Has it gone?" Reymond asked, looking at his brothers, "Has it gone?" he repeated to their pale faces. Chastity shook his head. The roar, out in the distance, seemed blessedly far away. Diligence sniffed the air; the stink had lingered behind the creature, a great sand-coloured beast with a black shaggy mane, briefly exposed in the light for them all to see. A lion.

"It hunts our prize," Humility said, shrugging his pack back on.

Diligence looked round. "It will return, and soon. We'd best run. Follow me." He set off in a comfortable lope, that Reymond knew he would not keep up for very long. They were all exhausted by this point, and the dawn was still some hours off.

It was circling them. They could hear it in the distance. Reymond jogged a little faster, catching up with Chastity. "What are we going to do?" he asked.

Chastity sighed. "Not sure if Humility has a plan, yes?"

Humility appeared as tired as the rest of them as they jogged onward into the night. It was hard to read any expression on his face. The smell was getting worse, the beast was getting closer.

"Humility?" Reymond called, his voice surprisingly loud in the desert air. Humility held up his hand, and the knights came to a ragged halt.

They adopted a rough circle, steel outwards. Humility in the middle. "Let it come," he said. "We must kill it, or it will take our prize."

Diligence fitted an arrow to his bow, Humility hissed. "Stay your arrows. Swords only." Reymond was not sure why this command was given, but it did not fill him with confidence.

There was a burbling growl to his left, then a roar. The beast ran out of the night, leaping towards the circle, directly at Kindness. Charity thrust him out of the way, staggering as he was swiped by a massive paw, all claws. He went down heavily on the sand.

Reymond dashed in, thrust with his sword and scored a hit in the meat of the beast's shoulder. It rounded on him and his sword was torn from his grasp, still sticking from the creature's hide. It thrust its head at him, jaw alarmingly wide, descending with hideous finality.

Chastity's arms seized Reymond round the waist as he tackled him out of the way. They tumbled down an incline in a shower of sand. There was a great hissing, spitting and squealing. As Reymond righted himself, he saw Diligence withdraw his own blade from the creature, followed by a gout of blood.

Diligence neatly stepped aside, under the beast's swiping paw. Humility took a great overhand swing at its hindquarters, and the beast yowled in pain.

Reymond staggered towards it, feet slipping up the incline, groping for a sword that wasn't there. His ears were ringing. He felt wetness running down one arm and his breath hitched in his chest.

Kindness wasn't moving. Reymond saw Temperance hanging back, looking for an opening, his sword poised. Charity's sword glanced off the beast's head, and, as it rounded on him, Diligence stepped in, slashing at its throat. Blood spurted. The creature sat back on its haunches, shaking its great head and as one Diligence and Charity plunged their swords into its chest, extinguishing it forever.

Reymond was relieved to see that Kindness was breathing, but had an egg-sized lump on his forehead. Feeling dizzy, Reymond sat heavily beside the priest and slowly toppled to one side. The last thing he saw was Temperance with his arm around Chastity, leading him up the hill.

†

Jules had left the others behind some time ago. His bow was strung, the scent of the beast was in his nostrils. He moved across the sand with an easy lope. There was no way that they could catch the beast; it was as if it somehow sensed them. He topped a rise and dropped to his belly as he saw the beast below him at the oasis lapping at the water, with the occasional glance around, alert to danger. It was a white or cream colour, standing many hands tall; a beautiful specimen. A horse in appearance, except for the spiral horn that jutted from its forehead. One of the last, if not the last, of its kind. The Hunter felt a sense of awe in its presence, but it did not stop him fitting an arrow to his bow. The twang caused the beast to look up from where it was drinking, an instant before the arrow struck it.

It turned in a circle, neighing wildly as the hunter loosed a second arrow which winged its way after the first. The unicorn bolted, the second arrow jutting from its flank, but the beast stumbled, and it was the third arrow that took it in the neck. It tossed its head as it collapsed slowly onto the sand.

The hunter ran towards it, dropping the bow and drawing his sword. He couldn't stand to see the creature in such pain. His heart was breaking. Tears streamed down his face. He hadn't understood, he hadn't known. He'd slain beauty, slaughtered innocence. His sword arced down and still the beast would not die. There was suddenly a second blade, thrust deep into the chest, extinguishing the life beneath it.

He stared wonderingly at Patience. His comrade looked stunned. They both had tears running down their faces. The others caught up at last.

"We all must blood our blades," Humility said and each man did so in turn, even though the creature was already dead. The Hunter knew that nothing he did in life from this point on would atone for this crime. Reymond raged against the others, took some calming down. Humilty looked down at the beast, pride visibly swelling his breast. They had done this. They could now complete the ritual. Temperance hungrily slashed open the beast, eager for the next part of the ritual, eager to taste the heart of the creature, to embrace the strength and longevity the Prophet had promised. The brothers gathered round as Humility started the fateful ritual. Overhead, a crow circled.

# Ma'Arra, The Holy Land 1098

CROWS CIRCLED IN the sky, cawing to each other, spreading the news of the great feast to come. The army of crusaders was both larger and better prepared than last time. Reymond hurried across the camp, seeking Charity to find out what their orders were. It seemed that this time the full might of the crusader army would fall on Ma'Arra. Reymond was tired; a few months terrorising the local populace while not moving a step closer to Jerusalem had been frustrating, although he walked with a lighter, more eager step today. There were still a few obstacles to remove between Antioch and Jerusalem, but they were on their way again.

The Tafurs now made up a goodly proportion of the army. Many had eschewed armour, going barefoot and dressed in sackcloth. Reymond and the others of the 7, as well as the few knights and men-at-arms remaining from Charles's men, looked out of place marching alongside the holy madmen.

They returned to Ma'Arra, which had changed little in the intervening months. The bodies previously piled up outside the walls had been moved, at least, and the local crows watched from the walls and a few scraggly trees. They flapped away outraged when the bugles of the crusaders sounded. Their harsh cries resounded from the walls, which were fully manned. The city was putting up a spirited defence.

The 7 were now protected, with long lives guaranteed, prowess in battle a promise from the ritual. But nightmares of the hunt still woke Reymond in the night. By the circles under the eyes of the brotherhood, he could tell he wasn't the only one. Jules seemed the worst affected. He had withdrawn into himself, moving only when necessary, going through the motions. Reymond hoped his friend would be able to find his way back to his old self soon.

They bedded in to the previous camp that had been set up some months earlier. Reymond was kept busy running errands. The 7 were chosen, along with a detachment of Normandy's men, to guard the princes as they toured the walls. Curthose chose the south wall, protected by a ditch, as the point of attack and in the afternoon the first siege ladders were moved into position.

Standing in line, Reymond tapped his thumb and jiggled his foot. Jules had told them that he had been assigned a different, secret role, and was missing but the other five stood at Reymond's side. Tafur was grinning like he'd just pulled off some immense trick. Charles looked more sombre, and Reymond was glad for the calming presence of Andros.

The flags were raised, and waved, and they started off, slow at first but once they were up to speed they fanned out. Some sixth sense made Reymond raise his shield, deflecting an arrow that would have taken him in the chest. Another was driven into the ground a step in front of him. He found he was roaring a prayer. They reached the ditch and scrambled across it. Reymond was half-expecting it to be filled with some sort of burning pitch or oil, but it was a hastily-dug affair. Arrows zipped past like angry birds and one glanced off his helmet, snapping his head to one side. For a moment he saw stars.

Now they'd made the wall no-one seemed sure what to do. Reymond shouted "Ladders! Ladders!" and the shout was taken up by the men around him. Five foot away a man was felled by a large rock, causing a geyser of blood to splash up the wall. Whilst he was staring at the blood splatter Reymond noticed bits of brain had embedded themselves on the coarse wall.

There was a *pffft* and the man standing next to Reymond, his mouth wide in mid-shout, swallowed an arrow and fell heavily. Reymond glanced down at him. One second a walking, talking man, the next second so much meat.

The ladders were placed against the wall and the usual jostle took place for men to earn the dubious honour of climbing first. Reymond watched the man who won the brief argument climb to the top of the ladder and receive a mortal sword wound for his 'honour'. The ladders were toppled, men jumped clear, some crunching to the ground.

Reymond heard the bugles, voices calling them to retreat. Another mad dash back to the safety of their lines. Whilst Reymond was drinking his fill of water he wondered if he'd seen an enemy today. He couldn't consciously recall.

After an evening of prayers and fasts Reymond and Andros were chosen to help fill in the ditch. This meant running with barrows full of debris to dump into the ditch, and returning with the empty barrow to be filled again. Constantly running in and out of the killing zone didn't fill him with enthusiasm. The others had been given carpentry duty and were off to build a siege tower. There was still no sign of Jules, and Reymond guessed he was still working on his secret project.

Late in the afternoon, as Reymond guided the wobbly barrow back from the pit for what seemed like the hundredth time, the trumpets announced that more crusaders had arrived from the north, and were attacking that wall. This led to a lessening of the arrows from the south wall, and Reymond breathed easier as he conveyed the pile of debris into the ditch.

Later, stood at a safe distance, he shielded his eyes and tried to see the enemy. They were nothing more than small moving blobs at this distance. Reymond imagined what it must have been like for them, recalling the dark days trapped inside Antioch.

When he returned to camp, rubbing the encrusted salt and dirt from his face he was surprised to find Tafur arguing with the sergeant. It was an incongruous sight, tall and thin versus short and stout, although both men had impressive voices.

"Hold it, hold it! What is going on here?" He broke the two men apart before they could punch each other. The nearby Tafurs looked ready for blood, the rest of the men looked in equal part angry and confused.

"Ah, a sensible man," the sergeant said. "A sensible man, like Reymond here, will tell you that when I say we've got no food, I mean we've got *no* food."

"There is always food. The princes do not starve."

"Go and bloody ask them, then!"

Reymond could see Tafur was ready to retort. He jumped in first.

"Why is there no food?" he asked, in his most reasonable voice.

The sergeant was calming down a little bit.

"All foraged out. What our leaders neglected to mention was that our next chance at real food lies within those walls."

"Well that settles it, then," Tafur said, in a voice that was a touch too loud. "We're getting over those walls, and we're getting whatever there is to eat in there." He cast a significant look at both Reymond and the sergeant, then, sweeping his ragged cloak behind him, he stalked off back to camp.

"What was that really about?" Reymond asked the sergeant, who shrugged.

"We'll be inside the walls soon, lad." The sergeant turned, not waiting for an answer.

Reymond watched him walk away the broad back, surmounted by neck that was a roll of fat and a tanned bald head.

Reymond flopped down next to the campfire, which still smouldered from when they'd cooked up what herbs and tubers they had scavenged. He gripped the skin of his belly and tried to pinch it, but there wasn't enough fat there to do so. He sighed, daydreaming about rabbits. Jules stared into the middle distance, lost in his own thoughts. Even the irrepressible Andros seemed slack and full of lassitude. He wondered where the others were right now. Another winter in the Holy Land.

He filled his belly with water, grateful that at least they had plenty of that. He spotted Jobert and Charles returning and relaxed down onto his elbows staring at the painted blue sky.

Charles broke the silence as he arrived. "We need to get into the unit with the siege tower," he said. "Curthose is planning on putting men on the wall. Those that volunteer are promised a greater share."

"And?" Reymond asked. He wasn't sure if he was interested. He wanted to see Jerusalem, and 'glorious charges' had a habit of becoming death knells.

"And? And we'll get rich!"

Reymond looked to his friends, Andros seemed interested, Jules looked as if his attention was far away across the desert.

"What if we don't want to get rich? Camels and needles."

Charles frowned. "So you'd prefer to sit idly by whilst others get rich?"

Reymond sat up, shaded his eyes and shrugged.

"It is our duty to God, the holy cause, the cross and to Christ," Sebastien said. His intervention was unexpected; Reymond hadn't spotted his approach.

"It's our duty to get rich?" he asked the young man, who was staring at the city.

"What?" Sebastien looked surprised. "No, it is our duty to eliminate this obstacle so we may fulfil our oath to reach the sepulchre in Jerusalem. We will fight where we are needed. If we are needed on the walls, that is where we'll fight."

Sebastien wandered away some twenty feet and sat, staring at the city. Those were apparently his final words on the subject.

"Looks like we're volunteering," Charles said scrambling to his feet to go and look for a commander. Reymond sighed. He was too hot, and too tired, to do anything about it.

Later, sat listening to Sebastien mumbling through yet another ceremony alone in his tent, Reymond found it difficult to sleep. He tossed and turned, unable to get comfortable. He heard one or other of the 7 cry out in his sleep.

When he eventually did sleep his dreams were strange and he awoke in a foul temper. Cross with the world and all in it.

As the box on wheels squeaked and groaned its way to the wall, Reymond cursed all men who asked for volunteers and the fools that volunteered for them. His mood had deteriorated, which he hadn't thought possible. The 7 were putting their backs into creeping the siege tower ever closer to the wall, while arrows thudded into its sides and flying rocks gouged white marks on the fresh wood, making the siege tower rock alarmingly. When something the size and colour of a large rock exploded at his feet he didn't pay it much attention. But when the air hummed and the first sting caused his arm to jerk, like a needle touching a raw nerve, he took notice.

The men around him danced in paroxysms of pain as wasp after wasp took out their anger at having their nest destroyed. Some men made a run for it, only to be scythed down by flocks of arrows. Some fell to the floor and rolled around, some were struck by rocks. Orders were shouted and Reymond gritted his teeth, poured his entire waterskin over his head, and kept pushing the tower forward, twitching every time he was stung.

With a shuddering crunch the siege tower hit the wall. The men in the top threw rocks at the defenders, buying their sappers time to undermine the wall. At the same time ladders protected by mantlets were deployed and volunteers clambered up them onto the walls. Reymond was one of the first, he didn't know why. As he climbed he saw one of the other ladders covered in a white cloud, like an explosion of flour. He heard men screaming as the quicklime got into their eyes and corroded their skin. Some of them chose to leap off the ladders to their deaths rather than endure the pain, or the very real chance they'd be permanently blind.

He felt a flush creep up his neck, and his ears burned. He was grinding his teeth as he felt a scream building. As he leapt over the top he gave vent to it, shouting in frustrated rage.

How dare they throw wasps, how dare they shoot his friends, how dare they exist as a barrier to his advance to the Holy City?

Reymond chopped a man's head clean off and before the body had fallen he ran through a second. A third stabbed him through the arm but this didn't slow Reymond down. He head-butted his assailant, feeling a satisfying crunch as his iron helm connected with the man's face. His sword took another man's leg off at the knee, and his backswing sliced another through the neck.

Reymond was blind to anything but the enemies in front of him, but he could hear a wailing scream. The last man went down before him, cleft through the shoulder, Reymond's blade parting his ribcage. The rest had fled, the city wall belonged to the crusaders.

Reymond was stopped at the top of the stairs, denied in chasing the fleeing defenders by Andros, who shouted at him. But he couldn't hear him and Reymond pulled Andros's hands away, giving him a violent shove. Andros slipped, and fell.

Reymond turned to see the sergeant stood at the top of the steps. His fist struck Reymond full in the face, forcing him down onto his backside on the bloodied stone. The wailing stopped abruptly, and as Reymond put his hand to his cheek, which was already swelling, he could hear a high pitched whistling in his ears and taste iron on his tongue. He realised the screaming had been coming from him.

Andros had regained his feet and was glaring at him, but he couldn't see any more of his brotherhood. The bulk of the sergeant blocked out the sun. "Here lad," he said, offering Reymond his hand.

Reymond allowed the shorter man to pull him up. Looking around, he saw that the walls were empty of enemies, and the Saracen had withdrawn. Evening had fallen. The sergeant nodded towards Reymond's arm. "You should get that seen to, lad," he said.

Reymond looked down; the sleeve of his tunic was soaked red. He felt the throb of his cut flesh as he wrapped a rag around the wound. As he was doing so the Tafurs swarmed up the ladders, and their 'king' strode over to Reymond and Andros, who was standing close by, looking sullen.

"Let's get some food!" Tafur ordered.

"We are to await the princes to negotiate a surrender," the sergeant told him.

"That could take hours. Look down there; there are houses within reach. Food, riches. Let's take what we can, while we can," Tafur insisted.

"We must wait!" Reymond cried, feeling himself flushing again, but Tafur and his men didn't stop. How dare they ignore him? The sergeant moved to block them, eyes narrowed at the expression on Tafur's face as he stepped in their way.

Tafur drew himself to his full height. "Out of my way. Do you not know I am a prince?"

Several of Tafur's men stood ready to back him up. One, wild-eyed, dressed in sackcloth and ashes – one of the 'Holy Warriors' who fought without any armour and often carried on fighting with even the most horrendous injuries, in an ecstasy of battle, fingered a wicked looking mace. Tafur's most-trusted man-at-arms, dressed in a motley of discarded and repurposed armour, loosened his sword. A third, a filth-encrusted beggar in rags, wandered over to the side of the tower and leaned out to look down the inside wall. Reymond put his hand on his sword and took a step toward the sergeant to lend him his support.

"I follow Robert Curthose and his orders were to stand

here," the sergeant stated.

Tafur signalled to his men who reached out to grab the sergeant to move him out of the way. The sergeant stepped back, out of their reach. "Get off!" he said, and stood atop the stairs in a pugilist pose. The Tafurs spread out in front of him and between the sergeant and Reymond. Reymond glanced at Andros and they made ready to fight, if the Tafurs attacked the sergeant Reymond was ready to back him up.

"Tafur, stop this," Reymond hissed. Tafur gave him a mild glance.

"I mean to go into the city, if he doesn't get out of the way, make him," he said to his men.

Sackloth & Ashes grinned a mouth full of blackened stumps and stepped forward to shove the sergeant out of the way. The sergeant grabbed the Tafur's arm, pivoted and knelt, and the man was thrown a few metres across the stones to land with an awkward thump. As the sergeant stood again, the man in rags drew a dagger and the man-at-arms pulled out his sword, which the sergeant concentrated on. Reymond half drew his own sword but was not fast enough.

"Look out!" Reymond shouted and the sergeant half turned towards him as the rag-wearing Tafur behind him thrust. The sergeant's eyes went wide and his mouth worked but no words nor sound came out. He toppled slowly to the side and Tafur and his men marched past down the stairs.

Reymond reached the bald man's side and, with horror, saw that the Tafurs, in a moment of treachery, had succeeded in doing what no Saracen ever had. They'd given the sergeant his first wound of the war. They'd killed him.

Reymond stood at the top of the stairs, wondering where Jules was; he didn't seem to be amongst the men on the wall. He had no idea where Charles and Jobert were; they could have been burned by the quicklime for all he knew. Sebastien, despite his little speech earlier, was also nowhere to be seen. Andros, who'd been standing with him a few minutes ago, was nowhere to be seen either. Reymond's blood boiled. The Tafurs would pay.

He had no authority over Tafur but he had to try to make him stop. As he followed them down the steps, a woman's scream echoed from below. Reymond increased his pace, hurrying to catch up with the others.

The first house on the street had its door kicked in. A dead child slumped on the threshold. There were crashes, screams, angry cries as men dressed in the motley of Tafurs ran past. Reymond walked into the first house, stepping carefully over the dead child. His cheeks were wet; he hadn't been aware until now that he had been crying.

There was a strange noise coming from the room he entered, and as his eyes adjusted to the gloom he saw a man, back to him, dressed in crusader gear. The man held an older child, a knife pressed to her throat, and beneath him a dead woman.

"Christ, man, this is wrong!" Reymond cried. The man, his face contorted with animal passion, rounded on him with the dagger. Reymond ducked out of the way. His blade sang as he ran the man through, kicked him free and let him drop to the floor. He fell to his knees to help the girl, shocked to discover she was already bleeding out, her throat slashed even as he'd moved to help her.

A mighty crash came from outside. It sounded like a house collapsing, but it was followed by raucous laughter. Reymond stooped to pick up his sword, still bloody from the crusader's gut, and he stumbled. The man on the floor, the man he had just killed, was Andros.

"No, no, no," he moaned, shaking his head vehemently. This couldn't be right. It must be a mistake. There was another loud crash, a cheer, and sobbing which raised in pitch and turned to screaming. The feeling he had upon the wall had returned. He was blind to anything but his rage. Reymond rushed outside. Someone, everyone, would pay for this madness.

At the threshold he was physically sick, he wanted his

happy-go-lucky friend to tell him that things weren't serious. He wanted his serious friend to tell him this was all a joke. He wanted the sergeant to order him to stand down. He wanted Charles to tell him the enemy had surrendered and the city was under the protection of the princes. He wanted the killing to stop.

He ran blindly through the streets, to the centre of Ma'Arra, where there were still pockets of fighting. There was a smoky, greasy smell in the air, redolent of burned flesh. His empty stomach grumbled. He strode around a corner and several ragged Tafurs turned, weapons raised, only to be lowered when they recognised him.

Le Roi Tafur, the man he knew as Temperance, was revealed. Standing a little behind his men and above them, on a set of stone steps. In his hand was a hunk of meat, dripping with fat and blood. His mouth was smeared, grease dripped down his ragged tunic. Many of his men had meat on daggers and sticks, or in their bare hands. Reymond looked to the fire burning next to the steps and was horrified to see the bodies piled up on it; he gagged and turned with dawning comprehension to Le Roi Tafur.

"Why looked so shocked," the man he knew as Temperance said. "They are but animals. We are hungry. It is just."

Reymond raised his sword and took a step towards Le Roi Tafur. He could feel his face twisting with hate and anger. The men in front of him raised their weapons. He would never best the half a dozen men protecting Le Roi Tafur, but a redness was descending on his vision. He screamed incoherently and charged at the small band. He cut three of them down before he was felled by a glancing blow on his helmet and a sword thrust through the ribs.

As his vision cleared he saw the scene, upside down. Le Roi Tafur stood looking down at him with an expression of pity. "Wrath is a sin, my friend," he said calmly.

Reymond coughed blood, and his eyes dimmed.

# Somewhere in Western Europe 1154

THERE WAS A crimson throbbing. His breathing was ragged, like he'd been running hard. He had his eyes closed. He tried to remember where he was, who he was. There was a blank in his memory. His head echoed with aftershocks of confused, jumbled images, dead faces accusing; his skin tingled, his muscles remembered deep abuse. He was sure that he had been tortured, and yet he was not in a torture chamber. The blankness in his mind was disturbing.

He opened his eyes and stared at the dead woman. Who was she? She had been hacked to death, and beyond. The sword was in his hand, dripping. He had murdered her, then. Who was she? If he could remember who she was perhaps it would remind him who he was.

The bedroom was large and richly furnished. His clothing was expensive. His sword was cruciform – he had a flash of it plunging into a horse's breast. He shook his head; where was his cross? He knelt by the woman and stared into her unseeing eyes. There was a trail of blood. He followed it to a simple wooden door, and fumbled the door open. He was in a small room set at the end of a stone corridor. Minimal light shone through high, narrow windows. He glanced back into the room, but there were no clues there that he could see, except the room was a chaotic jumble, the aftermath of a fight, or a tantrum...

He crept down the corridor, his bare feet, sticky with gore, gripping the stones, his breath misting on the air. He reached a staircase, the walls decorated with unfamiliar banners. Two mastiffs awoke at his step and bounded over to him as he entered the hall. He greeted them absently; they saw he had no treats and slunk back to the fireplace. A smouldering fire weakly illuminated the hall. He had no memory of this place.

He saw leftover food on the floor, bones that had been gnawed by the dogs, and he had a flash of men holding dripping meat. The smell of burning and blood. The sound of weapons clashing, of screams in the night. He had been wounded and brought to somewhere to convalesce, he realised. And yet when he felt his head and his ribs, where he had a vague memory of violence, he was whole, unmarked.

"What is happening?"

Only the dogs could hear him and they had no answers.

He decided to explore further, to see if he could find someone to tell him where and who he was. He wandered the halls until he came across more bloody footprints, a room, a young boy ripped open by a great sword blow yet lying as if sleeping peacefully within. He had another flash: a young boy in his mother's arms, an arrow piercing his chest, the women's ululations haunting his dreams. He spent some time staring at the boy, willing memory to come, but it would not.

He continued searching. He found what he assumed to be the servant's quarters, and an old man trying to crawl away, still alive. The old man started as his hand fell upon him and turned him over. He too was sword-struck. A blow to the back that seemed to have paralysed his legs.

"My Lord, please!" The man said.

"Who am I?"

"My Lord?" The man blinked, confused.

"Tell me who I am."

"Luis Alvarrez, my lord... Please no more? Please don't kill me."

The name meant nothing to him. Less than nothing. He

knew it was not his name. It seemed to awaken his memories though. Memories that belonged to a different time and place. Recollection roared back in, his life, and death. How could this be? He remembered a masked man, in a lurid scarlet room, parading his victims in front of him. All those that had fallen to his blade.

He remembered Andros.

He remembered the boy and the all-consuming rage.

He felt his face: it was not *his* face. He stared at his tanned stranger's hands.

And now he had awoken, stolen into another man's life. What had happened to the man? All his instincts screamed at him to get away. Before anyone could expose him. To just leave.

The old man resumed his crawl. Reymond dropped the sword. What had become of him? He could remember nothing of waking, but apparently he'd killed this man, Alvarez's, wife and son? And servant. He looked up and saw that the man was leaving a smear of blood as he dragged his body across the stone floor.

The solid thwack of his sword against his leg caused him to look down and he was surprised to see that he was mounted on a tan horse. He swivelled and could see no buildings in any direction. He'd blacked out, obviously, but he was wearing the same clothes as Alvarez still. As the sun rose he wondered where the other six were. Reymond realised he was a long way from the Holy Land and his instincts told him that he was a long time, a lifetime, away from the man he once was. He aimed the horse west, thinking that eventually he would come to the sea. He wondered what language he'd spoken when he'd conversed with the servant. It had come naturally to him, and yet now, thinking back, it had seemed foreign. He had been born in France, but how could he converse freely with an Iberian servant without first learning the language?

He was in a mountainous country he had no knowledge of at all. He gave the horse its head as he marvelled at what had happened to him, what was happening right now. He was alive. He was in a different body. Where was he? *When* was he? Were the others also alive? Why had he killed those people? He rode in a daze. He remembered the words Sebastien used before the ritual.

"This will bind our blood together, forever."

Forever? He shuddered. It had seemed blasphemous then, more so now. The Prophet had said it was part of God's plan, but how could that be? He should never have got involved, never performed such Satanic rights. Magic? It was the Devil's work.

The horse snorted and Reymond looked up. Coming towards him were three men on horseback, leading a mule.

"Good day." They spoke in a language Reymond had no right to know.

"Good day," he said, nodding to them. "Can you tell me where I am, please? I have been travelling through the night and appear to have become a little lost. Where does this road lead?"

The three men exchanged glances and the oldest hawked, spat on the ground and looked Reymond directly in the eye. "That way," he said, pointing back the way they'd come, "lies the monastery of San Sebastian."

"My thanks."

The man who'd spoke grunted, scratched under an armpit and without further conversation the three strangers moved off.

Reymond set his horse for the monastery. Perhaps there he could ask a priest for forgiveness. He rode with his thoughts in turmoil, a dark suspicion falling upon him. In a few hours he was at the monastery, where the monks greeted him as a friend.

Washing his hands in a brass bowl he was relieved to see that he had no obvious horns or other marks of the evil one, and yet he had come back from the dead. He had killed a child? A woman? Hadn't he? Had he? He must find the others, especially Sebastien. The prophet would know what to do.

The monks invited him in for a meal. He would be Luis Alvarez to them. He wished he'd spent more time in the house he'd woken up in, time to find letters or any documents that would have given him more information. He felt compelled to leave, to hide from the people who would have known Luis Alvarez the best, a subconscious desire to be as far from them as possible. The monks chatted about gardening and bees, but Reymond needed knowledge and he had to ask.

"How goes the crusade?"

The monks exchanged glances. "Not well I'm afraid," a senior monk replied. "We have heard that the Saracen have taken Damascus, some months ago."

"Taken Damascus?" Reymond thought frantically. It was obvious much had happened in the Holy Land since the fall of Ma'Arra, but he felt these simple monks were not the men to ask for a full picture. He needed to seek out the others of his brotherhood, but he was not sure how to go about doing so. Perhaps he needed to get to the Holy Land.

"It seems that they will need all the fighting men they can muster," he said. "How could I join the crusaders?"

"I am sure that by God's grace a man such as yourself could get to the Holy Land via Rome. But it is a long and arduous journey."

Reymond nodded. It was going to be a challenging voyage but he felt it was one he must make if he was going to make any sense of this at all. Waking up in someone else's house, someone else's body seemed like a dream. He accepted the monk's offer for a bed for the night.

Later, he was ill-prepared for the nightmares. His screams of torment and anguish woke the monastery, but he was unable to share with them the cause of his disturbance. He remembered the deaths he had caused in this body now. His dreaming mind supplying all the hideous details.

He left at dawn, after a mostly sleepless night, prepared to make the long journey for answers; he was aware that the monks seemed relieved that he was leaving. He strapped his sword on, mounted his horse and turned towards the north.

# New York, USA 1992

FISHER TOOK A room in SoHo, in an artist's residence. Costly but exclusive. His work hadn't changed over the last ten years, but this would be his last job. He was tired and getting slow, although he could still beat men half his age, the years were beginning to add a load he could no longer ignore. He was currently working for an anonymous collector, with two specialists helping him.

Antiquities were generally kept in museums, and Fisher occasionally worked for governments who wanted their antiquities back. Sometimes he worked for private collectors. He had become expert in taking things from one place to another, sometimes taking things no-one wanted taken, and sometimes taking them to places no-one wanted things taken to. It was specialist work.

Nowadays he received his briefs in encrypted emails, from random accounts. When he received an email labelled: "Remember Iran," he assumed it was work, but he got a surprise when he opened it.

Fisher
You owe me. Time for me to collect on that oath. I hope you still have the book. Meet me at the bench on Worth Street, next to Columbus Park. 19:00 tonight.
Patience

This had to be a joke. He'd told few people in his life about what had happened in Iran. Fewer still knew about the oath, and no-one knew about the book, which was secured in the deposit box of a bank in London. He checked the ammo in his handgun, pocketed an extra clip, and made ready to leave. He would be early, but he wanted to scope the place out.

When he arrived he walked all around the park, making a note of all the buildings overlooking the bench. He spent some time researching them, to discover that they were mostly apartments and a court house. He found a local coffeehouse and sat there until ten minutes to seven, sipping a coffee. Then he took a walk to the park, circling the area of the bench. A man he didn't recognise was sitting there jiggling a foot and glancing often at a watch. As he approached the man looked up, caught his eye, and nodded.

The man looked foreign, possibly the way he was dressed, but he was olive complexioned. He held himself taut, as if ready to explode into violence, scowling at the world like it had done him wrong. He tapped his finger against his thumbnail, a habit Fisher has seen before but couldn't place. There was a long case next to him on the bench, and Fisher sat down beside it.

"Fisher," the man said. It wasn't a question.

"Yes. Who are you?"

"I am... I know this is going to be difficult for you. I am Patience." The man opened the case, revealing the sword with the cross-shaped hilt that Fisher remembered so well. The one he wasn't able to find when the enigmatic Patience died during the dash across the desert. At the time he'd thought it odd. Now he assumed it had been left behind somewhere in the Iranian wastes.

"Where did you get that?"

"It was given to me in 1098 by the leader of my order. The Holy Order of the Cruciform Sword, more commonly known as the Knights of Virtue, or the 7. A man we called Humility."

Fisher scrutinised the man closely. It was obvious he felt he was speaking the truth. Which was crazy.

"So you are over a thousand years old?"

"In spirit yes. In this body, less than a year. This man's spirit will return when the seventh year of possession ends, unless the body is slain first."

Fisher rested his hand on his gun. It was a solid, reassuring weight at the small of his back.

"OK, you realise this sounds batshit, right?"

"Yes. It has always been difficult to convince people that the curse is a real thing."

"Let me get this straight. You're Patience? A man I personally buried years ago in a desert town on the other side of the world?" The man nodded and opened his mouth to speak, but Fisher pressed on. "And you're a demon, possessing people for periods of seven years? And you just happen to choose this moment to come and talk to me?"

"It is not the first time I have been called a demon. I would like to think I am not. But perhaps it is a label that fits." His mouth turned down as he contemplated this. "I return at odd times. I do not know why, or how, I awake into someone else's life, always with the sword, with the knowledge from the last time and all the times before, all the way back to my first life. I know I rescued you near Urmia, that you were shot twice, here and here." He pointed to the permanently angry reminders of puckered, shiny skin, hidden beneath Fisher's clothes. "I know I was killed with my own sword, through the stomach. I remember our conversations, although not word for word. I saved your life, more than once. You swore an oath to me."

"I thought you were dying. I thought Patience was dying... He *was* dying, he died... You are not him." Fisher shook his head emphatically.

The man cocked his head to one side. "I can tell you more. Answer any question you have. The oath binds you to me. I can compel you if necessary, but I would rather not."

"Assuming what you say is true – and I don't buy it for a

second – then what do you want?"

"I want the book. And for you, in the future, to fulfil your oath to me."

"The book? I sold that years ago," Fisher lied smoothly.

"I do not believe you. And I believe your heart is telling you it is I, but your head has yet to be convinced."

"Okay, even if, and it's a big if, I believe yer...then why the urgency, you keep coming back right? Why d'ya need me to do anything?"

The man stood and took a couple of steps. Fisher waited.

"It gets worse," he said, not turning around. "Every incarnation I become a little more soiled. The curse compels me to hunt the others and murder them." He turned around and stared intently. Fisher wondered if he should say something.

"When we return I don't know what happens to the spirit of the person whose body I inhabit. I assume they just go elsewhere for a time. But when the body dies then I go back to hell. What I assume to be hell. Where I am punished for all the sins I have committed, all the deaths on my conscience. If the body dies, the former spirit also dies." The man claiming to be Patience stared into the distance.

Fisher wondered what vistas the man's inner eye was gazing upon. "That means ya kill innocent people when ya kill the others?"

"Exactly that. Not only do I have to kill my brothers: although it is a degraded version of them, they are still my friends. I also end up killing innocents, and not just the ones we inhabit. There are always casualties. Like the tribesmen I killed to rescue you."

"Yeah about that. I'm still not convinced." Fisher shrugged.

"Let me tell you a story."

Fisher listened as the man told the full details of Fisher and Patience's time together in Iran. He included details that no-one else could possibly know. At the end Fisher still couldn't quite believe it, although he couldn't explain how this man, this stranger, could know so much.

"You've given me a lot to think about," he said, trying to pass it off, being polite. He wanted to think it through, find the hidden con.

"I am thinking that by tomorrow you will have explained things away in your head, come up with a narrative that will paint me as crazy, or worse, yourself. This is the truth," the man said.

Fisher shook his head. He couldn't see the angle, but he knew it must be false. He found himself agreeing to meet the man again, despite his reluctance. He was beginning to think of him as Patience now.

As he stood up to leave, he looked the man straight in the eye. "I buried the man called Patience. He is dead."

"Call me Reymond."

Fisher wondered at the name, pronounced with a Gallic inflection.

"Are you saying you are one of the famous Raymonds of the Crusades?"

"Of the Crusades yes. Famous? No, I am not one of the Princes. I was a farmer's son until I took the cross."

That phrase echoed with Fisher. He recalled a conversation, after he'd stared down the barrel of an assault rifle and watched a man take out half a dozen tribesmen single-handedly.

The whole conversation of the previous hour was thrown beneath the spotlight of his questioning mind. After the two men shook hands and Fisher walked away, he couldn't shake the fact that the man had been Patience. It was impossible, but it was true. He shivered, feeling that he was in the presence of something truly supernatural for the first time in his life.

# Ma-arat al-Nu'man, Syria 2012

LANDING ON THE rocky coastline of northern Syria wasn't high on the list of things Mari would ever like to do again. Their journey from Cyprus at night, avoiding patrols, had been hair-raising but they'd made it. A two- or three-day hike and they'd be at Ma'arat al-Nu'man – if they could avoid the Syrian army, and the rebels.

Mari marvelled that the two men were so calm as they trekked through the scrubby hills, towards a town that may or may not have been under siege in this incomprehensible civil war. She jumped at every sound, her pulse galloping. Jets roared; she heard the crump of artillery and the rattle of automatic weapons and small arms fire. It had been her constant background for the last two days. They slept in the open, taking it in turns to stand watch. She wondered at the fact the two men were so nonchalant. What were they thinking?

†

The constant rattle of firearms large and small echoed through the city. They had been crawling along, sticking to streets free of both army and rebels, staying under cover as much as possible. The streets all looked the same, except for the occasional square. Three, four storey buildings, shop fronts on the lower floors with apartments above, many now sporting breeze block defences. Everything was a drab beige. Many buildings were already rubble and the street was adrift in sand.

Reymond consulted the map. "We're close," he said. She knew where they were going but trusted that Reymond knew where they were.

From a street or two over she heard a rabble shouting in Arabic. Somewhere further away there was a high-pitched metal whine, a counterpoint to the trundle of a tank. An RPG exploded. They heard a man screaming. War.

Mari shuffled closer. "How the Hell did you talk me into this? It's insane!" she spat in a low whisper.

"We couldn't stop you, if I remember correctly," Reymond responded.

"If I had a time machine, I'd go back to that earlier me and give her a slap. What the fuck was I thinking?"

"The building we want is over there," Reymond said, pointing across the square. "Behind the mosque. We'll have to run for it."

Mari turned to Reymond, opened her mouth to say something, but he ran, at a crouch, into the square. He dodged from bench to bush to burned-out car, and made it across to the other side. As he turned, using the mosque wall as cover, Mari ran at a crouch, Fisher waited on the other side of the square. Mari reached Reymond's side, breathless, and watched as Fisher made the sprint.

Reymond had just mumbled something reassuring to her when Fisher stumbled and fell. He didn't get up.

"Stay here," Reymond said grimly. He dropped the carryall containing the swords and shucked his rucksack, then ran at a crouch towards his fallen friend. Mari tried to look in every direction at once. There was a sniper, but where? Could she do anything about it, even if she could spot it?

The bullets from the sniper rifle puffed up the dirt around Reymond. He reached Fisher and lifted him onto his shoulders with a grunt of effort that she could hear even at this distance. Fisher wasn't a small man, and built like a rugby player.

Reymond staggered back towards the mosque. She saw the door open a few feet away as Reymond ran towards Mari, she hoped that was a good sign.

Fisher was still breathing. He bled from a gut wound. Mari was relieved to discover that the mosque was a makeshift hospital. They carried Fisher inside and dumped him on a pallet acting as a bed, ripping away the clothes from his wound. It pulsed blood slowly. Mari had no way to know if the bullet had hit anything vital.

Two women in headscarves and a man in a simple white shift approached cautiously. Reymond tried to make them understand, first in English, then in French, then broken Arabic, that they must save his friend. Mari was stunned, she couldn't understand what was happening.

"Mari?" Reymond said gently. She turned to look at him. "Stay with him."

She nodded, distracted. Reymond put his hand on her shoulder. "Will you be alright?"

She nodded again. "Yes. Yeah, I'll be fine. Fine."

"Look after her too," he said to the man and the veiled women. He grabbed his sword and a gun and left the mosque without looking back.

†

The door took three kicks to open. It wasn't the most subtle of entrances. Reymond stalked through the ramshackle rooms, sunlight stabbed through gaps in the windows like God's fingers, dust swirled seeking an escape. He let his sword point the direction, making his way up the stairs and into a room that had sigils painted on the wall. Most of them were burned out now; just the ones representing Wrath and Pride remained. Sebastien waited for him.

"You look different," he said in greeting.

"You look the same," Reymond replied.

"It has been a long time."

"Almost a thousand years. Do you want to say something, not just chat?" Reymond took up a fighting stance, chanting Alouette silently in his head.

"I punished him, you know," Sebastien said. Reymond raised his eyebrows. Sebastien stared into the far distance, a thousand-year stare. "I punished Tafur, for killing you. He never saw Jerusalem. None of us did. Andros was killed by a woman, Jules wandered into the desert and died of thirst. Jobert was killed in battle, as was Charles, Tafur I punished in Ma'Arra. I was sorry he killed you."

"Not as sorry as I was," Reymond said through gritted teeth.

"Did you ever make it to Jerusalem? You were always so keen."

"No, I never did. I would still like to. It will be one of many regrets."

Sebastien snapped back to the present.

"I have an offer. Please, hear me out."

Reymond felt a slow throb behind his eyes, a dull insistent ache. His heart beat fast and his hand trembled. He clenched his fists. "Go on."

"Just leave. Walk out of here. I'll end the curse if you give me the book. I assume that's how you found me? You have the book? When the seven years elapse this time, it will be your last."

"How?" Reymond tried to keep his eyes on the sorcerer and evaluate the fighting space at the same time. Outside the noise got ever louder, the battle ever closer. An explosion rocked the building, dust cascaded from above as the plaster of the ceiling cracked. The two men ignored it.

"I alter the spell, take you out of the equation. It will mean making sacrifices, changes, allowances. But it can be done." Sebastien nodded, as if Reymond had already agreed.

"What have you done? What is the spell?"

"My dear Reymond, I was led to believe you had the book.

I thought you'd have worked it out. I have given myself eternal life –"

"At what cost?" Reymond interrupted, some of his cold, hard anger spilling out. A machine gun rattled close by; there was another, much louder, explosion and the machine gun fell silent. The shutters sprang open and swung wildly, screeching. Somewhere in the distance Reymond could hear the flapping of wings.

"I have to renew it, when things become... *difficult*. To stave off disease or repair injury." Sebastien sounded surprised to be asked.

"And that's when we return?"

"Yes Reymond. That's when you return."

"And you're just going to, what, write me out of it next time?" Reymond asked, disbelieving.

"If you take this offer, yes." Sebastien looked earnest.

"And what will that mean to the others?"

"There will be a change. I'm not sure how." Sebastien shrugged, obviously not caring about the cost to the others. Their conversation was interrupted as bullets sprayed through the wall, the building peppered with shots meant for another enemy. Fingers of sunlight poked through the swirling dust. Both men had ducked instinctively, and now both stood.

"Forget it. I'm here as much to give them rest as me." Reymond took a couple of steps forward.

Sebastien sighed, lifting his sword. He spoke in a low voice, in a language Reymond didn't know.

They exchanged a few blows, testing each other, and Reymond withdrew, confused. Sebastien seemed to make little effort and yet he moved so fast. Blood was already dripping down Reymond's arm from where he was a fraction too late on a block. Reymond shook his head. Sebastien's low tone didn't change. Reymond noticed an amulet in the shape of a sword hanging around the sorcerer's neck.

Reymond circled the smaller man warily, looking for an

opening. The noise of a tank outside drowned out all other sounds. There was a crump and again the whole building seemed to leap sideways and the front disintegrated as a large section of ceiling tumbled down and smashed through the floor. Reymond leapt over the sudden hole.

They met in the centre of the room and their blades clashed again. Reymond disengaged awkwardly, leaping away as a splash of blood hit the wooden floor, black in the dim light, squirting from a serious but not fatal wound high on his ribs. Smoke and dust blotted out the sun that should be streaming in the gaping hole in the wall. Sebastien's droning incantation had not changed. There was another burst of gunfire and the bullets pecked a line of holes in the far wall, obliterating the sigils. Incongruously Reymond could hear the beating of wings. He hoped it was not death. He wasn't ready, he was so close; his veins burned, his heart on the brink of explosion, he moved faster than he had ever done before.

Reymond's chest heaved as his rage came to the boil. He was over-matched and he knew it. Frustration stoked the flames of his anger.

He roared and flung himself at Sebastien, who sidestepped the charge, scoring Reymond lightly as he stumbled past. Sebastien was playing with him, and that made him even more angry. His awareness, his centring, all his plans fled as the rage took him. In three seconds, three brief moments of eternity, he went from towering anger with the strength of his arm as servant to wrath to lying on the floor, pushed over like a child, sword flung five feet away across the room.

Outside, a cacophony: men screamed, metal clanged like a drum played by a monkey on speed, and somewhere close by a building collapsed. The floor listed drunkenly.

Sebastien levelled his sword at Reymond's throat as Reymond squirmed backwards.

As Sebastien lifted the sword and closed his mouth and the dirgeful incantation stopped, a shot rang out. He stumbled forward a step or two and the sword wavered, Reymond took his chance, leaping up to tackle him.

As he grabbed Sebastien's arm he reversed the sword, ramming it through the blond man's chest. Sebastien's eyes opened wide, rolled up in his head, and he slumped to the floor, struggling no more.

Mari stood in the doorway, clutching Fisher's gun. Her eyes were as wide as Sebastien's had been.

"Are you okay?" she asked as Reymond tried to stand, slipping in the pool of blood collecting on the floor. He was soaked to the skin in gore.

He smiled at Mari. "You really are making a habit of saving me, aren't you?"

The battle swirled outside, and moved away. It still sounded close, but maybe a street or two away now.

Mari let out a long shuddering breath. "Fisher is stable but they want us to move him. I came to look for you. I'm glad I got here when I did."

"So am I." Reymond collected the swords. There was a sudden bright light and the wall painted with obliterated sigils burst into flames.

"We'd best get out of here," he said.

The man from the mosque convinced them they must get Fisher away. The battle for the city was winding down, and the rebels seemed to be winning. Being around after that point invited kidnap, or worse. Reymond swapped all their guns and the money they were carrying in US dollars for a clapped out car with no back seat and bald tyres.

The men from the mosque helped them manoeuvre Fisher

into the car. He was heavily sedated, a drip given to Mari to hold, they placed him on the back seat. The men from the mosque withdrew without a word and Mari, still making sure Fisher was comfortable, wasn't even strapped in when Reymond started the car and slammed his foot down. As they raced down the streets, weaving in and out of the rubble, Mari stared out at burning apartment buildings, burning tanks and burning bodies. She coughed on the greasy toxic smoke.

Mari sat in the front passenger seat, stony faced. They'd followed the road out of town until they were driving through sparse landscape. Eventually Reymond pulled off the road and pointed the car at the hills until they threw up a cloud of dust, grinding their way across the desert. Once they were out of sight of the highway, Reymond jerked the car to a stop.

Mari still stared straight ahead, oblivious to her surroundings. Fisher lay in the back in a slick of blood, still breathing. Mari knew he was a tough old bird, but she hoped that the journey back to civilisation wouldn't kill him.

Reymond climbed out of the car, leaving the door open. He took the swords and the book from the boot, and stalked off into the desert. When he returned, Mari hadn't moved. He opened the door and gently guided her out. When she was stood by the car he slapped her, hard.

"What the fuck?"

"Mari?" She rewarded him with a corker of a right hook, snapping his head to the side. For an instant, he staggered.

"Don't ever hit a lady." Mari folded her arms.

"I thought you needed a shock."

"Why?"

"You were kind of zoned out and I need you," he said simply.

"Need me? What for?" She narrowed her eyes.

"It's best if I show you." He headed into the desert once

more. Mari followed.

Some way from the car, they came to the large circle he had cut into the soft ground and, inside, the cloth which held the seven swords.

"It is impossible for me to work this alone," Reymond admitted.

"Work what?" she asked.

"Fisher was supposed to do this. It would have fulfilled his oath." Now the moment was here it looked like Reymond couldn't wait. His foot was already jiggling, he was tapping his finger in impatience.

Mari crossed her arms again and gave him a sceptical look.

"This can't wait," he said.

"So I've gathered. What do you want me to do, Reymond?"

"If I've interpreted the sorcerer's book correctly and what Sebastien said about the sacrifices fits in the way I think it does. Help me perform a ritual and end the curse."

Mari nodded.

"I need you to kill me."

"What? Reymond, no!"

"As part of the ritual, I have to die."

"This is some sort of sick joke?" Her face turned red, her eyes screwed up.

"There is no joke. I wish it was. To reverse the curse, all of the original 7 have to die. That includes me. I have all the swords. They need to be used to kill me."

"Reymond, I can't – my father."

"It's what I want. It's the rest I crave. A restoration of the balance. Your father will come back once my spirit has flown."

"No." Her voice went very quiet. She shook her head.

"Mari, please! If this doesn't happen very soon I'll leave this body. I can feel it coming. If I leave without completing this then I'll return. The others will return, evil will return... This will never end."

"But you killed Sebastien! It was his spell causing the

problem, his renewing it that brought you all back. I heard him," Mari insisted. "And if I kill you I might kill my father, if you leave the body he'll be back. He'll be back."

Reymond shook his head.

"Do you even know what you're asking?" Mari was panicked. It was a lot to take in, especially after the last couple of days. "What if you are dead, what if papa doesn't come back? What about me? What about Fisher? We'll be stuck in the desert, in a war zone. How am I supposed to get past the patrols by myself?"

Reymond shrugged.

"Arsehole! You want me to stab you to death?"

"In a very specific way."

"That's why we're out in the middle of the desert? I won't do it." She cut the air with her hand in an emphatic gesture of denial.

"Then you are condemning me, and the others. And all this, everything I've done, everything you have helped me do, has been a waste of time. Fisher was prepared to do it. Who else could I ask? Mari, I need you to do this."

Mari shook her head, the tears ran down her face. She turned and ran into the hills.

How stupid to run away, like a little girl. How infantile. Mari cursed herself as she climbed the hill, thorny plants scratching her legs and hands. She could hardly see where she was going; it was both dark and she had to continuously swipe angry tears away from her eyes. How could he? After all the struggles, to just give up. Just like her mother. Her foot came down into a rabbit hole, wrenching her ankle, and she gracelessly slid down the hill for ten feet or so.

"Oh for fuck's sake!" she shouted as loud as she could. "Get a grip, Mari!"

She found a handkerchief, blew her nose and wiped her eyes. She sniffed mightily, and as the silence of the desert descended like a blanket she heard a beautiful singing.

Reymond. It must be Reymond.

She couldn't make out the words at all. They were sung in a foreign language, but his voice was high and clear. Unashamed. There was a glow in the night, back in the direction she had come from.

The glow grew stronger. She decided she'd behaved badly and felt she should apologise, but she didn't know how she felt about Reymond wanting to give up, and the possibility that in order for him to end the curse her father may be lost in the void forever.

No, if she was honest with herself, she did know; she was furious. She was just finding her feet when sunlight bathed the hill. Mari felt a warm glow on her cheek. Contentment and a feeling of peace flew through her briefly, fading with the sudden burst of light.

She made her way softly and slowly down the hill, until she could see Reymond cross-legged, holding a brightly glowing object which he put to one side. Strong chanting took the place of the memory of song. The cawing of crows accompanied her down the hill.

Reymond had removed his clothing and washed himself with water from a blue glass bottle that looked like a genie should live in it. Mari stopped five foot away, irresolute, unsure where to look. Reymond's body was hard, muscled, scarred. Mari had seen it before, of course; her father had sometimes worked stripped down to his trousers, but now he seemed more primal, clad in nature and shadow. He had many more scars than she'd noticed her father had borne. He broke off his chant, staring at her.

He appeared completely unselfconscious. He bent, picked up the glowing object which was his sword and strolled over to her. He placed the blade in her unresisting hands, and guided it until the tip pointed directly at his heart. The sword seemed to be lighter than a feather, made of light and prayer. All the other blades had been subsumed within it as he'd sung sad songs of purity.

"Reymond, I – "

"Shhh." He smiled.

"But – "

Reymond walked forward onto the blade. It sliced effortlessly, through flesh, muscle, sinew, and life. He slumped, still reaching for Mari's hand, still smiling, and in the distance she heard galloping hooves.

Shocked, Mari let go of the sword. Reymond stumbled into her arms and they both fell. The sword vanished. Reymond gazed at her.

In a small voice, he said, "Merci." Then his eyes closed and his face took on a beatific calmness that Mari could not mistake for the animation of life.

She bent over him, her tears a benediction upon his face. The air shimmered; a dawn glow suffused the hillside. A gentle snort and the sound of hooves behind her made her spin around, dropping Reymond in the process. There was nothing there. The crows leapt into the air with a great beating of wings and a many-throated call. Darkness reasserted itself, and as she turned back she saw her father's body at rest. She looked up, and through her tears, as the last glow became a memory, she saw the stars blaze into life in the sky above her.

# Acknowledgements

IT MAY BE my name on the cover but a book is a collaborative project from start to finish and there a lot of people that need a nod of acknowledgement for being a helping hand along the way. I started writing this book in 2013 but the true genesis of Reymond goes back to a tabletop campaign about a decade earlier so thanks to Rik, Jon, Simon, Les and Matt.

There have been plenty of drafts and a couple of rounds of beta reading so thanks to all those who have given their opinion and valuable insights – Eva Rosander, Gav Watkins, Dave Gullen, Eric Nash, Maria Herring and Justin Newland.

Much thanks must go to Joanne Hall who not only accepted the book on behalf of Grimbold (thanks also to Sammy Smith here) but also did the first, and most painful, edit. Talking of edits much, much thanks to Kate Coe who did a terrific job of making this book a novel.

I'd like to thank my mum and sisters, Denise & Carol, who have been so enthusiastic about my writing and came to my first book launch.

And last, but certainly not least, I couldn't write without the support of my partner Claire who earns my undying gratitude for putting up with me being dreamy (thinking about writing), scribbling notes at odd times and sequestering myself away at my desk to stare at the blank pages in horror, or, worse, stare at my own prose in horror.

And to you gentle reader, if you have reached this far, I thank you.

# A Selection of Other Titles from Kristell Ink

## Terra Nullius by Kate Coe and Ellen Crosháin (eds.)

Land belonging to no-one. An anthology of speculative fiction that explores the colonisation of our Solar System and far beyond, where pioneers carve out a new existence under other stars. New worlds and new challenges bring out rich stories filled with alien races and strange technology, but against this backdrop there's the many facets of human emotion as colonists struggle to make a new home.

This is human life on the final frontier.

## Children of the Shaman by Jessica Rydill

When their aunt is taken ill, thirteen-year old Annat and her brother are sent from their small coastal town to live with their unknown father. Like Annat, Yuda is a Shaman; a Wanderer with magical powers, able to enter other worlds. As Annat learns more about her powers, the children join their father on a remarkable train journey to the frozen north and find a land of mystery and intrigue, threatened by dark forces and beset by senseless murders that have halted construction of a new tunnel. But Annat's doll, her only remembrance of her dead mother, may hold a dark secret - and when her brother Malchik is kidnapped, Annat and her father must travel onwards to find him before it is too late.

Between uncertain allies, shadowed enemies and hostile surroundings, it is only in the magical kingdom of La Souterraine that they can find answers - and it may be that only a Shaman can save the family and the Goddess.

## BLOOD BANK by Zoë Markham

Benjamin is a programmer moonlighting as a security guard at Dystopia, a seedy club that caters to the down-and-outs, the desperates, the addicts. He's been building his reputation, saving for a way out - but when he rescues a young woman from the nearby estate, he may just have stepped too far out of line...

Lucy is ordinary; a girl with a deadbeat boyfriend, a normal life and college studies. But when her world takes an odd twist, she starts to wonder about the people she's meeting, the situations she's in, the odd aversions and attacks happening around her. They're just coincidences...aren't they?

And Zack is in deep trouble. He's losing his girlfriend, drowning in debt, and has dwindling job prospects - and that's not the worst of it. His debt is to people who won't ever forget it, and who want the things closest to Zack's heart: his blood - and his life.

In the heart of Swindon, an ancient order hides in plain sight, spreading their influence through the streets like a disease. But despite their widespread power they are catching up with the modern world: the vampires are going online, and the Order is about to become more powerful than even they would have dreamed...

kristell-ink.com

Lightning Source UK Ltd.
Milton Keynes UK
UKHW010627050721
386659UK00001B/190